"There are a lot of bubbas in this area who would be pissed off to discover that a girl wasn't what they thought she was," Jake commented. "If Tala was dating someone else, could be he wasn't as understanding as Luke."

It was obvious from her expression that Neve had already thought of that.

"What did her parents say?" Audrey asked.

"That they moved here for a fresh start. Tala started hormones when they lived in Bangor, and apparently was bullied incessantly, which led to a suicide attempt. Her parents thought bringing her to a new town where no one knew her history would be the best thing for her."

"So they brought her to Edgeport?" Jake lifted his cup and shook his head. "They were *so* wrong."

Praise for

Kate Kessler

It Takes One

"Deliciously twisted and genre-bending, Kate Kessler's positively riveting *It Takes One* boasts a knockout concept and a thoroughly unique and exciting protagonist, a savvy criminal psychologist with murderous skeletons in her own closet."

—Sara Blaedel

"A book that kept calling to me when I should have been doing something else. Hard to put down, compulsive reading."

—Rachel Abbott

"*It Takes One* is a gripping roller-coaster ride of shock and suspense....Kate Kessler excels at creating an atmosphere of fear and suspense."

—Kate Rhodes

"This first in a series combines an intriguing mystery with a terrific cast of characters. Fans of Nancy Pickard or Lisa Unger will find much to like in Kessler. Expect her to become very popular very quickly."

—*Booklist* (starred review)

Two Can Play

"Readers can't help but enjoy solving the mystery along with Audrey right up to the final, unexpected twist."

—*RT Book Reviews*

"A smart crime novel that will engage readers."

—*Publishers Weekly*

FOUR

OF A

KIND

By Kate Kessler

AUDREY HARTE NOVELS
It Takes One
Two Can Play
Three Strikes
Four of a Kind

FOUR OF A KIND

AN AUDREY HARTE NOVEL

KATE KESSLER

REDHOOK

www.redhookbooks.com

Copyright © 2018 by Kathryn Smith
Excerpt from *The Walls* copyright © 2017 by Hollie Overton

Author photograph by Kathryn Smith
Cover design by Crystal Ben and Wendy Chan
Cover images by Shutterstock
Cover copyright © 2018 by Hachette Book Group, Inc.

Redhook Books/Orbit
Hachette Book Group
1290 Avenue of the Americas
New York, NY 10104
hachettebookgroup.com

First Edition: March 2018

Redhook is an imprint of Orbit, a division of Hachette Book Group.
The Redhook name and logo are trademarks of Hachette Book Group, Inc.

The publisher is not responsible for websites (or their content) that are not owned by the publisher.

The Hachette Speakers Bureau provides a wide range of authors for speaking events. To find out more, go to www.hachettespeakersbureau.com or call (866) 376-6591.

Library of Congress Cataloging-in-Publication Data has been applied for.

ISBNs: 978-0-316-43899-5 (trade paperback), 978-0-316-43902-2 (ebook)

Printed in the United States of America

LSC-C

10 9 8 7 6 5 4 3 2 1

This book is for Steve—always

AMBER ALERT

ISSUED FOR: MAINE
Tala Lewis

- Missing Date: **February 17**
- Missing From: **Eastrock, ME**
- Age Now: **17 years old**
- Sex: **Female**
- Race: **Filipino**
- Hair Color: **Dark Brown**
- Eye Color: **Brown**
- Height: **5 feet 9 inches**
- Weight: **130 pounds**
- Description: **The child was last seen wearing a purple coat, black sweater, jeans and black boots.**
- **Anyone having any information should call 911.**

March 31, 2017

POLICE EXPAND SEARCH FOR MISSING TEEN:

MISSING EASTROCK GIRL MAY HAVE GONE TO NEW YORK, FRIENDS SAY

By Mark Picard, Herald *staff writer*

EASTROCK—Police are widening the search for missing Eastrock teenager Tala Lewis.

"We're exploring the possibility that Tala may have left the state," said state trooper Detective Neve Graham. "Obviously, we just want to bring Tala home."

Tala, 17, was last seen February 17 after spending time with friends. Those same friends say she was supposed to meet them that night, but never showed.

"She was happy that day," said best friend Kendra Granger. "We hung out with friends and made plans to go to New York after graduation. She said she couldn't wait to get out of here."

"I can't believe she'd just take off," said friend Luke Pelletier. "But the only place she'd go is New York. She wouldn't leave her friends for any other reason."

While friends and family have a hard time believing Tala would leave without word, police say that
many runaways eventually end up in larger cities
where they can blend in and avoid attention.

Tala was last seen wearing a sweater, coat and
boots. She is 5'9" tall with dark hair and eyes.
Anyone with information should call 911 or the
Maine State Police.

CHAPTER ONE

April 26, 2017

There were three words Neve Graham hated to hear. They echoed in her ears as a twig snapped beneath the sole of her boot. *They found something.*

It was late April, but there were still patches of snow in the heavily sheltered woods, despite it being a sunny day. Another few rains and it would be gone soon. New shoots of life burst through the dirt, rotting vegetation giving away to something vibrant and green, despite the stubborn snow.

God, she hated spring. It smelled like death to her, all that decay stripped bare by the slow but relentless thaw.

"You see it yet?" called a voice.

Neve turned. Coming along the path toward her was Charlotte deBaie, death investigator for the area. "Just got here," she replied. "Can I carry some of that?"

Charlotte waved her away as they started down the rough path down the rocky hill. "Do you think it's her?"

"It's someone." When she'd gotten the call earlier, she'd been told that hikers had found human remains at the Edgeport state park, commonly referred to simply as "the Falls" by locals. The area only had one missing person, but that was one too many as far as Neve was concerned. Part of her wanted to give the family closure, but there was no goddamn way she looked forward to making that visit.

Maybe it was a tourist. A lone hiker who hadn't told anyone where they were going. It was possible—it happened occasionally.

Charlotte's boot skidded on a loose rock. Neve reached up to steady her. She really didn't want to break the larger woman's fall at the bottom of the bank. Plus, the guys would make lesbian jokes for the next month, regardless of the fact that both Neve and Charlotte were in relationships with men.

When they finally reached bottom, they had to pick their way along the rocky terrain bordering the river to where the falls growled and splashed. A young man was sitting partway up the steep incline. Neve recognized him as Gareth Hughes, one of the caretakers of the park. He was pale and perched on a rock about ten feet below the bridge that allowed hikers to cross over the falls.

"Climbed all that way down just to climb up again," Charlotte muttered, watching where she stepped. "Sounds about right."

Neve smiled slightly. "Better to come down the path than that." She pointed where Gareth sat. That was just an invitation for a broken neck, which was what had probably happened to the person he'd found. There was a path from the parking lot to the upper level of the falls as well, but it was tricky terrain.

Finally, they reached the base of the falls, where they were soon joined by Gareth's brother, Owen, and Neve's fellow state trooper Vickie Moore, who was in uniform and the first on the scene. There were others as well, but Neve was primary since it was a female body. She'd been looking for Tala Lewis for two months, ever since the girl went missing.

Neve and Charlotte suited up to preserve the scene and made their way twenty feet up the side of the falls. The rocks and vegetation were wet from melt and rushing water, making it a slippery mess.

"Be careful," Neve cautioned as her own toe slipped on a slimy patch. Damn booties.

"Not my first rodeo, girlie," Charlotte replied, deftly avoiding the same spot. Somehow, she managed to look cool and graceful while a tiny trickle of sweat ran down Neve's back.

Gareth reached down to give her a hand up the last couple of feet. Then, when Neve stepped to the side, he helped Charlotte as well. The bridge was only a few feet away—a good place for anyone else to stand so as not to contaminate the scene any more than it already was.

"Where is it?" Neve asked the younger man.

He pointed to a pile of rocks that looked as though it had been part of a landslide at one time. Behind them, Neve saw alders, more rocks, and a boot. A boot that looked as though it might still have a foot in it. She swallowed. She'd been doing this job for ten years now, and it never got any easier.

She and Charlotte approached in single file, Neve stepping on the hard rocks in an attempt to preserve the scene as much as possible. She paused on top of the largest boulder and looked down.

Shit.

The body had been a young woman at one time. It was surrounded and still partially covered by rocks. Long black hair stuck to the scalp and tangled with debris on the ground. She wore a puffy purple jacket, ripped and stained with blood, and jeans stuffed into black boots. Her skin was almost the same color as her coat, with patches of red. *Freezer burn*, Neve thought. It wasn't the bloat that got to her—or even the smell. Thank God it was still too cool for bug activity, and the rocks had kept her covered until meltoff started. No, what got to Neve was the grimace, and there always seemed to be a grimace. It was the one reminder that what they were looking at used to be alive. The girl's revealed a slightly crooked eyetooth.

Charlotte began taking photos with her phone. "It's her, isn't it?"

Neve nodded, her throat tight. They both knew they'd have to compare dental records before they could say anything publicly, but there was no doubt in her mind. "It's Tala Lewis."

And it was obvious her death *hadn't* been an accident.

The moment Audrey Harte saw the unmarked police car pull into the drive, she knew something bad had happened. Detective Neve Graham was a friend, but things had been strained between them ever since Neve made it clear she didn't fully trust Audrey, or her fiancé, Jake. It wasn't that Audrey blamed her; Neve had every reason to be wary as a cop, but *not* as a friend. Audrey would never betray her that way.

So if Neve was there, unannounced, then something bad had

happened. Audrey turned away from the workers building an extension onto the old farmhouse that would soon be her Grace Ridge facility for troubled teens and walked toward the spot where Neve had parked under an ancient apple tree. There would be blossoms on the tree in a few weeks, toward the end of May, but for now it was thick with buds. It was obvious back there, on what locals referred to as "the Ridge," that spring had truly arrived.

Neve climbed out of the car and shut the door. She wore a black pantsuit and white shirt that indicated she was on duty. Was it Jake? Audrey's mother? No, someone would have called her, unless it was really bad.

"What's wrong?" Audrey demanded, closing the distance between them with long strides.

Neve leaned against the car. Her dark hair was back in a tight bun, but curls had managed to escape regardless. They had met as children, and Neve had been the first black person Audrey had ever seen that wasn't on television. Audrey was also the first person Neve ever met whose eyes were different colors. They'd been fascinated by each other, and became pretty good friends.

Then Neve's father arrested Audrey and her best friend for murder and put an end to that.

Neve crossed her arms over the chest of her button-down. "We found a body this morning."

Audrey's shoulders sagged. "Tala Lewis?"

Neve nodded. She looked defeated. "Yeah."

"Shit. Alisha is going to be heartbroken." Alisha was Jake's niece, who'd been good friends with the girl who'd disappeared a couple of months ago. Alisha clung to the hope that her friend had taken off to New York or LA to pursue her dreams of becoming an actress. She was convinced that Tala would send word as soon as she was settled in, even though the girl was much more considerate than that and would never let people worry about her.

"I'm going to ask you not to say anything to her until we know for sure. I haven't talked to the parents yet."

"Of course." She didn't like keeping secrets from Alisha, but she couldn't be expected not to share the news with friends, and her mother—Jake's sister, Yancy—had a reputation as a gossip. It would be all over town before suppertime.

Neve was silent for a moment, giving Audrey a chance to study her. She looked exhausted; there were dark circles under her wide eyes, and tension in her brow. "What else?" she prompted. It was obvious now that Neve had sought her out not because of Alisha, but because she needed to talk. "Is it Bailey?" Bailey was the daughter of Neve's boyfriend and was currently incarcerated at a juvenile facility, awaiting trial for the murder of her stepmother, Maggie. The same Maggie whose father Audrey had helped kill.

It all felt so very incestuous.

"No. She's good. The lawyers are optimistic." She shifted against the car, turning so that her back was against the driver's door. "The body we found had been stabbed. Multiple times."

"The body" rather than Tala. Either Neve was being very diligent about not committing to the victim's identity, or she was trying to be impersonal. "I don't suppose there's any way it could have been accidental?"

Neve gave her a sharp look, as if questioning her intelligence. "We found her back the Falls. Someone had taken the time to cover the body with rocks."

Audrey leaned against the car as well. A cool breeze ruffled her hair. "So now you have to tell the parents their daughter was murdered."

"By someone who seems to know the area and had the thought to leave her in a spot where she was very unlikely to be found. If it wasn't for the park guys doing some work, we might not have found her. Once the warm weather hit..."

She didn't have to explain any further. Audrey had worked with the police enough—and watched enough TV—to have an idea what bugs and animals could do to a corpse.

"You're thinking it was someone local."

Neve sighed. "I hate the cases with murdered kids. I thought when I left New York I was leaving this kind of stuff behind."

Audrey didn't know exactly what had happened, but she knew Neve had been shot and almost died, and that her parents had begged her to give up the city, because her father had almost been killed on the job years earlier. It was the reason they'd moved to Edgeport.

"It's been getting worse," Neve continued.

"Since I came home," Audrey supplied, because of course it was all about her.

"Shut up." Neve scowled at her. "You coming home didn't have anything to do with what Bailey did, or this. It's just that I've been much more affected by crimes involving kids because of it."

"Welcome to my world." Audrey had started into her career as a forensic juvenile psychologist because of her own background, but it soon became more than that. She wanted to help kids, but now her life was so full of wounded and even criminal teenagers that she sometimes wondered if she'd become desensitized to the very issues she wanted to help solve.

"No. You're trying to help these kids. I'm the bad guy. I had to arrest Bailey." She closed her eyes and leaned her head back. "I don't want to be my frigging father."

Ah. Audrey supposed she ought to have seen that one coming, but Neve didn't talk much about her father, or what she thought of him. Really, Audrey was the last person fit to comment on the mental and emotional health of Everett Graham.

"You're not your father any more than I'm mine."

Neve shot her an arch glance. "*Seriously?*"

"Hey, I might be like him, but I'm also a fully grown woman capable of making my own decisions. I'm not my father, and you're a better cop than your father ever was. At least you care." That might have been overstepping, but Neve didn't seem to mind.

"She was stabbed to death, Audrey. I've never seen anything so brutal."

Audrey's lips compressed. It was obvious Neve was affected by this case if she felt she needed to discuss it when she oughtn't. "It was personal."

Neve nodded. "Very. If this was one of those criminal shows we'd be discussing overkill."

Audrey liked procedurals. "So, what are you going to do?"

Neve sighed and tilted her head back as she met her gaze. "Wait for ID to be confirmed and the autopsy results to come in, and then I'm afraid I'm going to have to start looking for a murderer."

Audrey's smile was grim. "I've got an alibi."

CHAPTER TWO

Did you hear they found a body?"

Alisha Tripp's head whipped up so fast a spasm ran down her neck. She stared into heavily lined wide eyes. Lucy Villeneuve plunked her skinny jean–clad ass into the seat beside her on the bus. Lucy lived close to Ryme, which was on the other side of Edgeport from Eastrock, where the high school was located, which meant Alisha was probably going to have to listen to Lucy for her entire ride home, as Alisha's stop was first.

Lucy was something like what Alisha's mother was accused of being—a gossip.

"No," she replied, which was true. Even if it weren't, she wouldn't tell Lucy.

"Kendra's mother said she saw the cops going back the park road this morning—meat wagon too."

Alisha grimaced. "Meat wagon" was one of those terms that unsettled her stomach, kind of like "genital warts," or "trust me." Or maybe it was the idea of them finding someone that made her feel queasy.

Now that she took a good look at Lucy, she could tell the girl's expression wasn't eager at all, but concerned, and she immediately felt bad. Lucy, Kendra Granger, and Tala had been best friends since Tala moved to Eastrock last summer. Of course Lucy would be worried that the body they'd found was Tala—Alisha was.

She and Tala hadn't started becoming friends until just before Christmas, but they'd become close incredibly fast. Alisha hadn't had a best friend since Bailey was sent away. She had lots of friends, but not one she would trust with her secrets, not until Tala. And Tala had trusted her too.

"Tala would never go back the Falls," she muttered. "Not by herself."

"Maybe she wasn't by herself," Lucy suggested with a lift of her eyebrow. "Randy was around that night."

Alisha frowned. She knew what Lucy was implying. Tala never would have gone off with a loser like Randy Dyer. Would she? "Don't be stupid."

The other girl slumped against the bus seat, her body turned toward Alisha, who set her book bag between them as a way of maintaining her own space. "I don't *want* it to be Tala, you know. I just want them to find *something*."

"I know," Alisha murmured. "Me too."

"And poor Luke. This has been absolutely *tragic* for him."

That wouldn't be the word Alisha would choose, but it was appropriate. Luke Pelletier and Tala had been dating for almost two months when she disappeared. Of all of them, he'd taken her disappearance the hardest—the most personal. Why would she just up and desert her friends and family? Her boyfriend? People said she went to New York, but Alisha couldn't believe

Tala wouldn't at least let her parents know she was okay. She wasn't that selfish or unthinking.

She turned her attention toward the back of the bus, where Luke sat. He lived in Edgeport too. He sat by himself—the space where Tala used to sit empty—and stared out the window. Something pinched in Alisha's chest at the sight of him. Suddenly, he turned his head. She didn't look away fast enough. She forced a little smile when his gaze met hers. Surprisingly, he smiled back. It wasn't much, just a twitch at one corner of his mouth, but it was something. Then he went back to staring out the window.

She wondered if he'd heard they'd found a body.

"Kendra's been a mess," Lucy was saying. "I mean, so have I, but Ken's been really wrecked. I stayed over at her place the other night and I woke up in the middle of the night. She was standing by the window, crying. I was like, 'What's wrong?' and she told me she was upset about Tala. That she just felt so bad all she could do was cry."

Alisha looked the other girl in the eye. "She probably wouldn't like you telling me that."

Lucy shrugged. "Are you going to say anything to her?"

"No." She wasn't a shit-disturber.

"Then it doesn't fucking matter, does it?"

At that precise moment, Alisha decided she didn't much care for Lucy, and like her uncle Jake and her great-grandmother, when she decided she didn't like someone, there was no changing her mind. "You're a lousy friend, Luce."

The girl's face flushed, and her eyes glittered. "Fuck you, Alisha." She grabbed her stuff and stood up—never mind that the bus was moving. For a second, Alisha imagined what might happen if they had to come to a sudden stop. She watched as Lucy stomped to the back of the bus and dropped into the empty spot next to Luke. He didn't even look at her.

Alisha turned away and pulled her phone out of her bag. She texted her uncle Jake. He'd know if they'd actually found a body back the Falls, and if he didn't know, then Audrey would. They would tell her the truth.

She just wasn't sure the truth was what she wanted to hear.

Neve was having lunch the next day at Gracie's, the local tavern, when her phone. Normally, she had lunch at the field office in Machias, but there was no point in driving over there when the brunt of her work was in her hometown. She'd only end up having to deal with reporters who had gotten wind they'd found a body. The ones skulking about town were bad enough, but she could avoid them.

She glanced at the screen before answering the call. It was the coroner's office in Augusta.

"Hello?" She sucked ketchup off her thumb.

"Hey, doll." It was Annette Martin from the medical examiner's office. "Am I interrupting your lunch?"

"Nah. I'm good." She could eat onion rings and talk at the same time. "What's up?"

"Well, the body you sent me definitely belongs to your missing girl."

"Tala Lewis?" She needed to be sure.

"Unless you've got another one I don't know about."

Neve closed her eyes. *Shit.* She had expected this outcome, but it was still…what? Disappointing? Enraging? A pisser? "Give it to me."

"COD was deep lacerations to the neck, torso, and abdomen. Basically, the poor thing was stabbed to death. I counted forty-one points of entry. She bled out."

"Jesus."

"I recovered the tip of a blade from one of the rib wounds. T he size and shape make me think hunting knife, but of course, we'll know more once it's processed."

A hunting knife—the second most common household item in Edgeport after a rifle. Practically every male, and many females, owned at least one. Gideon owned at least two.

She didn't like thinking of her boyfriend and murder at the same time.

"It appears that she was killed where you found her," Annette continued. "She had defensive wounds on her hands and arms. Judging from what we found at the scene, I'd say she bled out as her attacker covered her with rocks. Of course, runoff took away trace evidence."

Of course. "How long has she been dead?"

"Judging from decomp and state of the body, I'd say she's been out there for at least two months."

So she was probably killed the night she disappeared, or shortly thereafter. "Why would a teenage girl climb the falls in the middle of winter?" It would have been cold—icy. If the climb had been difficult the day before, it would have been doubly so in February.

"Could have been a party. She might have been drinking." T he Falls was a popular party spot, given its remote location. "Tox screens won't be back till next week. Maybe she was dared to? When I was that age I would have done almost anything a boy asked."

"Yeah," Neve agreed dryly. It almost always came back to a boy. "Me too. Anything else I should know about?"

"Well, I don't know if it was simply part of the stabbing, or intentional, but her penis was completely severed."

"Her *what*?"

"Penis." There was a pause. "You didn't know Tala Lewis was transgender?"

"No." Jesus H. "The family never said anything about it."

"That's a pretty significant detail to leave out when police are investigating your child's disappearance."

"Tell me about it." A tickle of anger rose up in Neve's chest. She didn't like it when people withheld information. She didn't care if the family thought it was unimportant, or private. She should have been told that Tala was transitioning, because now it was much more possible that the murder was sexually moti-vated, or a hate crime. If she'd had that detail two months ago, she might have conducted her investigation differently.

"Any evidence of sexual assault?"

"There's evidence of activity, but nothing that leads me to believe it was forced. I didn't find any sperm or fluids, but given the time of death and that she's been outside in freezing temperatures, I'm not surprised."

So probably a hate crime, though not necessarily. "Thanks, Nettie. If there's nothing else, I'll let you go."

"I'll ring you back when I have more."

Neve hung up and shoved her phone into her purse. T hen she swung the bag over her shoulder, rose from her chair, and made her way to the bar. She shoved a twenty across the polished surface. Jake Tripp, Audrey's fiancé and owner of Gracie's, was working behind the bar. He was tall and lean, with brown hair that always seemed to flop over his high forehead, and piercing hazel eyes. He would have been too pretty if not for those eyes. She'd seen hardened ex-cons with more open gazes. Honestly, Neve didn't find Jake all that attractive, and there was something about his relationship with Audrey that gave her pause. The two of them seemed to breathe each other. She was pretty sure that wasn't healthy. But it worked for them. She just hoped Audrey didn't ruin her career—and herself— by getting too involved in Tripp business. She couldn't prove it, but she was fairly certain Jake had something to do with the prison death of Matt Jones the year before. No one missed Jones, but that wasn't the point.

"Need a receipt?" he asked. He always seemed to be assessing—reading people. He probably would have made a great cop if he didn't consider himself outside the law.

She nodded, and he quickly punched some keys on the cash register. He tore off the strip of paper that printed out and handed it to her. "I get the feeling saying 'Have a nice day' would be wasted on you."

Her smile was grim. "You wouldn't be wrong. Thanks anyway." She shoved the receipt in her jacket pocket and walked out into the sunny spring day. She slipped on her sunglasses as she slid behind the wheel of the Impala. She hadn't been looking forward to telling the Lewises that their daughter was dead, and now she looked forward to it even less because they had hidden important information from her. Information that might have played a part in their child's murder.

It made her wonder what else they might be hiding.

Audrey came home from Grace Ridge to find Jake and Alisha at the table looking at bridal magazines.

"Seriously?" she asked as she hung her bag on one of the dining room chairs.

Jake grinned at her as he looked up, his eyes crinkling at the corners in that way she found utterly sexy. He'd been a little odd with her earlier—distant—but now he seemed more himself, thankfully. "I came home early and Lish wanted help picking out a dress."

"Not like you were here to help," his niece added with mock disappointment. "Uncle Jake says I can have whatever I want." There was a glint in her gaze that gave Audrey pause. The kid had something on her mind, and Audrey knew what it was.

"I don't doubt that." Jake loved the girl as if she were his own, and spoiled her twice as much. "Have you found anything yet?"

"One or two," Alisha replied with a shrug. "Nothing I'm in love with."

Audrey sat down at the table and pulled a magazine from the pile. To be honest, she had fallen willing victim to the bridal scene herself. She'd found her dress in a magazine just before Christmas and a local shop that had it in stock. "How was school?"

Out of the corner of her eye, she caught Jake sending her a sideways glance, but she kept her attention on Alisha, who was still flipping through the magazine.

Another shrug. "Everyone was talking about the body they found back the Falls."

"Yeah? What were they saying?"

The girl met her gaze. "That it's Tala. That someone killed her." Her wide eyes brimmed with tears, but they didn't fall. She was a lot like her great-grandmother, Gracie, who would have rather swallowed glass than let anyone see her cry.

Audrey would have reached out for Alisha's hand, but Jake beat her to it. His niece squeezed his fingers but looked at Audrey. "Have you talked to Neve?"

She shook her head. "Not today, no."

As if summoned, Neve's car pulled into the drive at that moment. Jake's expression turned grim as he looked out the window. "My dar, I think you'd best put some steel in your spine." It was something Gracie used to say when she thought someone needed to prepare for the worst.

Audrey answered the door when Neve knocked so she didn't have to see the expression on Alisha's face. When she saw Neve's she knew the news was as bad as they feared.

"Alisha's here," she said in a low voice.

Neve nodded. "I was hoping she might be. Can I come in?" And then, when Audrey stepped back to let her inside, she asked, "Is it okay if I tell her?"

"She's going to have questions."

"I'll tell her all I can."

"Then sure." Really, if the choices were for her to hear it right from Neve, or at school the next day, she'd rather have Alisha informed. It was never easy finding out a friend was dead, let alone murdered. Unfortunately, that would be something Audrey and Alisha now had in common.

Neve shrugged out of her blazer as she walked into the kitchen. Alisha watched her with an anxious gaze. "Was it Tala they found?" she blurted.

Jake turned his head so that all three of them stared at Neve. She draped her jacket over the back of a chair and sat down next to Alisha. "I'm sorry to say it was, honey."

Audrey watched as the girl dug her nails into her palms but was otherwise still. "How did she die?"

Neve cleared her throat. "She was stabbed."

Alisha's jaw tightened. "Did...did animals get her?"

Jesus, Audrey thought. Was that how Alisha had been picturing her friend these past few months? Eaten by animals? She supposed there were worse things that could have happened.

A gentle smile softened Neve's features. "No."

Alisha nodded stiffly. "Good. Does Luke know?"

"Not that I know of. I just came from talking to her parents."

"Oh." The teenager didn't seem to know what to do with that information, probably because the idea of the kind of pain that came with losing a child was just outside her imagination. It was outside Audrey's too, for the most part.

"Alisha, can I ask you a couple of questions about Tala?" Neve asked.

Alisha looked to her uncle first, and when he nodded, she

glanced at Audrey. "Do you want us to leave the room?" Audrey asked her.

She shook her head. "No."

"I'll put the kettle on." It was what you did when people came calling, or there was a tragedy. Tea was the universal balm for emotional upheaval.

"You've been friends with Tala for a few months, yeah?" Neve asked. Audrey smiled at her use of present tense. Just because someone was gone didn't mean what you felt for them stopped. God knew she sometimes wished it did.

"Yeah. She wasn't hanging out with Kendra and Lucy as much as she used to."

"Do you know why?"

"Kendra used to date Luke. I think Tala was uncomfortable with that."

"Because Tala was dating Luke?"

Alisha nodded. "Kendra was always bringing up things from when Luke and her were together. She'd say, 'Remember that time…?' and it would be something stupid that none of the rest of us knew about. And she'd always comment on things that he liked."

Audrey and Neve shared a glance. "Letting Tala know she got there first."

Alisha frowned. "Yeah, well Tala didn't like it. She was insecure about Kendra. I don't know why. Tala was way prettier than her. Nicer too."

The kettle whistled, so Audrey quickly got cups, milk, and sugar out and dumped some loose leaves in Gracie's old teapot. Then she set it all on the table. Neve waited until she sat down to continue with her questions. "Luke told me that he and Tala broke up just before she died. Is that true?"

Wide blue eyes lifted to meet Neve's gaze. "She didn't just die. She didn't have a stroke. She was murdered."

Neve's serene expression never wavered. "Would it make you feel better if I used that word instead?"

Alisha seemed to think about it, then reluctantly shook her head. "No." She dumped sugar into her cup. "Yeah, they broke up a day or two before. Luke was a mess. He wouldn't talk to anyone on the ride home from school. I thought he was going to cry." She looked like this was something that personally offended her. "I couldn't believe Tala had done that to *him*."

Audrey was very careful not to react, but it was obvious from her tone and body language that Alisha thought highly of Luke—maybe too highly.

"Did the breakup have anything to do with the fact that Tala was transgender?"

Jake set down his cup. "She was what?"

Neve barely glanced at him. "Transgender."

"Really?" He turned to Audrey.

She shrugged. "It's the first I've heard of it." She thought about the tall, lithe Filipina girl Alisha had brought to the house on several occasions and couldn't come up with one single thing that might have outed her as trans. In the grand scheme, it didn't matter at all. However, in a murder investigation it mattered *a lot*.

Neve was still focused on Alisha, whose round cheeks had gone pink. "Did Luke know?"

Alisha hesitated, then nodded. "He did. It freaked him out at first, but he liked her and he said it didn't matter."

"So why did they break up? Was one of them seeing someone else?"

"I don't know. Tala was supposed to call me that night, but…she didn't." A single tear slipped from Alisha's eye, but she quickly brushed it away. Audrey wanted to go to her and hug her, but she stayed where she was—holding Jake's hand under the table as they watched his niece go through something neither one of them could fix.

"I do know that Tala was worried about sex," Alisha offered. She turned to Audrey. "She had that stuff—what do you call it when you hate your body?"

"Body dysmorphia," Audrey supplied. "It's when someone is obsessed with what they perceive as flaws in their own appearance."

The girl nodded. "Tala hated her body. I thought she looked amazing, but she can't—couldn't—get surgery for another couple of years, or something, so she still had all her guy junk. She hated it."

"It's common," Audrey remarked. "Poor kid. Was she in therapy, Lish?"

"Yeah. I think she had to be. It was all part of eventually getting surgery."

"So, you don't know why they broke up?" Neve asked, drawing back the table's attention.

Alisha stared at her. "You think Luke killed her?"

Neve shook her head. "I didn't say that."

"You don't have to." Alisha flushed. "He didn't kill Tala because of her dick. He knew about it and he didn't care."

Jake's eyebrows rose, but he said nothing. Audrey realized then that her fiancé was someone who wouldn't feel the same way were he in that situation. Lucky for her she'd been born physically female, then. Then again, Audrey couldn't say she was such an open-minded individual that it wouldn't matter to her either. She supposed you could eventually get past it, if you loved the person enough, and you *wanted* to get past it.

"But he was angry that she broke up with him."

"You don't kill somebody because they tell you you're through," Alisha snapped. "Luke's not Bailey." And on that stunner, she shoved back her chair, got up, and stormed out of the room. A few moments later, a door slammed upstairs. She'd gone up to Jake's old room, where she slept when she spent the night.

"Wow," Neve said, reaching for her tea. "The kid makes a good dig." She didn't sound offended, but rather surprised.

Audrey was surprised too. Bailey had been Alisha's best friend. Alisha stood by her through the entire ordeal after Bailey killed Maggie, who had been both her abuser and girlfriend, for lack of a better term. That she would use Bailey's name to make such a callous remark spoke as to how much she thought of Luke.

Jake looked impressed. "I didn't think she had it in her." And then, "Sorry about that."

Neve waved a hand. "Clearly she's not who I should talk to if I want dirt on Luke." She glanced at Audrey. "Shit. I just realized. Isn't he your cousin or something?"

"Yeah, on Mum's side. I don't really know the kid—and I'd

be the last person to get my nose out of joint if you thought he killed that girl. Do you really think he did?"

She leaned over the table, clutching her cup in both hands. "Whoever killed this girl did so with a lot of rage—the kind that's personal."

Audrey nodded. "Genital mutilation?"

"Fuck around," Jake growled. "Do we really need to know?"

Last fall Jake had found the body of a biker who had been shot. Before that, he waited on the beach with Maggie's corpse until the cops arrived. She wouldn't have thought of him as spleeny. But then, all men seemed to get that way as soon as they knew a penis was in jeopardy.

"I can't give details," Neve said. "In your professional opinion, why would the parents neglect to tell me their daughter was transgender? Why didn't anyone think it was important to give that information to the police?"

"I would imagine it's because they were trying to be considerate of Tala. If she had been born a biological female, no one would think to mention that to you. Since Tala was a girl in every way but her physicality, her family and friends thought of her and treated her as a girl."

Neve seemed to consider this. "It still pisses me off."

"There are a lot of bubbas in this area who would be pissed off to discover that a girl wasn't what they thought she was," Jake commented. "If Tala was dating someone else, could be he wasn't as understanding as Luke."

It was obvious from her expression that Neve had already thought of that.

"What did her parents say?" Audrey asked.

"That they moved here for a fresh start. Tala started hormones when they lived in Bangor, and apparently was bullied incessantly, which led to a suicide attempt. Her parents thought bringing her to a new town where no one knew her history would be the best thing for her."

"So they brought her to Edgeport?" Jake lifted his cup and shook his head. "They were *so* wrong."

CHAPTER THREE

When the office administrator for Eastrock High School called Audrey the next morning asking if she could come by for a meeting with the principal, she thought maybe Alisha had gotten into trouble, but then she reminded herself that Yancy, the girl's mother, or Jake would get calls before anyone reached out to her. She was the third emergency contact on Alisha's list.

So she had no idea what the school wanted with her when she walked into the office at two thirty that afternoon. But she wondered if it had anything to do with Tala Lewis and the news van circling the property.

EHS had been home to some of the best and worst moments of her post–juvenile delinquent life. There had been the occasional trip to the office for fighting; she'd be expelled now for that kind of stuff, but back then it had been time in the office, detention, or a day's suspension. She probably would have gotten in a lot more trouble if she hadn't established herself as an overachiever. She'd understood that being considered academically superior and a hard worker was what would get her out of Edgeport—and she *needed* to get out of Maine. She needed to go somewhere far away where no one knew about her past. Where she could reinvent herself as whoever she wanted to be.

Kind of like Tala Lewis.

A young woman—whom Audrey didn't recognize—smiled as she approached the front desk. "Dr. Harte?" she asked.

"Yes," Audrey replied, a little surprised that the woman knew her. At one time she'd believed herself notorious enough that everyone up and down the shore knew who she was. When had that changed?

"I'm Tilly," the woman said. "Have a seat. I'll let Principal Welton know you're here."

Audrey walked over to the waiting area, but she didn't sit. Instead, she looked the pictures hanging on the wall—various awards won by the school and its students, mentions of alumni in newspapers. Should she be put out that there was nothing about her that she could see? She'd had her own TV show at one time, when she lived in LA. Surely that was worth a mention? There was a grainy old photo of her younger brother, David, on stage as Danny in *Grease* from his senior year, but nothing about her.

Then again, she didn't see anything about Jake or Neve up there either, so she was in good company, she supposed. Her brother had always inspired adoration in those who knew him, so it was no surprise that he was displayed so prominently.

"Dr. Harte? Please come in."

Audrey turned. She hadn't met Beverly Welton before this, but she'd seen her around the area—the combined towns of Edgeport, Ryme, and Eastrock, while fairly large in area, were not that big in population. Eastrock was the largest, and still everyone in it pretty much knew everyone else. The populace had been talking about the new principal, who moved to town when her predecessor had a heart attack. She was a good-looking woman—and so was her wife. There were times when Audrey questioned her own decision to remain in a place that thought lesbians were exotic. But Edgeport was where Jake was, where her family was, and she felt it was where her future was, as much as she hated to admit it.

She shook hands with the woman before following her into the office. They weren't alone. Already there was Nurse Taylor, who was sister to Edgeport treasure Binky, and who had been at the school since Audrey went there almost two decades earlier; a man Audrey didn't recognize; and Micheline Poirier, with whom Audrey had gone to school and who had gone on to become the school guidance counselor.

"You haven't met Mr. Robson," Principal Welton said. "He's with the school board. Please, sit."

Audrey said hello to them all and took the empty seat next to Micheline. She didn't like being the only one in a group who didn't know what was going on, but she put on her professional face and forced herself to wait patiently for the principal to explain.

"Dr. Harte, your background is in juvenile psychology, yes?" Welton asked, leaning her forearms on the top of her desk.

"My focus has always been on forensic juvenile psychology, but I have worked with kids who weren't criminals."

"And you have also worked with children who may have witness to or been affected by a crime?"

Audrey thought she saw where this was going. "Yes." She didn't elaborate.

Robson shifted in his seat. "You are no doubt aware that police found the body of Tala Lewis?"

"I am."

"You are good friends with Detective Neve Graham, are you not?" That was from Nurse Taylor.

Audrey wasn't certain she'd call her friendship with Neve "good" or close, but as far as friends went, Neve was one of the few she had. "Complicated" was probably a better answer, but then that applied to pretty much all of Audrey's relationships. "Yes."

"Then you probably know she thinks someone murdered the girl."

Audrey arched a brow at her tone—like there was some question as to Neve's judgment. This was beginning to feel more like testimony than a conversation. "Multiple stab wounds are usually an indication of foul play, yeah."

The old girl's face paled. She looked away.

Welton cleared her throat. "I'd like to employ your services as a therapist, Dr. Harte. Would you be interested in spending a few days here over the next week or two to talk to our students as they attempt to work though this tragic event?"

"I haven't actually done much work in grief counseling," Audrey revealed. "I'm not sure I can provide what you want."

The principal smiled. "What we want is someone to help our students process what has happened to their classmate and their feelings about it. They may have questions as to why someone would do such a thing, and I—*we*—believe you are more qualified than any of us to aid in that process and answer those questions."

And if Audrey was the one talking to the kids, the faculty wouldn't have to answer questions that made them uncomfortable. It was a good opportunity to do her job and get to know the teens of the area. And hey, if she could help even one or two who were ignorant about gender fluidity find tolerance and understanding, she'd consider her job done.

"I can do that," she told the small group staring at her. "But if I enter into a professional relationship with any of these students, everything they tell me is protected by doctor-patient privilege. You won't be privy to any of it unless I think one of them is a danger to themselves or others."

Nurse Taylor made a small noise that let Audrey know *exactly* what she thought of that. Principal Welton inclined her head. "Of course. Our first and foremost concern is the children."

Audrey nodded, unsure of whether she quite believed that. She told them her hourly rate and watched as Robson and Welton exchanged glances. She was prepared to negotiate, but not much. Her time was her time. When Robson nodded, the principal smiled triumphantly. "Excellent. Let's start with twenty hours a week for the next two weeks and see how it goes, shall we? Are you fine with submitting a bill for reimbursement?"

She said she was, and that was it. She had a therapy gig. Earlier in the year she'd gotten her license to practice in Maine and began brushing up on her clinical skills. When she worked with Angeline, a lot of her time had been spent researching and doing interviews. It was a lot easier to just sit there and ask questions when you didn't have to offer something in return. Lately, however, she'd realized she wanted to do more. This was a good opportunity to dust off those skills.

With everything agreed upon for the time being, Audrey got up, shook hands with everyone—even crotchety old Nurse Taylor—and left the office. It was a few minutes before school let out, and a beautiful day, so she waited out front for Alisha. Final bell rang and there was nothing, and then the doors burst open and kids spilled out like bees over a hive.

When Alisha finally came out, she was with a tall, dark-haired boy Audrey recognized as Luke Pelletier. They were followed by three boys whom she didn't recognize, but whose parents she probably knew.

"Hey, Luke," one of them called. "Are you a faggot if your girlfriend has a dick?"

Oh, Jesus. People said teenage girls were mean, but boys were just bad.

Luke said nothing, but Alisha's face flushed red. To Audrey's surprise, she kept her mouth shut. Audrey didn't like that. Alisha stood up for her friends. If she was quiet, it meant she was intimidated.

Audrey started walking toward them.

"Hey, did you kill her because she wouldn't suck your dick, or because she wouldn't let you suck hers?" another of the boys asked, then laughed at his own brilliance.

"Did you kill the last person who refused to suck yours?" Audrey asked.

Alisha and Luke came to a stop, the boys behind them too. They all stared at her.

"Who the fuck are you?" the boy demanded, all zits and frown.

One of his buddies elbowed him. "That's Audrey Harte. She killed Clint Jones way back."

Way back? Audrey arched a brow. It hadn't been *that* fucking long ago. She looked each one of the boys in the eye. "And it wasn't because he wouldn't suck my dick." Then, to Alisha and Luke, she said, "Let's go."

Luke didn't protest. He didn't say anything, just followed Audrey to her car. Alisha smiled at her. "Thanks for that. T hey're on our bus."

Audrey nodded. Sometimes being a murderer had its perks, but she wasn't going to say that in front of Luke Pelletier, because if she called someone guilty based on looks alone, she'd have the kid in jail already.

"I'm surprised you didn't drop me off first," Alisha commented as they pulled out of the Pelletiers' driveway.

"He's your friend," Audrey replied. "I guess he's family, but I don't know the kid. I figured he'd be more comfortable if you were along for the ride."

Right. His comfort, that was what Audrey had been thinking about. "You could have just dropped both of us at my place. Mom would have driven him home later."

"Your mother's at work."

Alisha rolled her eyes. "He just found out his girlfriend—my friend—was murdered. Boning each other isn't exactly high on either of our lists."

"Boning is the least of it. He's a suspect, Lish. You think your mother would appreciate me leaving you alone with a suspected killer?"

"I'm alone with an actual killer all the time. Like, right now, for instance."

Audrey didn't take her eyes off the road, but Alisha saw her eyebrow twitch. "First Bailey, now me, huh? You must really like this kid, to take swings at two people who care about you."

Her tone was so calm, so understanding that Alisha immediately regretted her remark. Uncle Jake told her once that she shouldn't get into a pissing contest with a skunk. At the time she hadn't understood what he meant; now she thought she might. Audrey was the last person she should mouth off to—or try to manipulate in any way. It was just going to come back and bite her on the ass.

"He's my friend. I've known him since kindergarten."

"And that makes him incapable of murder?"

"No. Who he is makes him incapable of it. He can't even kill a spider."

"Everyone's capable of murder given the right circumstances."

"No, Audrey, they're really not." She was getting pissed off now. "I know you and Uncle Jake—even my mom—probably think that's some kind of defect, but there are some people in the world who are actually incapable of killing another person. They're called normal."

Audrey gave a snort of laughter. "Yeah, you like him all right."

Alisha flopped back against the passenger seat and stared out the window. "You are so bent sometimes."

"Maybe, but I'm right, aren't I?" Audrey's voice was softer now. "You like him. *Really* like him."

She didn't know what to say, so she said nothing, which was the wrong thing where Audrey was concerned, because it was like she could read Alisha's mind most times. Maybe she could make sense of what Alisha was feeling.

She did like Luke, but she couldn't *like* him. That was the major rule of friendship—you didn't date your friend's ex-boyfriend. She didn't know if death changed the rules, but it didn't matter, because even if she did have a thing for Luke, he was still in love with Tala.

"He didn't kill her," she insisted.

"Okay," Audrey agreed after a pause.

"Are you going to help Neve find out who did? You figured out about Bailey, and Tori Scott, and you helped Mackenzie find her father."

"And got beaten up and shot, and practically caused my sister to miscarry. Not exactly incentives there, sweetie. Besides, Neve doesn't want my help. If she does, she'll have no problem asking for it."

"But you have to do something."

"I *am* doing something. I'm going to be spending a few days at the school in case any students need to talk about Tala and what happened."

A flicker of hope blossomed in Alisha's chest. "You can find out if anyone at school knows anything."

"Even if they do, what they tell me is protected—it can't be used in court."

Her hope evaporated and turned into something sharp and dark. "What fucking good are you, then?"

Audrey slammed on the brakes so hard, Alisha's seat belt snapped up against her, biting into her chest. They were stopped right in the middle of the road—not that there was any traffic at the moment.

"Okay, I know you're upset and that you've lost a friend, but don't you *ever* talk to me like that again, got it?"

Alisha opened her mouth to say something smart-ass, but all that came out was a sob. She burst into humiliating tears and buried her face in her hands. It was all so frustrating. Her friend was dead and no one seemed to care, and the few people who did care couldn't seem to see past Luke.

And she felt totally shitty about all of it.

A warm hand wrapped around the fist clenched in her lap as the car began moving again. It was almost as if Audrey were giving her strength through osmosis.

"I'm sorry," Alisha said, her voice thick with snot and tears. She grabbed a napkin out of the glove compartment to blow her nose.

"I know you are, my dar." It was a term of endearment her great-grandmother had used; her uncles and her mother used it as well, especially when talking to Alisha. It made her feel better hearing Audrey say it. "I wish I could make this better for you, but I can't. I wish I could fix it. Hell, I wish I could bring her back for you."

Alisha knew all of that. "They cut her up and left her out there all alone. She died in pain and afraid." Just the idea of it made her want to puke.

Audrey's grip on her hand tightened. "I know, sweetie. I know. It's a terrible, horrible thing, and I can't make sense of it either. From what little I know about Tala, she seemed to be a sweet girl who was liked by everyone who knew her."

"Not everyone," Alisha reminded her, turning her face toward the window. Her tears were gone—dried up by anger and her feelings of uselessness. If Audrey wouldn't look for Tala's killer, then Alisha was left with no choice—she'd have to look for the motherfucker herself.

CHAPTER FOUR

Ghe said *what?*" Jake's nostrils flared a bit as he turned toward her. They were in the kitchen, making dinner. He was wearing old jeans, a gray T-shirt, and suspenders. "Grandpa chic," his brother Lincoln called it. Audrey thought it was cute—on him.

"She said, 'What fucking good are you, then?' Seriously, it felt like someone punched me in the chest. Then it pissed me off." All she'd shown to Alisha was her anger, though. She'd never let the girl know how hurt she'd been by her tone and words. Alisha was a good kid, and she'd feel guilty enough about it later as it was.

Jake's jaw clenched. "I'm going to have a sit-down with that kid. It's one thing to mouth off at Neve, but not to you."

Audrey shrugged, trying to seem more over it than she honestly was. "She's got a crush on Luke. She's afraid he's going to get in trouble."

He set down the knife he'd been using to cut potatoes. "What would Gran say?"

Not fair of him to play the Gracie card. "She'd say it was no excuse."

He went back to slicing potatoes. "Lish has always been given a lot of freedom to speak her mind, but there's a difference between being frank and being an ass."

"She just found out her friend was murdered. Cut her some slack."

"I've been giving her plenty of slack for the last couple of months. She's not herself."

"Probably because she feels guilty for lusting after Tala's guy. She's a teenager—you remember how much that sucked."

"Yeah." He sighed and dumped the potato slices into a casserole dish along with butter and chopped garlic. "I do. I still want to have a talk with her."

"Wait a couple of days. You know she'll be over here sometime in the next twenty-four hours like nothing ever happened."

Jake nodded. "Speaking of messed-up teenagers, I saw you got a call from a lawyer's office. Did they set a court date for Bailey?"

"July twelfth. She's being tried as a juvenile, thank God."

"Was there any question? I mean, she's just barely seventeen."

"Apparently the prosecutor was throwing it around. I think he was trying to make a statement. Severity of the crime and all that."

"I'm glad it didn't stick. Poor kid's been through enough. I can't imagine what sort of mess Maggie made of her."

Maggie, Audrey's childhood best friend, accomplice in murder, and worst enemy. "Mess was the only thing Maggie knew."

She'd reconciled many of her feelings regarding Maggie. She might even go so far as to say she'd made peace with her.

Might.

"Never thought you'd be lackadaisical where she was concerned."

"Me neither. Maybe there's hope for me after all." She smiled when she said it.

"You want to chop onions or tomatoes?" he asked.

"I'll take the onions." They bothered his eyes way worse than hers.

Their domestic harmony was interrupted by a car pulling into the drive.

"Alisha or Neve?" Jake asked before turning to look.

Audrey listened. When a car door slammed she smiled triumphantly. "Neve."

He started walking toward the door. "I think you're right."

She was. A few moments later Neve walked in, again wearing her on-duty outfit of dark pants, white shirt, and blazer. She looked tired. "Hey there," she said. "Sorry to just show up like this, but I wanted your opinion on something—professionally."

Audrey washed her hands to get rid of the onion smell. "Okay."

"Do autopsy photos brother you?"

Wiping her hands on a towel, she shrugged. "They're never pleasant, but I'm pretty good at detaching. Let's go into the dining room."

In the next room, Neve sat down at the table and set a folder on top of it. "I hear you're going to be doing some work at the school."

Audrey joined her. "God, news travels fast in this place."

Neve smiled, revealing teeth that seemed impossibly white. They had to be veneers. "I stopped by to talk to Principal Welton and ran into Micheline. She told me." The smile faded a little. "Are you going to tell me if you hear anything criminal?"

"Not unless I think someone's in danger. You know the rules."

Neve sighed. "Yeah, I just don't like them. What if one of those kids did it? Are you going to protect them?"

Audrey met her direct gaze with one of her own. "I would have liked it if someone had protected me."

Neve looked as though she hadn't considered that. She probably hadn't. "Good point." She slid the file folder toward her. "As a forensic psychologist, tell me what kind of person you think did that."

After a deep breath, Audrey opened the file. There, in full color, was Tala Lewis's naked corpse on the autopsy table. She'd been cleaned up and her wounds were clearly visible. There were so many of them, mostly focused around her breasts, abdomen, and groin. Between her legs had gotten the worst of it.

"That's a lot of anger."

"Tell me about it. Charlotte found a piece of the blade—it broke off inside her. It takes a lot of strength to stab someone that many times."

"And rage. I'm no profiler, but from the damage done to the sexual organs, I'd say this person was really pissed off that Tala was transgender. But at the same time, they removed the very part of her that she herself longed to be rid of."

"Not like that, I don't imagine," Neve remarked dryly.

That went without saying. "Was there sexual assault?"

"No signs of it."

"That seems odd to me—that there was no assault—given the sexual nature of the stabbing."

"Maybe he couldn't get it up."

"Or it wasn't the point." Audrey looked at the body in the photo. Death eventually made monsters of everyone, even the beautiful. "They didn't touch her face."

"Not a mark. She had defensive wounds on her hands and arms, a contusion on the back of her skull, and bruising on her right shoulder and both thighs." At Audrey's questioning glance she continued, "Her attacker took her down and held her there. Knelt or sat on her legs. Put a hand on her shoulder for leverage."

"Or so they could get close. They wanted to watch her suffer."

"That's not the kind of thing a stranger does, unless it's a serial."

"This doesn't feel methodical enough to be a serial, unless he's new to it. Even then, it feels personal to me."

"Me too." Neve leaned forward. "What does it say to you when a killer leaves something in the victim's mouth?"

"Depends on what it is. But shoving something in a person's mouth is a way to silence them: literally gag them. I once studied a case of a kid who used to shove his victims' fingers in their own throats to show how they made him sick. What did they put in Tala's mouth?"

Neve lifted her chin. "Look at the last photo."

Audrey did. It took a second for her to realize what it was. She looked at Neve in horror.

"Her penis."

The last people to see Tala Lewis alive were Luke Pelletier, her family, and Kendra Granger. Tala had been a fairly popular girl by virtue of still being relatively new at the high school, and had many friends, but the one everyone seemed to agree had been her best friend was Kendra. If anyone knew why Tala was in the park the night she died, it was Kendra.

Neve and Vickie were heading over to Eastrock to interview the girl when Neve's cell rang. She took the call through the car's Bluetooth. "Graham. What's up?"

"Hey, Detective." It was Malcolm, another trooper on Neve's team working the murder investigation. "They found a glove in the parking lot at the top of the falls. It had blood on it. They're testing for a match against Tala Lewis now."

"Could you tell if the glove belonged to a man or a woman?"

"It was one of those knit ones that stretch."

"What color?"

"Gray."

So, still gender neutral. Might be Tala's. They didn't find gloves on the body, which was unusual given the time of year she'd been killed, but there had been wool fibers in the wounds on her hands. "You got photos?"

"Ay-huh. Sent them to you just a couple of seconds ago." As if on cue, Neve's phone buzzed with a notification.

"Great. Any luck finding the knife?"

"None. I'm thinking the killer took it with him. We've been through the entire park—even the river."

"Keep looking. It might have gotten caught up in meltwater." It might have been two days since they'd found the body, but she'd been out there a little over two months. They'd had flooding lately too. If the killer had tossed the knife, it could be in the ocean by now, or somewhere along the miles of river edge.

Or, it could be caught up on a rock, just waiting to be found. Regardless, it would be pretty clean by now, but there could still be identifying marks. They had lots of area to cover before giving up the search on the girl's personal items.

"Will do. Anything else?"

"Talk to the folks who live along that road. Maybe one of them will remember something from the night Tala disappeared." According to Annette, it seemed the girl had been murdered the same night. Annette based this on the condition—and contents—of the stomach and digestive tract, and the amount of microbial activity before the body froze and after it started to thaw.

"On my way. Catch you back later."

Neve disconnected. "What are you looking at?" she asked Vickie after a quick sideways glance.

"Kendra Granger's Twitter feed." Vickie swiped the screen of her phone. "The day we confirmed it was Tala Lewis, she posted, 'Too sad 4 words. Good-bye, Tala. You'll always be my best friend' and then that arrow-three thing that makes a heart."

"The less-than sign," Neve corrected before she could stop herself. "Any responses?"

"Yeah. Mostly dramatic outpourings of love and support, but there are a few nasty ones—stuff like how Tala deserved to die, calling her a faggot."

"Get some screen shots." Even though tech could document it all with no problem, Neve liked to have as much primary information as possible. "What about Tala's account?"

"Oh, that's blown up. Lots of people leaving memories and condolences, and of course, the assholes coming out of the woodwork to bash her. I hope her family hasn't seen it. I've grabbed copies of those for you too."

"Thanks. Make note of the names and accounts of all the users who posted something—good or bad. The replies too. T he killer might have trouble keeping his mouth shut."

"It's mostly just kids."

"Kids are just as capable of killing as adults." Didn't she know it.

"Right. Sorry. You really think this is a hate crime?"

"There was a lot of hate involved; whether it was based on Tala's gender, I don't know. I just know we can't ignore it."

"The parents couldn't tell you anything?"

Neve shook her head. "They hadn't told anyone about Tala's transitioning, and Tala hadn't told them about any bullying. In fact, as far as they were concerned, their daughter was finally happy with who she was becoming, and was living a life like any other normal teenage girl."

"Did they actually say 'normal'?"

"Yeah. I think the Lewises were having a harder time accepting the change than they even know."

"It must be hard. You have a baby, it's a boy and you think of it that way, and then, fifteen, sixteen years in, the kid says you've had it all wrong."

"It usually comes to light well before the teens, I think." She'd been doing a lot of reading on the subject, and watching videos, so she could better understand what Tala had been going through. From what she'd seen and read, transgender kids had a hard time of it, not just with being accepted by others but accepting themselves as well. Alisha and Audrey had mentioned body dysmorphia, and Neve now had a better understanding of the disorder. It had to be a terrible thing. As a teen, she'd had her own bout of being uncomfortable in her own skin. As the only black girl for miles, she'd spent a lot of time wishing her skin were lighter, that her hair were different. There had even been times when she was angry at her mother for being black, and at her father for having married her. All she wanted was to be like the other girls at school.

And she had no doubt that was something she and Tala Lewis had in common. But Neve had made a few friends who accepted her, and it seemed Tala had as well.

The Granger house was located on one of the "good" streets in Eastrock. It was a neighborhood where centuries-old houses had been well maintained and updated over the years. It was where the "old" families lived, where the few doctors, lawyers, and business owners of the area tended to live. The lawns were perfect, and there were several cars in each of the paved drives. The Grangers lived on the north end of the street, in a big Victorian painted a warm, rosy peach with white trim.

Neve parked behind a red Range Rover and got out of the car, Vickie with her. When she knocked on the door, it was opened by a young man who looked to be in his early twenties—Kendra's brother, Kyle. He was a good-looking kid, if you liked frat-boy types. He was wearing low-slung jeans and a gray T-shirt with a faded logo on the front. His green gaze sparkled as it met Neve's, and his grin could only be described as flirtatious.

"Detective Graham," he drawled. "Been a while. You look good."

Neve almost rolled her eyes. In the background, she could hear a television blaring and male voices laughing. "Thanks, Kyle." She didn't return the compliment but noticed he smelled of beer. "Is your sister home?"

"Yeah."

When he didn't step back or invite her in, Neve raised a brow. "I'd like to speak to her."

"Sorry, but the parental units aren't here."

"What difference does that make?"

He looked a little smug. "You can't question her without our parents here."

He obviously watched too much TV. "She's not under arrest, Kyle. I just want to talk to her—and I can do that whether your parents are here or not. Now, are you going to let me in, or do I have to acknowledge that joint behind your ear?"

Horror stiffened Kyle's handsome features. His hand immediately shot up to his ear, where the thin rollie rested. His cheeks flushed, but he still managed to meet her gaze as he stepped back, waving his arm with a flourish. "Come on in."

With a satisfied smile, Neve stepped over the threshold into the foyer of the house. Inside, she could smell vanilla and furniture polish mixed with the subtle but distinctive scent of pot.

Kyle pulled out his phone and swiped his thumbs over the screen. A moment later, he looked up. "She'll be right down." Then he turned his back on them and walked away.

"How do you suppose he keeps his pants from falling down?" Vickie asked in a low whisper, leaning close to Neve's shoulder.

"Hangs them on his ego, I imagine." Neve glanced around at all the rich wood and gleaming floor. She felt like the hired help being made to stand there in the entry hall, and that was so not her comfort zone, so she walked farther into the house, her fellow trooper just a few steps behind. She was just about to enter a small, parlorlike room at the foot of the winding stairs when she heard what sounded like a small herd of wild animals approach. Two girls ran down the staircase toward her—Kendra and Lucy Villeneuve, whom Neve had previously nicknamed "Kendra's shadow" when first investigating Tala's disappearance. Talking to both girls would definitely save her a trip to Lucy's house.

Neve opened her mouth to speak, but Kendra cut her off. "Did you find him?" She demanded. "Did you arrest Randy Dyer?"

Alisha was watching a movie in the living room and eating store-bought pizza when the glare of headlights swept through the front window. It was too early for her mother to be home from work at the resort a little farther back their road, and the vehicle didn't sound like Jake's or Audrey's. Frowning, she left her pizza on the table and got up off the couch.

Since being abducted by a nut job last year, she was much more cautious than she used to be. The screen door was locked as well as the inside door, and she knew where the key to the gun cabinet was.

She peered out the window in the door. There, under the bright light of the porch, hands in his pockets, was Luke. Alisha's heart gave a surprised thump at the sight of him. What was he doing on her steps? Why had she decided to change into sweats and a T-shirt? And did she have pepperoni breath?

She opened the door. When his gaze fell on her, Luke smiled. Then she unlocked the second door and let him in.

"Hi," he said, stepping over the threshold.

"Hi." She so had pepperoni breath. "What's up?"

He shrugged. "I was going nuts at home, y'know? I had to get out, and you're the only person who hasn't started looking at me differently since they found Tala."

"Because she was trans? This place is full of small-minded assholes."

His gaze locked with hers. He had the prettiest blue eyes. "And because they think I killed her."

"That's just stupid. Anyone who knows you knows the truth."

Luke smiled, but it looked like it took effort. "Thanks. I'm sorry to just show up. Do you have people here?"

"No, it's just me. Mom's at work. You want some pizza?"

"Sure." He followed her as she went to grab him a plate. "I wasn't sure you'd be home. I thought maybe you'd gone to Kendra's."

Everyone knew the Grangers were out of town and that Kendra and her brother were having friends over. Alisha hadn't felt like going. To be honest, she was pissed. Kendra was supposed to have been Tala's best friend, so what the fuck was she doing partying two days after finding out Tala had been murdered?

"Didn't feel like it," she replied, taking a plate from the cupboard. "How about you?"

"Same. And you know what an asshole her brother is. He's friends with Tal's brother. I can't handle it right now."

"Right." She slapped a slice of pizza onto the plate and handed it to him. "Soda?"

"Sure. Kyle hit on her one night at Kendra's."

"Really?" Tala hadn't told her that.

Luke nodded. "I was there. He came on strong, but she just blew him off. Guess he's forgotten all about it now."

"Doubtful."

He looked her in the eye. "Do you think there's something wrong with me for liking her?"

Alisha swallowed. Part of her wanted to punch him for being stupid enough to ask that, but another part wanted to hug him. And another part...hurt. "No. I think you're just more...enlightened than most of the hillbillies around here." She handed him a can of soda from the fridge. "Let's go to the living room."

He followed after her. Alisha was very aware of him behind her, and of how small the room now seemed with him in it.

"What are you watching?"

"*Blade Runner*. Have you seen it?"

"Are you kidding? It's a classic. Play it up."

They sat together on the sofa and watched the rest of the movie, adding commentary where it seemed needed. When it came time for more pizza, Luke got up and got slices for both of them.

When the credits began to roll, he leaned back against the sofa, his body angled toward her. "You know, Tala never wanted to watch sci-fi movies."

"Why not?"

"She thought they made her seem boyish."

Alisha found that incredibly sad—and stupid. She shook her head. "I like sci-fi. Do I seem like a boy to you?"

"No," he replied, watching her intently. "You don't."

She swallowed, her heart tripping over itself in her chest. "Do you still miss her?"

Luke nodded. "Sure. Not like I did, though. When she first disappeared I was angry and hurt, y'know? Like, I took it personally. Then that started to fade away. Now, though, knowing someone killed her? It's different. I just feel really sad. And still pissed off, but not at her. She didn't deserve to die like that."

"No. She didn't. It feels weird, knowing I'll never talk to her again."

"Yeah. I wish I could, just so I could tell her I'm sorry for being such a jerk when she dumped me. She was right to do it, I know that now."

"Really?"

He took a drink of soda. "One night she came over to my place—my parents were out. We were going to...we were going to have sex. But, when I saw her naked..." He cleared his throat, still looking at the floor. "I couldn't do it. I mean, I literally *couldn't*." He lifted his gaze to hers. In the glow of the TV his cheeks were flushed, his eyes filled with shame.

It took Alisha a moment to totally understand what it was he was saying. Her own cheeks warmed. "You mean because she hadn't had surgery?"

Luke nodded. "As a person—as her friend—I didn't care how she'd been born, but as her boyfriend...Shit. I cared, Lish. I cared a lot and I'm an asshole for it."

She reached across the couch and wrapped her fingers around his wrist. "That doesn't make you an asshole." But poor Tala. She must have been crushed. She hated her body so much, and then to be rejected by her boyfriend...Alisha's heart broke for them both.

He hung his head. "I just wish I could have been *better* for her."

"You were the best you could be." God, she sounded like Audrey.

"Yeah, well, it wasn't good enough, was it?"

"If she weren't dead, would you ask me that question?"

Luke hesitated. His eyes widened. "No."

"And did you ever use her to get yourself off?"

He looked offended. "*No*. I've never done that with anyone."

Why did that fill her with such relief? "Did you ever think
of her as anything other than a girl?"

He gave an emphatic shake of his head. "No. Not even that
night. It was weird because in my heart I knew she was a girl,
but I just couldn't get past..." He flushed again, his features
tightening. "I couldn't touch her."

Alisha stared at him. "I don't know what to say to make you
feel better. Honestly, I get that it would be freaky. I don't know
how I would have handled it."

"Really?"

She nodded. "I'd like to think I'd be okay and all open-
minded, but it's not like I have much experience." She laughed
self-consciously.

He watched her for a moment—long enough to make her
uncomfortable. Then, he smiled. "Thanks for making me feel
better."

She shrugged. "I didn't do anything."

"Yeah, you did. You always make everything better. It's like
your superpower, or something."

"Right," she scoffed.

"Seriously, you're awesome."

"So awesome I'm single." She instantly felt stupid for saying it. He was staring at her now and her chest was so tight she could barely breathe.

"Any guy would be lucky to have you."

Alisha forced a smile, because there was only one guy she wanted at that moment, and she was ashamed of herself for it. "Want to watch another movie?" she asked.

He rose to his feet. "Let's go for a drive."

At that moment she heard Audrey's voice in the back of her head: *Everyone's capable of murder given the right circumstances.*

Not Luke. Alisha knew deep in her heart that Luke wasn't capable of killing someone—not even if his own life depended on it. He wasn't like Audrey, or Uncle Jake, or even her. Which was why she turned off the TV and went with him. He needed someone to watch his back.

CHAPTER FIVE

Audrey didn't normally go to Gracie's on Friday night, but as the weather got nicer and tourists began rolling through town, Jake started spending more and more time at the tavern. If she wanted to see her fiancé, she had to occasionally polish a stool at the bar with her butt.

The parking lot was full and the old house that had had several additions built onto it over the years was full of people—only a couple of tables were open, and the place vibrated with music and conversation. Almost a year ago, Audrey had walked into this place and found her father passed out in the corner; now he helped out working behind the bar when Jake needed him. More important, he was sober.

John Harte—Rusty because of his once-ginger hair—set a plate of onion rings on the bar in front of her. They were her favorite and he knew it.

"I had dinner," she told him. She'd been trying to watch her calories the last few months since clothes had started to feel tight after Christmas. They were feeling tight again. Jake simply fed her too well.

He shrugged and snatched one of the rings off the plate and took a bite. "So did I. You want another drink?"

It was only cola, so she nodded and helped herself to the fried perfection in front of her. Willpower only went so far.

"Talked to your sister lately?"

Audrey sighed. There had been family drama—to put it mildly—around Thanksgiving that made things a little strained between her and her big sister, Jessica. They were working things out, but their parents worried because the girls had been estranged after Audrey killed Clint. They didn't want that to happen again. Audrey tried to tell them it was okay— she didn't want her father having another heart attack—but they still fussed.

"I called her before I came here," she told him. "Spoke to the girls too. Mackenzie is coming to visit on Memorial Day weekend."

"The girls will be excited." Isabelle and Olivia, Jessica's daughters, were always thrilled when their big sister came to visit.

Audrey took another onion ring. "She's a great kid."

"Speaking of great kids, you're going to stay out of this murder business, right?"

She swallowed and wiped her greasy fingers on a napkin. "T he school's hired me to talk to students having a hard time with it."

Her father shook his shaggy head. He needed a haircut. "Jesus H. Christ. And you said yes, didn't you?"

She nodded. "Well, yeah."

"Of course you did. I knew you wouldn't be able to stay out

of it. I told your mother you'd be neck-deep in it before we knew it."

"Dad." She stared at him, silently willing his heart to stay calm and not freak out. "I'm just counseling kids."

"Mm. Right. We'll see how long it stays that way. One of them will say something that gets that head of yours churning, and then you'll start sticking your face in where it doesn't belong and that Graham girl will let you."

"Hey, Rusty," called Binky Taylor, town institution and jovial drunk, from a few stools down. "Gimme a beer, will ya?"

Her father hesitated but then turned away, grumbling. Audrey sighed in relief. Her father was always giving her a hard time for being nosy. He blamed it on the Pelletier side of the family—her mother's side—but it seemed to Audrey that he had his own share of busybodiness. Not like he could keep his face out of her business.

A commotion in the stage area of the building made her turn her head. Randy Dyer and some of his friends were being rowdy, laughing and shoving one another around. Lincoln, Jake's brother, who was waiting tables in that area, approached them with a frown on his face. Recently Linc had been trying to get his act together—to the point where Jake had hired him back part time at Gracie's. In January he'd started taking hospitality courses at the local community college, and just a few weeks ago he'd cut his trademark rock-star hair. Apparently he'd stopped smoking hash too. Audrey had to wonder how much of this transformation was owed to his career goals and how much thanks went to his girlfriend, Marnie. She was a little older than Lincoln, divorced, and really seemed to have her act together.

Audrey watched as Randy gave Lincoln a shove. Stupid kid. You'd think he'd know better than to push a Tripp. Lincoln actually slapped the kid upside the head, grabbed his arm, twisted it behind his back, and steered him toward the exit. Randy's struggles only made Linc apply more pressure. She could hear the kid's protests of pain over the southern rock playing. Not her favorite music, but it seemed to make people drink.

Suddenly, Jake was there. He'd been in the office out back but had obviously seen the altercation on the security screens. Audrey watched him with a little smile on her face as he met his brother on his way back in from tossing Randy out. She loved it when he looked serious and badass. Loved the way his faded black tee pulled across his back, and the way his jeans hung on his hips. He was lean, but sinewy and deceptively strong. She wanted to walk up to him and bury her face in the hollow of his neck and take a deep breath.

"Jesus, get a room," her father growled.

She laughed. Jake turned his head at the sound, looking right at her. He flashed that smile that was for her alone as he walked toward her. "I didn't know you were going to be here," he said before kissing her.

She shrugged. "I was bored, so I thought I'd come down." She jerked her chin toward Lincoln. "What was that all about?"

"Drunk assholes. Dyer was shooting his mouth off about the Lewis girl, apparently."

Audrey tilted her head. "Really. What did he say?"

Her father leaned across the bar. "Told you."

She whipped her head toward him with a glare. "Stop eaves-dropping."

He shrugged and went back to wiping glasses.

"He accuse you of getting involved in the case?" Jake asked with a small smile.

"Of course." She saw the way he looked at her. "I'm not going to—if I can avoid it."

"Might as well ask the sun not to shine." Since he was still smiling, she didn't take offense.

"FIGHT!" The shout broke through the conversation and the music, pulling all attention toward the door. A small group of young men pushed their way to the exit.

"Fuck around," Jake said, his jaw tight as he followed after them. Audrey was hot on his heels.

"Stay here," she said to her father, who had started to follow. The only thing he loved as much as a drink was a fight, and if he jumped into the fray her mother would never forgive her, or Jake for letting it happen. Anne Harte treated her bull of a husband like he was made of china these days.

Outside, the gravel lot was full of cars, lit by two powerful lights on tall poles. There was one out back too. After Jake got jumped behind the place that fall, he'd decided to invest in better lighting.

In the middle of the lot Randy Dyer and Luke Pelletier were pounding on each other, and trying to stop the bloodshed was Alisha. Randy was older and bigger, but he was also drunker, and Luke was decidedly angrier, which made them fairly well matched.

Until Randy pulled a knife.

"Is that the one you used to kill Tala?" Alisha demanded.

Randy turned toward her. The sight of a blade in such close proximity to his niece was all Jake needed to be spurred into action. Audrey didn't even try to stop him. He moved too fast for her anyway. One second he was just a few feet ahead of her and the next he was behind Randy with one arm around his neck, the other restraining his knife hand.

Audrey saw the look on Alisha's face and moved to intercept her. Never mind that she'd gotten into a fight in this same parking lot not even a year ago—she wasn't going to let Alisha do something that might make her the victim of revenge at a later date. She caught the girl by the shoulder and pulled her back just as Neve's car pulled into the lot.

Luke's nose was bleeding, so Audrey gave him a tissue as Neve and Vickie approached them. Neve had her cop face on.

"What's going on?" She asked.

Neither Audrey nor Jake looked at the boys for explanation; they turned to Alisha. Her face was flushed, her jaw clenched and eyes glittering. Audrey knew the look. "What happened?" she asked the girl.

"We were going for a drive," she replied, nodding at Luke. "We stopped here because I wanted onion rings, and saw Randy. He started mouthing off at us."

"What about?" Neve asked.

Alisha glanced at her before dropping her gaze to the ground. "Tala."

"Who took the first swing?"

"I did," Luke admitted. "Randy said something to Alisha and I hit him."

"What did he say?"

Luke hung his head.

Jake tightened his hold around Randy's neck. "What did you say, asshole?"

Alisha sighed. "He said I must have a dick because that was the only kind of girl Luke liked. Then he grabbed me and asked if he could see it."

Someone in the gathered crowd laughed. A couple of some-ones. Neve shot a hard look in their direction before turning back to the situation. Audrey kept her gaze on Jake, who said something in Randy's ear that made the younger man blanch. Things hadn't turned out so well for the last person who threatened someone Jake cared about.

"I think you're coming with me, Randy," Neve said.

"I was defending myself," he said. "You can't fucking arrest me for that."

She nodded at the knife in his hand. "There's that."

"Switchblades aren't illegal anymore, Officer," he replied with a smirk.

Neve smirked back. "Unless you threaten someone with it, asshole. Plus, you assaulted Alisha, and I want to talk to you about the night you assaulted Tala Lewis."

That surprised him. In fact, he looked horrified. "I didn't do nothin' to that freak."

"That's not what I heard. Now, you want to come with us, or should I drive you home and do this in front of your father?"

Now Randy looked downright panicked. Everyone knew what a son of a bitch Teddy Dyer was. Audrey knew his younger brother Dwayne, who, while no peach, was known to be the best of the lot, and even then he drank too much, liked his drugs, and had more kids scattered around the countryside than there were wild blueberries.

"I'll go with you," he replied, grudgingly.

Neve smiled. "Thought so. Don't worry. I'll drive you home after." She turned to Vickie. "Help Mr. Dyer to the car, please." Then she turned to Audrey.

"What?" Audrey asked, reluctantly turning her attention away from Jake, who was watching Randy like he'd enjoy five minutes alone with him.

"You think he's dangerous?"

For a second, she thought Neve meant Jake. She shrugged. "He pulled a knife, and he looked to me like he was prepared to use it. Did he really assault Tala?"

"According to Kendra Granger, he did. By the way, she's probably going to talk to you at the school. I told her you'd be there."

Audrey met her gaze. "I'm not spying on these kids for you."

"I'm not asking you to do anything." Neve clapped her on the shoulder and began to walk away. "With your track record, I figure all I have to do is let you do your thing and eventually you'll piss the killer off enough that they'll come after you."

"Very funny," Audrey replied, but Neve was already gone.

"Do you own a lot of knives, Randy?" Neve asked. They were in the field office in Eastrock. She didn't want to be there. She wanted to be home with Gideon watching something on TV, drinking beer and fooling around, but instead, she was wasting her time with an ignorant yahoo who looked at her like she was dirt under his boot.

"Yeah," he replied. "So fucking what? It's not a crime."

"You own a lot of hunting knives?"

"I got a couple."

"Ever break one?"

He looked at her like he thought it was a stupid question. "No."

Not like she expected him to admit it. She sat down at the table across from him. The file with crime scene photos of Tala Lewis lay unopened in front of her. "Tell me about your relationship with Tala Lewis."

His belligerent expression didn't change. "We didn't have no relationship."

"No? Then tell me about your bullying of Tala Lewis."

Randy shrugged. "There's no law against telling someone what you think of them, is there?"

"Not unless it becomes harassment. I'd say you definitely harassed Tala. According to her friends you constantly confronted her in public."

"Him."

"Excuse me?"

"I confronted *him* in public."

"Tala Lewis was a girl. She identified as female."

He snorted. "You ever know a girl with a dick?"

"Yes, actually." Back when she worked in New York, she'd

met several. "Let me ask you this, Randy, why did you care if Tala had a penis or not?"

"Because that made him a guy, not a girl. And he was walking around pretending to be a girl. You know the fucking chink would use the girls' bathroom at school?"

"Yes, because she was a girl." *You fucking moron.* She didn't say that part out loud. Nor did she school him that Tala wasn't Chinese. "So you didn't like her because she was transgender and nonwhite."

"I didn't like *him* because he was a fucking freak."

"How did you find out Tala was trans, Randy?"

"What?" He actually looked surprised. "I heard."

Neve sat back in her chair with a little smile. "No, you didn't hear it. Nobody but her closest friends knew, and they didn't tell anyone. I think you found out another way, didn't you?"

He squirmed in his chair.

"I hear that you hit on Tala at a party. I think you made a play—maybe got handsy—and discovered for yourself that Tala's anatomy wasn't what you expected. She pushed you away but not before you realized the truth."

"I never touched her...him." His red face suggested otherwise. "And I didn't make a play."

"You did," Neve insisted. Instinct told her she was right on this one. "You grabbed her, or pressed up against her, and you realized something wasn't quite right."

Randy shook his head. "Nah."

"Then why did your friends all laugh when they found out Tala was trans? Not at her, but at *you*?"

The flush in his cheeks evaporated, leaving him pale. "They know?"

Neve nodded. "The whole town knows—or they soon will. You might as well tell me the truth." She watched him roll that around in his narrow little mind. This wasn't the first time she'd dealt with Randy. The first time, he'd used the word "nigger" in front of her. The second time, she arrested him for picking a fight with a Native American kid who hadn't done anything but be not-white. She couldn't stand the ignorant little bastard.

"Fine. I saw her around some, and ran into her at a party. I gave her a few drinks and a little smoke and then I made my play."

Funny how he switched to using "she" as a pronoun when he talked about assault. "So, what? You stuck your hand down her pants, rubbed up against her?"

He was blushing again. "I put my hand under her skirt. She tried to push me away, but I thought she was playing."

Neve's fists clenched. "Little clarification for you, asshat, when a girl pushes you away she doesn't want you."

A grimace contorted his narrow features. "Yeah, well, I didn't want her either. Not after grabbing a handful of dick."

"That's not what I heard. I heard you came sniffing around a few times, and it was only after she told you off that you started getting mean." She actually hadn't heard this, but based on what she knew about Randy, she figured she knew how it played out.

He didn't say anything, and Neve knew she was right.

"You didn't reject her. Tala rejected you."

Still nothing, but his jaw tightened. She watched the muscle in his cheek flex, and that was answer enough.

"Where were you the night of February seventeenth, Randy?"

Scowling, he looked up. "That was two months ago. I don't remember."

"It was a Friday, does that help?"

"I was probably with my friends. We go sledding a lot in the winter." By sledding he meant snowmobiling, not flying downhill on a toboggan. Neve shuddered to think of how drunk or stoned and reckless the bunch of them probably were when they tore around on the machines.

"So if I ask people on Park Road if they saw your old beater driving back toward the Falls that night, they're going to tell me no?"

He didn't hesitate. "I don't drive back there in the winter anymore. Got stuck too many times." He looked almost smug.

"Which one of your friends drives when you go back there, then?"

"Jimmy Dodsworth."

"So if I ask the folks on the road, will they have seen Jimmy's vehicle?"

This time, he paused. "Maybe. I don't know. I'm not his fucking keeper."

"Mm. I hear you thought Tala Lewis deserved to die."

He scowled at her. "Where'd you hear that?"

"Twitter." She showed him the screen shot of his—and a dozen other people's—tweets concerning the murder. "'It got what it deserved.' @RandyDyer_69 is you, isn't it? I mean, there's a photo of you on the profile page."

He shifted in his chair but managed to maintain his slouch. "Yeah, okay. I said that, but a lot of people said the same thing. You walk around pretending to be something you're not, you've got to be prepared to face the consequences, y'know?"

Neve folded her arms over her chest. "There are those who say race is determined by the father. My father is white. If I told you I was white, what would you say?"

Randy looked at her like it was a trick question.

Neve smiled tightly. "I identify as black—and you believe that because you see a black woman when you look at me. But I could call myself white, and you'd call me a liar, even though I can prove I'm half white. Tala Lewis identified as a girl, and you thought she was one until she stopped meeting your expectations of gender. You thinking she wasn't a girl doesn't make her less of one—and it sure as hell doesn't make you much of a person."

His scowl returned. "Hey—"

"You ever lose your temper, Randy?" She interrupted him, wanting to take advantage of his irritation.

"Doesn't everybody?"

"You like to fight."

He shrugged. "So?"

"Have you ever hurt anyone when you were angry?"

"Yeah, but I never stabbed nobody."

"I bet you wanted to, lover of knives that you are." She opened the file and slid it toward him. "Ever fantasize about doing something like this?"

His silence was more than answer enough. He stared at the photo of Tala's head and shoulders. There were stab wounds clearly visible, surrounded by bruising where the hilt of the knife had forcibly struck her flesh. Neve watched as he swallowed hard, never taking his gaze off the photo. He was pale, and his fingers shook, but he still reached out as though he wanted to touch the dead girl.

Neve pulled the file away and closed it. "You can go home now, Randy."

He looked surprised. "You're letting me go?"

Neve smiled as she stood. "I don't have anything to hold you on."

He also stood, frowning. "Not even the fight?"

"Nope." She could hold him, but she was more interested in what he'd do when she let him go. And then, of course, there was the obvious. "Oh, by the way, that girl you grabbed tonight? You know she's Jake Tripp's niece, right?"

Oh, the expression of panic on his face! For once Neve appreciated Jake's reputation. "She is?"

It was a small town, but Randy was at that age where he didn't pay too much attention to people younger than him, unless he thought they were hot. Alisha was a pretty girl, but maybe she wasn't his type—lucky for him. "Yeah. You might want to avoid Gracie's for a while. And him." At that moment, she actually appreciated Jake and what he was.

Then, after flashing Randy a sympathetic smile, she left him alone in the interview room. She was going the hell home.

CHAPTER SIX

Monday morning Audrey drove Alisha to school since it was also her first day of counseling. She had absolutely no idea what to expect but assumed that the brunt of students who came to see her were simply those taking advantage of being able to get out of class.

"I told Luke he should talk to you," Alisha informed her. "I don't know if he will, but..."

Audrey pulled into a parking spot. It was a beautiful day and she was suddenly filled with resentment for having to spend it inside the building. Funny how returning to her former high school could awaken those old feelings.

"I hope he does." Audrey gathered up her computer bag. "Want to do lunch together? Frank's is open." Fat Frank's was a local institution. A fast-food joint that was open seasonally from May till October, it had the best clams and lobster rolls in the area. It had been in business since the early seventies.

Alisha grinned. "Yeah! I'll meet you in the office."

"Sounds good. Spread the word that I'm totally not scary and I'll buy you ice cream."

As she got out of the car, Alisha laughed. "You are totally scary, but I'll do my best."

They approached the school together. Outside, kids lined the sidewalk that surrounded it. A couple of them were smoking, but the rest were simply standing around, slouching and talking. Alisha looked them over, like she was searching for someone.

"Luke is usually out here," she said. Then, to a group of guys standing near the entrance, she said, "Have you guys seen Luke?"

They looked uncomfortable. "He went inside," one replied. Audrey noticed the kid had a mullet. Was it 1985? Jesus, she hoped those things didn't come back into fashion.

"You're not exactly his type, Lish," another quipped, jabbing one of his buddies with an elbow. Obvious much?

Alisha narrowed her eyes. "I'm his friend, moron. That's something you wouldn't understand."

Audrey put her hand on the girl's arm. "Let's go inside." The boys were just being idiots, products of upbringing and peer pressure. They'd never let on if anything Alisha said to them actually made a difference. She might as well be talking to a row of porta-potties.

"I want to go by his locker," Alisha announced when they walked inside. Conversation buzzed in the corridors as groups of teenagers swarmed their lockers and classroom doors. "You don't have to come with me."

"I think I will, though. If you don't mind?"

Alisha shook her head. Audrey didn't say anything as she walked beside the girl. Luke Pelletier was her cousin, but more important, he meant something to Alisha. She wouldn't feel right going to work at the school without checking in on him, especially when she couldn't be certain if he was capable of murder. Alisha trusted in him, but the kid had backed the wrong horse before.

Audrey looked around as they walked. Her locker had been along this very hallway her senior year. The school had changed its colors since then. Back when she went there the lockers had been maroon, against gray walls. Now they were dark blue and the walls, while still gray, had white stenciled murals on them to brighten the place up. The scenes were all very sporty and academic, like some kind of cheerful propaganda.

They found Luke at his locker, surrounded by the three boys Audrey had witnessed harassing him the previous week. One of them gave Luke a hard shove, knocking him back. The row of lockers reverberated under the impact.

"Leave me the fuck alone!" Luke shouted.

The boys laughed. "You got no one to protect you now, *Perv*-ier. Where's your girlfriend and skank murderer when you need them?"

"Right here," Audrey said loudly, causing them to go very still. "And *skank*? Really? I've gotten worse insults from twelve-year-olds." It was true. She'd once interviewed an underage prostitute who called her some very colorful and inventive names.

The boys slowly turned to look at her. One of them looked belligerent, but the other two actually seemed vaguely nervous. She had to admit, she liked it. Just because her work centered on kids didn't mean she had to like every teenager that crossed her path. They were just as capable of being assholes as adults. The only difference was that kids could change and heal a lot easier than adults could.

"I'm not his girlfriend," Alisha said, her cheeks flushed.

"Oh, right. His girlfriend was a guy." The other two laughed at this.

Audrey stepped closer, leaning in and blocking him from the others because she had no desire to shame the kid in front of an audience. "You seem to be very hung up on that. Would you like to make an appointment with me to discuss whatever fears and concerns you have about your own sexuality?" Honestly, she was mostly serious. It was the same kid who was preoccupied with cock sucking the other day. "It will be confidential, I promise."

He swallowed as she backed away. She held his gaze. "Luke, Alisha, let's go."

Luke didn't need to be told twice; he fell into step beside them. They walked him to his homeroom before continuing on to Alisha's. He didn't say anything to them, just walked through the door, his head down. Not exactly polite, but given his situation, Audrey supposed she could give him a pass.

Alisha looked a little upset, though. "Thanks for defending Luke again."

Audrey shrugged. "I've never been big on bullies. I'll see you at lunch, kiddo."

She walked into the office just as the first bell rang. Within minutes, she was set up in a small room with a large overstuffed chair, love seat, and coffee table in it. There was even a window, letting in bright sunshine, and a bookcase full of old year-books. It all looked very inviting. Someone had even thought to put a box of tissues on the table.

"Is it okay?"

She turned. Micheline stood in the doorway, looking slightly anxious. Her eyes were bright and her round cheeks slightly flushed. "I wasn't sure what kind of setup you'd prefer, but I thought this would at least make the kids—and you—more comfortable."

Audrey smiled. "It's perfect, thanks. Miss White would never have thought of something like this."

The shorter woman smiled at the mention of their old guidance counselor. "Miss White would have been ticked off that the school hadn't asked her to do it. I'm happy to let someone with your training handle this awful situation. If you need anything else, let me know."

"I will, and thanks again."

Micheline smiled. "Your appointments are in a shared calendar that I just e-mailed to you. They can be made by the front desk, or you can make them yourself. Just make sure you put them in the calendar so the student doesn't get accused of skipping."

"Oh, fabulous. Thanks so much."

"Good luck." Micheline walked away without shutting the door. Audrey didn't mind—an open door was always more inviting than a closed one. After a visit from both Principal Welton and Vice Principal Robert Tyson to make sure everything was to her liking, she sat down in the chair and pulled out her phone to access the calendar Micheline had sent. She didn't have anything scheduled for first period, but her second-period appointment was Kendra Granger. Lucy Villeneuve was scheduled for Tuesday afternoon. She was alternating mornings and afternoons throughout the week so she could continue to work on Grace Ridge and wedding plans.

As the second bell for first period rang, Audrey's phone pinged. First period now had an appointment: Jamie Allen. She looked up when she spied someone in the doorway. Well, she'd be damned.

It was the kid who'd been picking on Luke at his locker. His lean cheeks were pale, making the freckles there all the more prominent.

"Hi," she said. "Jamie?"

He didn't move from the doorway. "Did you mean what you said, that whatever we talk about is private?"

She nodded. "Yeah. It is. Do you want to come in?"

He crossed the threshold and closed the door.

Audrey had just finished her notes on the not-so-surprisingly troubled Jamie Allen—bisexual and ashamed of it, youngest child of an unpredictable alcoholic and his exhausted wife—when Kendra Granger arrived for her session. She and Jamie had discussed his curiosity about Tala Lewis, so Audrey considered their talk to have fallen within the parameters set by the school board. She'd made another appointment for him the following Monday, and promised to e-mail him a list of books he might find helpful, since he insisted that his father would never allow him to go to a therapist on a regular basis. She also gave him her business card and the number of the local crisis line. It was all she could do. He didn't know what he was feeling, but he knew it really pissed him off that Luke and Tala had dated, and he wasn't sure which one of them he was more jealous of. He was just angry that he couldn't be himself and angry that Tala had been. Angry that he wasn't what his father wanted him to be. Angry that his father was a drunk—angry at everything.

Kendra, on the other hand, didn't look angry at all. She looked perfect. Her skin was flawless and so pale it had to be a bitch to find foundation to match—not that she needed it. Her eyes were a bright blue; her hair was a glossy dark brown. She wore jeans, boots, and a long-sleeve top, and looked as though she'd just stepped out of the pages of a teenage fashion magazine.

"Are you Dr. Harte?" she asked from the door.

Audrey smiled as she stood. "I am. Come in, Kendra."

The girl walked in, clutching the strap of her purse, and sat down on the love seat. "You don't look old enough to be a doctor."

"Thank you, but I assure you I am." Audrey went to the door and closed it before sitting down again.

The girl moved her purse to the other side of the couch, as though saving that seat for a friend. "My mother made this appointment for me. I'm not really sure what I'm supposed to talk about."

"Well, the school set this up so that anyone upset by Tala's death could discuss it."

"With you."

"Yes." Audrey tilted her head. "I get the feeling you think I was the wrong choice."

The girl shrugged and looked away. "No offense, but didn't you kill somebody once? Why would I want to talk about my friend who was murdered with someone who did the same thing?"

It wasn't as though Audrey hadn't considered this sort of response from some of the students. She'd lived with what she'd done to Clint for the past twenty years. But she was a little surprised to have it delivered to her in such a matter-of-fact tone. Kendra wasn't afraid of her, just wary.

"You don't have to discuss this with me at all," Audrey informed her. "I can't make you talk to me, and even if I could I have no desire to do that. But I also know what it's like to have had a friend killed, and what it's like to have to say good-bye knowing there are so many things I didn't get to say."

Kendra regarded her for a moment, as though weighing that against the crime that Audrey had committed. "What good is talking going to do? It can't bring her back."

"No," Audrey agreed. "But it might make you feel better. Do you want to give it a try? Or do you want to just go back to class?" The nosy side of her protested at this. She wanted to know what Kendra knew about Tala, her life, and her death. But she couldn't force Kendra to confide in her or to trust her.

"I don't see how it will make me feel better, but sitting here with you is better than Mr. Wilson's theories on the female reproductive system. I'm pretty sure he has no practical experience with it."

Audrey had to smile at that. "Then he hasn't changed much in the last fifteen years. Still, I'll take it as a compliment that you'd rather be here."

Another shrug, the universal teenage symbol of antipathy. "Take it however you want."

Audrey had dealt with her share of moody and surly teenagers, so Kendra's attitude didn't offend. And since the school was paying her her regular hourly rate, the girl could spend the next forty-five minutes however she liked. Audrey was still going to get paid for it. Sometimes, you just had to let it go.

Kendra lasted all of a minute. "She was my best friend and I hated her. How's that for a place to start?"

"An honest one?" Audrey smiled faintly. "You wouldn't be the first female to have felt that way about her best friend."

"Have you ever felt that way?"

Getting personal was a professional no-no, but sometimes you had to give a little bit in order to get. Especially with teenagers. "Yes. That friend I told you about who was killed was sometimes my best friend and sometimes my worst enemy. Why did you hate Tala?"

"Lots of stupid reasons. She was tall and thin. She had perfect boobs. She was gorgeous." Kendra paused. "She was so perfect and such a girl, and she'd been born a boy. How unfair is that?"

"Very, I guess," Audrey allowed. "I imagine she envied you for having been born a girl."

"She did. She said I had to do less work than she did. I didn't understand it until one night we were getting ready to go out.

It took her forever to get ready. Everything had to be perfect. *She* had to be perfect. Even though I cursed her out for taking so long, I still wished I'd looked as good as she did."

Audrey didn't comment on the fact that Kendra was gorgeous. She had a feeling the girl knew it, despite having been insecure around Tala. "But you were best friends despite that."

"Everybody loved her. She liked everybody she met, and she made people smile. She was funny and liked to make people laugh. She was really popular. A lot of guys wanted to get with her. We were all surprised when she picked Luke."

And a little hurt too, Audrey surmised, given the change in Kendra's tone. "Why's that?" From what she had seen, Luke Pelletier was a good-looking kid. If Alisha liked him, he had to have something going for him.

"Luke's pretty quiet. He's smart, likes to read. He'd rather watch a movie than go to a party. He likes to be alone. Tala liked to be the center of attention. They were, like, total opposites."

"Maybe that's what brought them together."

Kendra shrugged. "Didn't keep them together, though. She still dumped him. I didn't even know she was going to do it. We were *supposed* to be best friends. I told her when I broke up with him."

"You and Luke dated." She knew this already, but sometimes in her line of work it was helpful to pretend you had little or no prior knowledge.

A nod. "When he asked her out, she asked me if it was okay. Like I was going to be a bitch and say no."

"She respected your friendship enough to ask."

The girl's gaze was sharp enough to cut glass. "She wanted to cover her ass. I cause a scene, I'm the bad guy."

This anger toward Tala might have been alarming if Audrey hadn't once been a teenage girl. She'd spent a lot of time bouncing back and forth between loving and resenting Maggie when she was a teen. Even without their unique circumstances, she would have had moments.

"I was jealous and a bitch. When she told me she and Luke had broken up, I told her he obviously wasn't the great guy she thought he was." She looked down at her hands. "She looked like I'd hit her. Next thing I know, she's dead."

Audrey studied her, looking for any indication that she might have been with Tala when she died—or that she might have been the one to kill her. She'd built her career on studying kids who committed crimes or were victims of one, and she couldn't just turn that off, regardless of why the school had brought her on board. Still, she reminded herself of why she was there, which was to be a support to the kids who came to her, not treat them like suspects.

"Aren't you supposed to ask me how that makes me feel?" Kendra asked.

"I have a pretty good idea, but okay, how did that make you feel?"

"Like shit. She wanted to come over to my place, but I told her I was busy."

"Why?"

"I didn't want to listen to her crying over him, and I didn't want her to see that part of me was glad they were through."

"You still have feelings for Luke." So much of therapy was spent stating the obvious—she'd forgotten about that.

She laughed humorlessly. "Yeah. Mom doesn't think my feelings are real. She says I didn't want him, but I didn't want anyone else to want him either."

Nodding, Audrey smiled faintly. "I remember feeling the same way a time or two."

"Really?"

"It's true. You can be best friends with someone and still have negative feelings toward them, or be jealous of what you think they have that you don't."

"Tala called me a jealous cunt."

Audrey knew she shouldn't be surprised, but she was. Everything she'd ever heard about Tala had her painted as a sweet girl who rarely swore. "That must have hurt." And Tala must have been in a lot of pain to have said it.

"It did. I told her to fuck off, and—" She stopped.

Audrey watched her patiently, studying how her expression went from anger to horror and then regret. "And?"

Kendra cleared her throat. "I told her Luke had no problem getting it up for me."

Ah, the precision cruelty of a teenage girl. "Was that the last thing you said to her?"

Tears filled the girl's eyes as she bobbed her head in a jerky nod. "I've spent the last two months hoping that she's out there and that I haven't heard from her because she's pissed, or that she's miserable and thinking I hate her. Anything was better than thinking she was dead. She died hating me."

The poor girl was going to carry the guilt with her for a long time, Audrey thought.

A tear trickled down Kendra's cheek. "Most of the time I just really, really miss her. I just wish I could tell her that I'm sorry—for everything."

A hard lump formed in Audrey's throat as she offered the tissue box. She couldn't help but think of Maggie. "Yeah. I remember that part too."

CHAPTER SEVEN

Neve really wanted to talk to Luke Pelletier, but she didn't want to cause a spectacle by dragging the kid out of class. From what she'd gleaned from Audrey, he was getting picked on enough as it was, and she didn't want to add to that, even though he was a possible suspect.

Although she seemed to be the only person who thought he might be capable of killing Tala. Everyone else she spoke to seemed to think he was great.

But people had thought Ted Bundy was a nice guy too. And Tala Lewis's wounds had definitely been caused by someone with physical strength, but also strong emotions toward her. Neve knew all too well just how heated some people in the town could get when it came to someone being "different."

Lincoln Tripp had once hit on her because he'd "never been with a black girl before." She'd told him that she'd never been with a moron before either, and planned to keep it that way. Unfortunately, she did eventually succumb to his charms one drunken night. Most women her age in Edgeport had at some point. Lincoln could be a good guy when he wanted, but he was no Gideon.

She wondered how Audrey was getting along at the school. It drove her frigging nuts to think one of those kids might tell her something important to her investigation and that Audrey wouldn't share it because of privilege. She had to trust that Audrey would at least point her in the general direction if anything like that happened. But she and Audrey sometimes had ... *issues* where trust was concerned.

Her father hadn't helped matters when he stopped by the house that morning. Everett Graham had strong opinions where Audrey Harte was concerned, and he never hesitated to voice them.

"I'm not surprised she's got herself involved in the investigation," he commented, running a hand over his bristly square jaw. He was a tall, strong man with graying hair and piercing blue eyes. He was used to people doing what he wanted them to do, and he hated that Audrey had never actually confessed to being the one that killed Clint. Maggie took the blame for the killing blow.

"Dad, the school asked her to work there."

"She didn't say no, did she?"

"Because she's a juvenile psychologist. She wants to help the kids."

"She's a psychopath with a death fixation."

"She's not a psychopath." The other part she couldn't really argue. "And it doesn't really matter because there's nothing I can do about it."

"Nothing you can do about it? You're in charge of the investigation."

"Yes, I am. Please remember that and refrain from telling me what to do."

He looked offended. "I wasn't going to tell you how to do your job."

"You were, because you think you're the only cop who was ever good at it."

Stiffening, he stared down his slightly crooked nose at her. "I do not."

"Then it's just me you think you're better than."

"You're acting like a child."

"And the highlight of your career was arresting one." Two, actually, but whatever.

He'd walked out, slamming the door so hard the windows rattled. Gideon came into the kitchen with a worried look on his rugged face and hugged her. He knew how her father could push her buttons. Neve still felt a little guilty about getting into it with him, but experience told her that the old man had been maybe two minutes away from actually lecturing her on the lousy job she was doing. He couldn't help himself—he tried to butt in on every case, and then tried to make her work it like he would.

He would have delegated as much as possible—and he would have gone to the school and yanked Luke out of class. That was why Neve went to the Falls instead. They still hadn't found Tala's phone, and she wanted to take a look on her own.

It was a nice day, cool but sunny, and she was crouched on the bridge above the falls studying a stain on the wood. It looked like blood. CSU had gone over the site, so she assumed she'd hear if it was Tala's or not. They had found fabric matching her coat caught on a splinter on the handrail, so they knew Tala had been on the bridge that night. Could she have dropped her phone? They hadn't found it in the water, or on either side of the bed, but then they were still looking downstream. Still looking for the murder weapon as well. And that glove they'd found? There were two blood types on it—B positive and AB positive. Tala was AB, and Annette had confirmed the blood was hers, so the other contributor might have been the killer. She just hoped they were in the system.

Neve glanced down, over the side of the bridge. She took a small pair of binoculars from her pocket and put them to her eyes, scanning the rocks and trees below. She stopped and came back, focusing on a tree below where the bloodstain and fabric were. What was that? She moved slightly, adjusting her angle and trying to block the glare of the sun for a better look.

Was that a small backpack or purse? Her heart gave a little thump. It was, she was sure of it. But how the hell was she going to get it? It was too far below for her reach from where she was, and too high to reach from the ground.

She got Vickie on the radio. "See if you can get hold of Gareth, will you? Find out if he's got tree-climbing gear and tell him to get back here ASAP."

"You find something?"

Staring down at the tree, she tried to make out what it was. "Yeah, I think so."

A few minutes later, Vickie let her know that Gareth was on his way. Fortunately, he'd been working on one of the trails when she called him and had climbing equipment in his truck. Neve spotted him making his way down the steps a little while later, said gear slung over his shoulder. He was built in a similar way to Jake—tall and lean and ripped. Muscles in his forearms and biceps stood out beneath his tanned skin. Summer was still six weeks away and already he was the color of a walnut. By August he'd be as brown as her favorite leather jacket. She carefully picked her way down the side of the falls to meet him.

"You're my new favorite person," she told him.

He grinned, revealing a space where a canine tooth used to be. "Whatcha got?"

"This way." She led him into the other bridge that spanned the river, this one much lower than the one she'd just left. It led to the picnic area. It also was the only way to get to the tree she wanted him to climb.

Gareth had gloves with him to assist in the climb, so Neve didn't offer him a pair of the nitrile ones she had in her pocket. She pulled some on, however, as he secured his gear on the towering pine. She pointed to the general area he needed to get to and told him what to look for. It was barely visible from where she stood.

He didn't have to climb far, but it was higher than could have been reached by a regular ladder. Neve was pretty sure it would take her forever to do it, but Gareth scampered up the tree like a monkey. She remembered someone telling her that he used to work for the phone company, so maybe he just had a lot of practice. Regardless, he made it look easy and graceful. When he came back down, she saw that it was indeed a little backpack—the same kind Tala Lewis's parents said she'd had with her the night she disappeared.

Neve practically snatched it from his hands when he offered it to her. Having arrived, Vickie was right there beside her, eyes wide. "Is that hers?"

"I think so." Neve opened the bag. Inside was a wallet—with Tala's ID. Her driver's license had her new name on it, while the social security card still had her birth name—Matthew. There was also a lipstick, compact, tweezers, tampon, and cell phone.

"Why would a trans girl have a tampon?" Vickie asked.

Neve shrugged. "Maybe it made her feel more like a girl to have it? Think of how many times you've had a friend ask if you have a spare."

"Fair enough. You think the cell phone still works? It's been out here a couple of months."

"I don't know," Neve said. The phone was the same make and model as hers. A teenage girl's phone was her life—her diary, social gateway, entertainment center, and window to the world. It was the next best thing to actually being able to talk to Tala herself. "But I have a charger in my car."

When Alisha came to meet Audrey for lunch she had Luke with her. Audrey took one look at the kid, the dark circles under his eyes—compounded by the shiner developing around one—and his posture, and knew she couldn't leave him there alone. For Alisha's sake, she wanted to believe he had nothing to do with Tala's death, but even if he had, she didn't think she'd abandon him. He looked desperate, and she knew all too well the things desperate people were capable of doing.

"You okay?" she asked him.

He hesitated, then glanced at Alisha, who was digging through her bag for something, and quickly shook his head. Poor kid was a mess.

Audrey handed him her phone. "Call your mother for me."

He didn't ask why, didn't say anything. In fact, he hadn't spoken since walking into her temporary office. Once he'd entered the phone number on the screen, he handed the phone back to her. Audrey stepped out into the main office as she held it to her ear.

"Hello?"

"Linda? It's Audrey Harte."

"Audrey! How's that place of yours coming along? Your mother was telling me all about it at the Hannaford the other day."

Yes, she could only imagine the bragging her mother had done. Anne Harte was a sweet woman with a steel backbone and a pride in her children that bordered on ridiculous. "It's going great, thanks for asking. Listen, I'm at the high school right now with Alisha and Luke."

"The Tripp girl? She's been such a good friend to him lately."

"Linda, I want your permission to take Luke out of school today. I want to take the kids for lunch, and then maybe see if he wants to talk about things. I think he's being bullied. He's got a black eye."

"Those fucking little bastards." A sigh filled Audrey's ear. "Jesus Christ, who cares what Tala had in her pants. I'm just trying to raise my boy to be decent and modern, and some stupid redneck moron decides to make his life hell because of it."

That about summed it up. "So, can I take him?"

"You bet your ass you can. Let me talk to whoever's at the desk."

And that was how Audrey ended up taking both Alisha and Luke to lunch at Fat Frank's. And how she ended up with a teenage boy on her sofa at two in the afternoon, watching Netflix while he ate a bowl of ice cream as big as his head. Alisha hadn't been happy when Audrey sent her home, but she didn't want Luke censoring himself.

"You like this stuff?" he asked her. They were watching the latest Marvel offering.

"Yeah, I do," she replied with a smile. "You look surprised."

He shrugged. "You just don't look like the type of person who'd be into superheroes."

"I used to read more comics than my brother when we were kids. Guess whose powers I wanted."

He thought about it for a second. "Phoenix?"

"Nope."

"Storm?"

"Nuh-uh."

Another shrug. So easily defeated. "I give up. Who?"

"Wolverine."

He laughed, and her reaction to it could only be described as delighted relief. He hadn't been broken. Not yet.

"Thanks for letting me hang out here," he said. "School's a little crazy right now."

She dipped her chin. "Crazy? Luke, you're being bullied. T hat's not crazy, it's mean."

"Did you get bullied when you were in high school?"

"Not really. I had one friend who could be...difficult. My situation was different than yours, though."

A small, much-too-cynical-for-his-age smile curved his lips. "Because of what you did?"

"Yes."

"You weren't prey."

"I suppose not. I wasn't a predator, either, if that was your next question."

He set his bowl—now empty—on the coffee table on top of a magazine. "Is that okay?" At her nod, he continued. "Maybe I deserve to be bullied."

"Why would you think that?"

He stared at her, holding her gaze long enough that she began to feel as though he were peeling back layers and exposing all her dark corners. She didn't flinch. "Has Lish told you anything about me and Tala?"

Audrey shook her head. "Only that the two of you broke up just before she was killed."

The kid flinched. "She dumped me. She said I couldn't handle her being who she was."

"Could you?"

"No. I wanted to, but I couldn't." He told her what had happened when they actually tried to take their relationship to the next physical level. He blushed like crazy but maintained eye contact. "So, maybe I deserve being bullied. I was a coward too."

"It was a shock, and something that the two of you might have worked out if Tala hadn't been killed."

"She didn't want anything to do with me."

"She was hurt."

"She was pissed. She said I shouldn't have dated her if I was disgusted by her."

"Were you disgusted?"

"No. It was just...weird, y'know? She said I should get back together with Kendra and lose her number. She said she hated herself enough, she didn't need a boyfriend to hate her too."

"Luke, this all sounds pretty intense. Did anything else happen to make Tala react this way?" Hurt and defensive she could understand, but what he told her sounded like the girl had gone on the offensive.

He hesitated. "She told Kendra and Lucy what happened."

"Lucy Villeneuve?"

"Yeah. I don't know what they said to her, but they both told me that it was good that I knew 'where I stood' with Tala, and that maybe it was for the best that we broke up. I think they told her that I didn't want to be with her. I think they lied to her about me."

"Why would you think that?"

"Because they hated her." A pause. "And because Kendra hoped she and I could get back together."

Audrey frowned. She was getting a better picture of the situation now. "Sometimes girls act like that when they're hurt or jealous."

"No, they really hated her."

"So, you think they conspired to make sure the two of you didn't get back together?"

Luke hunched, pressing his elbows into his knees as he leaned closer. His face was pale and earnest. "I overheard them planning to kill her."

CHAPTER EIGHT

Audrey called Neve. She had to. Luke was okay with it, though a little reluctant because he didn't want to cause trouble.

He didn't want to cause trouble. She fought the urge to physically shake her head in disbelief. Not causing trouble was one thing, but how about saving his own ass? Not to mention the moral aspect of it.

"Luke, you need to tell Detective Graham about this. In fact, I'm surprised you haven't already."

"Why?"

She wanted to smack him upside the head, she really did. "Do you honestly think the girls might have hurt Tala?"

He blinked, and then his expression went from youthful blankness to a more adult tension. "I think they wanted to, yeah. You don't think they killed her, do you?"

He'd just told her that he'd overheard them discussing it. She remembered doing the same thing with Maggie—and then they'd done it. "I don't know, but you have to tell the police what you know—for Tala."

That put a little steel in his spine. "Right. Okay."

Audrey left him in the living room when she made the call. Fortunately, Neve was in the area, so she was there within fifteen minutes.

She came up the front steps in jeans, a henley, and hiking boots. She looked a little sweaty in the afternoon sun.

"Not on duty?" Audrey asked as she opened the door.

"I am, but we were digging around back the Falls today, so I left the heels and blazer at home." Neve turned toward her. "Hey, if you were a transgender girl, why would you have a tampon in your purse?"

"To make me feel and appear more feminine. Did Tala have one?"

"Mm. I wondered if it was what you just said, or if maybe she was carrying it for someone."

"Do you think it's important?"

"It is if that friend was with her the night she died." She stepped inside. The old floorboards creaked as if in greeting. "Where is he?"

Audrey closed the door and led the way to the living room, even though Neve knew where it was. "Luke, Detective Graham is here."

The kid actually stood up and offered his hand, though he looked a little nervous and his cheeks were pale. Neve accepted the handshake without any mockery and then offered him something. It was a cell phone. There was a crack in the upper left corner of the screen, and the case was purple with black polka dots. "Tala's cell?" He looked at her in wonder. "Where'd you get it?"

"Found it in her bag. Do you happen to know the password for it? I'm surprised it even powered on."

He nodded and tapped the screen a few times with his thumbs before handing it back to her. "It's zero-six-twenty-three—the day she began living as a girl." There was a smudge of black on his fingers.

"Thanks," Neve said. "Sorry, that's from when we finger-printed it."

And now Luke's prints were on it, should Neve decide to pull them as well, Audrey realized. Had the trooper done it on purpose?

He wiped his hand on the napkins Audrey had given him earlier. "Finding her phone. That's good, right?"

"It depends on what we find on it," Neve replied, putting the phone in a plastic bag and then into her purse. She pulled out a small voice recorder. "Do you mind if I record our chat?"

Luke swallowed and shook his head.

"Do you want me to stay?" Audrey asked.

Neve let Luke answer. "If you want." Which was teen speak for "Yes, please." Audrey hid her relief, because there was no way she would have left him alone with Neve. It wasn't that she didn't trust Neve as a person, but she was a cop, and her priority was solving a murder, while Audrey's was to protect vulnerable kids.

They all sat down. Audrey found herself taking a seat beside Luke this time. She didn't know if he was lying or not, but if he *was* lying, she bought it. Sometimes she was better at spotting bullshit than others, and sometimes she got played along with everyone else. Her profession didn't make her immune to human error. She'd learned that lesson the hard way over the last year.

"Just tell her what you told me about that day in class," she prompted.

Neve shot her a dark look, but Audrey just made a face at her. It wasn't like she was the kid's lawyer, or as though he was being questioned. He was giving a statement, and she'd remind Neve of that if necessary.

Luke nodded, oblivious to the exchange. He told Neve what he'd told Audrey about hearing Kendra and Lucy talking one day in law class about famous murder cases and how Kendra had been asking people how they'd kill someone. The teacher had been talking about a particular case from a few years ago.

"I'd use poison," Lucy had said. "It's less mess and harder to trace. Oh, wait! No, I'd use a food allergy, if they had one."

"Death by peanut," Stacey Hicks, Kendra's cousin, had quipped, and they all laughed.

Mason Stokes had said he'd probably use drugs—which surprised no one because he was the school drug dealer.

Neve's eyebrow twitched at that little tidbit. Obviously she hadn't been aware of Mason's extracurricular activities. "What happened next?"

Luke took a drink of the soda Audrey had gotten him before Neve's arrival. "They asked me how I would do it and I said I wouldn't, but Lucy called bullshit and said that if I hated someone enough or felt threatened enough, I could kill, so how would I do it? Finally, I told them I'd probably use a gun because it would be quick."

"Not if you're shot in the gut," Neve corrected. "It takes a long time to die from that." That was the only reason her father had survived when he'd been shot. Audrey knew this because Neve had told her.

"Okay, so you said you'd use a gun, then what?"

He drew a breath. "That's when Kendra said she'd like to stab somebody because she'd want them to know that she meant to kill them."

Audrey and Neve exchanged glances. Audrey sighed inwardly. And the kid had wondered if this was important information. Jesus, it was a good thing he was cute, because he sure as hell wasn't the brightest bulb in the fixture. Or maybe he just didn't want to think the girls capable of murder. Regardless, his naiveté would probably come back to bite him on the ass someday.

"And Mason said that was harsh, and asked who would she want to stab. She looked right at me and said, 'Tala.' I asked her why, and she just shrugged. Lucy looked at me and said, 'You know why, asshole.'" Luke looked from Neve to Audrey and back again.

Neve rubbed the back of her neck. "Do you know why?"

"Because Kendra wanted me back." His eyebrows knitted together. "Isn't that fucked up?"

"People have killed for less," Audrey said. "There were girls in Virginia who killed another because they said they didn't like her anymore."

"There was more to that one," Neve chimed in. "Okay, so Kendra said this in front of your classmates?"

Luke nodded. "Mr. Boudreau asked her if she had anything to contribute to the class discussion since she was so busy having her own, and she asked him why the killer hadn't just taken his wife's body out into the woods and let the animals have her rather than put her through a wood chipper that could have DNA on it. She said it would be better to let nature dispose of the corpse."

"Did she." It wasn't a question. "What did Mr. Boudreau say to that?"

"He said it was too bad she hadn't been there to consult the killer and asked if she had any objection to him continuing with his teaching."

Neve glanced at Audrey. "He hasn't changed much." They'd both had a class with him when they'd gone to the high school. "Was that the end of the conversation?"

"Yeah. Later, Kendra came up to me and said she'd only been joking about wanting to kill Tala. And that she was sorry for saying it."

"Is that why you never said anything about this before now?"

"I didn't think Tala was dead before you found her. I thought she'd run away." His shoulders slumped. "I'd hoped she had."

"You thought she'd run off to New York to become a model or something?"

Luke nodded. "I guess a part of me knew she wouldn't just take off, but I didn't want to think something bad had happened to her, y'know? I just kept hoping she'd come back so I could tell her I was sorry."

There were actual tears in the poor kid's eyes. Either he was being completely honest or he was a lot smarter than she gave him credit for being. "Do you have any other questions?" she asked Neve.

Neve lifted her chin. "How'd you get that black eye?"

"Kid at school. He called me a cocksucker and said that Tala was a freak that deserved to die. I hit him. He and his friends decided to hit back."

Neve's expression soured as she rose to her feet. "Bet you wanted to use one of those fast bullets of yours on him."

Luke shook his head and lifted his gaze to meet hers. The tears had completely dried up. "No, ma'am. People like him deserve to go slow."

Luke had dinner at Alisha's. Audrey had been reluctant to leave them alone, but Alisha hadn't given her much choice. Since her mother was still at work, Alisha made them hamburgers and French fries. Afterward, she drove Luke home even though she would've gladly spent the rest of the evening with him. They both had homework to do, and Luke needed to talk to his parents about the situation at school.

"Thanks for letting me hang out," Luke said from the passenger seat. "Sorry I'm not more fun to be around."

"I've been meaning to talk to you about that," Alisha replied dryly. "I really resent how you're allowing being bullied to drag you down."

He chuckled, and Alisha smiled in relief. She was worried about him, but she would never let on to him just how much.

"Well, still…" He shot a quick glance in her direction. "I'm lucky to have you as a friend."

Her cheeks warmed, even though the word "friend" made her stomach hurt. "You're welcome. I don't mean to pry, but did it help talking to Audrey?"

"Yeah. It did. She's pretty cool."

"She is. I'm really glad she's marrying my uncle."

"Oh, hey, do you mind if I turn this up?" he asked when a new song started to play on the radio. It was something from the eighties that Alisha didn't know the name of but had heard before many times. The two of them sang along as they drove. For three minutes it was as though nothing horrible had happened and life was normal.

The happy interlude came to an abrupt halt as they approached Luke's house.

"What the fuck is *she* doing here?" His tone was sharp, one that Alisha hadn't heard him use before.

She looked at the silver Jeep parked in his driveway. "Is that Kendra's car?"

"Yeah." He turned his head toward her. "Think we could just keep driving?"

"Sure." Alisha was happy to do just that. She liked having him all to herself, and she didn't feel like explaining to Kendra why she was with him.

But just as they were about to keep on going, both Kendra and Lucy appeared on the front step.

"Jesus, do they go everywhere together?" Luke asked. His dark brows pulled together. "I wish they'd just leave me alone."

"You want me to keep going?" Alisha asked. The girls would recognize her car and probably give her a hard time for it later, but she wasn't going to deliver Luke into the hands of people he didn't want to see.

"No. I don't want to make trouble for you. Just drop me off, thanks."

Alisha pulled into the driveway behind Kendra's Jeep. The girls had come down the steps and were walking toward them. Kendra intercepted Luke as soon as he opened the door and stepped out of the car. Lucy came around to the driver's-side window. Alisha didn't want to talk to her, but she also knew it would be rude to just drive away.

She pressed the button to lower the glass. "Hey," she said as Lucy leaned down. "What's up?"

"I was just about to ask you the same thing. We heard Luke left school with you at lunch."

It wasn't a question, so Alisha didn't feel like she had to respond. Still, it wasn't in her to let someone talk to her like she had done something wrong when she hadn't. She lifted an eyebrow. "And?"

Lucy actually looked surprised. "You know how Kendra feels about him."

"I do. I also have a pretty good idea of how he feels about her." The second it was out she knew she shouldn't have said it.

Lucy's eyes narrowed. "What the fuck's that supposed to mean?"

"Nothing. I have to go."

"Yeah. That's a good idea. Maybe think about staying away. Why stick around when you're not wanted?"

Alisha lifted her chin and looked Lucy dead in the eye. "You tell me." Again, she probably shouldn't have said it, but it felt good when she saw the look on Lucy's face. She put the car in reverse and started backing out of the drive, forcing the other girl to step away. The last thing she saw was Kendra following Luke into the house and Lucy trailing along after them.

Lucy had just basically told her to stay away from Luke. Had she delivered the same warning to Tala?

Monday night Neve went to bed still poking through Tala's phone. The cell was full of photos and texts—she never seemed to clear out her cache, which was both a blessing and a pain in the ass. She had more social media accounts than Neve thought possible, which made combing through it all a little tedious.

"No," Gideon said. "Put that thing away. You're not working at midnight."

Neve glanced up, about to ask for five more minutes, but he was standing there in the en suite doorway in nothing but a pair of pajama bottoms slung low on his lean hips. The man was delicious. And it had been a while since they'd taken time for themselves. Gideon was in construction, so spring and summer were his busiest months, and both of them had been preoccupied with Bailey's upcoming court date.

"You have something else in mind?" she asked with a coy arch of her brow.

He grinned. He was the most gorgeous thing she'd ever seen. And he was hers. All hers. She was well aware there were a lot of women in the area who were jealous of her, and she liked it.

Gideon walked toward her side of the bed, muscles shifting beneath his skin. He was like a cat, all sinew and grace. He yanked the sheets down, exposing Neve's tank top and boxers. A little thrill shot through her. Oh, yeah. It had been way too long.

He pressed his knee into the mattress, planting his hands on either side of her. She reached for him as he lowered his body to hers. Their lips came together hungrily as she ran her palms down the smooth curve of his spine. He had the sweetest little ass. She dug her fingers into each cheek as he ground his hips into hers. He pulled the neck of her tank top down, and lowered his head to her breast.

A long time—a *long* time—later, they lay entwined, stroking lazy circles on each other's backs with the tips of their fingers.

"Oh, my God, I needed that," Neve said.

"Mm-hm," he agreed in that low, sleepy way that made her want to bury her face in the crook of his neck and never leave. "Sure did. Why don't we do it more often?"

"Because we're idiots."

He chuckled. She kissed the crinkles that fanned out from his eye. "Did you talk to Bailey today?"

His laughter evaporated, making her instantly regret the question. "She says if she's released she wants to go live with her mother in Portland."

Neve hugged him close. "I'm sorry."

"You're not surprised, huh?"

"No. Would you want to come back here if you were her?"

"I guess not. I just assumed she'd want to be with us."

There was no denying the edge of hurt in his voice. "What did you tell her?"

"I told her we'd cross that bridge when we got there. I asked her to talk to Audrey about it, though. She's the only person I know with a similar situation."

Except Audrey had killed to protect the very person whose life Bailey had taken. Neve didn't say that, however. She just held him. "Well, we have to get her out first."

He shifted his head to meet her gaze. "You think we won't?"

It was gutting, the fear in his eyes. "I didn't say that. I think things look good, but you need to be prepared that the judge might decide she needs to do more work." There was always the chance that Bailey would have to serve more time. She just hoped the circumstances and all the work the kid had already done would make a difference. Hoped that they got a sympathetic judge.

"I know." He sighed. "But Stillwater was good for her. This place she's in now…she's having a hard time."

Stillwater was the facility Audrey had gone to after killing Clint, and it was where Bailey had spent the first ten months after her arrest, but it had closed earlier that year and she'd gotten sent to a facility near Augusta that had twice as many kids and half the compassion.

"She's going to be okay, babe. You have to believe that."

Gideon nodded. "I just wish I hadn't been so fucking blind. I wish she had told me."

"Maggie made sure she wouldn't. It's not your fault." But

how she wished she could dig up Maggie's corpse and bitch-slap her a few times for the hurt she'd brought down on Gideon and his kid. For the hurt she'd left in her wake like a trail of expensive perfume. Maggie had been one of those people who couldn't help but destroy everything they touched.

"We should have Jake and Audrey over some night. I want to thank them for all they've done."

Neve didn't like being in Jake's debt, but he and Audrey were there for them, whether they liked it or not. He had helped get Bailey a good lawyer—a really good one. And of course, Audrey had helped on the psychological side of things, finding someone to present a clear picture to the judge of just what sort of damage Maggie's abuse and manipulation had wrought. She'd even volunteered to testify on Bailey's behalf if it might help.

"Sure. I'll ask Audrey when a good time might be."

He hugged her close and pulled the sheet up over them. It was still a little cool at night, and they'd both worked up a sweat that was now turning to a chill.

"I love you," he said, pressing his lips to her hair.

Neve swallowed. Every time he said it felt like the first time, damn it. She was in so deep with this man she didn't know which way was up. It was terrifying and wonderful. "I love you too."

She rolled to her side so he could spoon her and listened as his breathing changed. He always fell asleep long before she did. He was one of those people who could close their eyes and start snoring. It usually took her a good thirty minutes or so to turn off her brain.

It was dark in the room, but there was a light on Tala's phone—tiny and unobtrusive, yet easy to focus on. Neve stared at it, willing it to tell her all the secrets it knew. She thought about Bailey and how she and Tala were the same age. Would they have been friends? Probably, especially since Alisha had befriended the girl. Alisha certainly seemed to attract the walking wounded—probably because she was a loyal friend. Neve would give the Tripp family that—if they liked you, they would do anything for you.

It was when they stopped liking you that was the problem.

But she didn't want to think about the Tripps. She needed to focus on finding who had killed Tala. Bailey had killed Maggie because of years of sexual abuse and manipulation. In Neve's experience there was always a reason. Even serial killers had their triggers. It was rare that murders, especially those as up-close as Tala's, were committed for no reason. There was always a motive.

So what had Tala done to motivate someone to kill her? Someone out there knew the answer, and there were clues in Tala's phone. There had to be. A teenager's phone was as good as or better than a diary. Every aspect of Tala's life was in that little plastic box, and the identity of her murderer was there too.

Neve just had to find it.

CHAPTER NINE

The clock said 3:15 a.m. Audrey was alone in bed. She reached over and found Jake's side cold to the touch. Frowning, she sat up. "Jake?"

No reply.

She lay there a moment and waited, but he didn't come. Knowing there was no way she was going back to sleep without finding out where he was, she threw back the blankets and slipped out of bed. Clad in a T-shirt and knit shorts, she padded barefoot from the room, the smooth hardwood cool beneath her feet.

She stood at the top of the stairs and looked down; there was the faint glow of a lamp underneath the door of Jake's office. The steps creaked slightly beneath her as she made her way down. At the bottom, she turned right and knocked softly on the door.

"Yeah?"

She turned the knob and pushed. Jake sat at his desk in a T-shirt and pajama bottoms. His hair was mussed and his cheeks were flushed. He looked tired and stressed.

"You okay?" she asked, leaning against the door frame.

He nodded. "Couldn't sleep, so I decided to catch up on some paperwork. You?"

"I woke up and you were gone." She smiled. "You know how nosy I am. I had to find out where you were."

He smiled back, but it looked forced. "Now you know. Go back to bed. I'll be up in a bit."

Audrey started. That sounded really...dismissive. "Right. Sorry to bother you."

He didn't say anything—he'd gone back to his paperwork. Hurt—and pissed—Audrey backed out of the room and closed the door. She was tempted to slam it—or at least get a little forceful with it, but she didn't.

What the hell was up with him? He'd been acting weird the last few days, and he kept telling her nothing was wrong, when it was obvious it was. For a man who was a really good liar, he was pathetically bad at hiding his distraction from her. Or maybe he wasn't even bothering trying to hide it. Why not just tell her he didn't want to talk about it?

They were supposed to be partners, weren't they? Hell, she talked to him about everything—probably even things he wished she'd wouldn't. His continued silence and bizarre behavior made it worse. Made her think that she was the cause of the problem.

Which totally fed into the deep-seated anxiety she had where he was concerned. They'd been connected since they were kids, and they always would be, but there were times when she didn't trust his feelings for her. Not because she didn't think they were real enough, but because he'd put them aside if he thought it was for the best. Years ago he'd made her think he didn't care about her so she'd leave and go to school. Was he having second thoughts about marrying her?

If he thought she could actually go back to sleep now, he was out of his ever-loving mind. She had a full day ahead of her and wanted to be on the ball. So, instead of stomping off and sulking like she wanted, she went back upstairs, used the bathroom, and crawled into bed with her tablet to do a little reading.

Jake didn't come to bed. When Audrey went downstairs a few hours later—after finally going back to sleep—she found a note saying he had to make a run for supplies for Gracie's and that he'd see her that night.

Audrey ripped the note into as many pieces as she could before throwing it in the trash. Then she made her way to his office once again. Whatever he'd been working on, it was gone now. The top of his desk was completely clear—freakishly so. One of the drawers was even locked. The only thing there was a pad he used to write down appointments or notes before putting them into his phone.

She stared at it a moment before grabbing a pencil from the WORLD'S BEST UNCLE mug Alisha had made for him when she was five. She ran the lead over the top sheet on the pad, letting it bring out what had been written on the one previous: *Ashley, Tuesday 11:15*. It was followed by a phone number with a Maine area code.

Who was Ashley? And why was he meeting her that morning when he was supposed to be getting supplies for the tavern? Jake wasn't the type to cheat. She wasn't worried about that—

even though she suffered from the same fear many women had that their significant other might find someone he liked better and leave. But that said more about her than Jake.

No, he didn't have another woman, but there was *something* going on.

Audrey tore the top page off the pad and put it in her pocket. Later, if it drove her crazy enough, and if she got mad enough, she just might call the phone number for herself, but for the time being she owed Jake his privacy. She'd already crossed a line by snooping, and even though she was hurt, she needed to respect him and trust that he would eventually share with her what was going on.

She didn't have any more time to dwell on it. She grabbed something quick for breakfast and made her coffee to go. Then she drove back the Ridge to check on how renovations were going. They were still on schedule and everything was looking great. She made some calls, talked to the contractors, and took some photos. Once she was done there, it was lunch time. She grabbed a bite and then went to the high school. She got there with ten minutes to spare before her first appointment.

Lucy Villeneuve was five minutes late by the time she breezed into the small office. She was a fashionably dressed young woman, with makeup skills that suggested too much time watching "gurus" on social media. Seriously, her eyebrows were sharp enough to cut glass.

"It was my mother's idea for me to talk to you," she said when she sat down. "Just so you know, I don't want to be here," she announced, echoing Kendra's earlier statement.

Don't let the door hit you in the ass... "Oh? Why not?"

The girl tilted her highlighted head. She ought to have blended out that contour a bit more. "Because talking about it's not going to bring Tala back, is it?"

Audrey shook her head. "No. It's not."

"And it's not like you can make me feel better."

Another shake. "Not immediately."

Lucy shrugged her slim shoulders. "So what's the point?"

Studying her, Audrey noted the acne not completely hidden beneath the layer of makeup, the teeth scrapes on the top of her right index finger, and the darkness of her roots. Lucy Villeneuve was a girl who spent a lot of time trying to be what she thought she ought to be. That didn't leave much time to like who she was.

"Were you and Tala good friends?"

"Me and her and Kendra were always together. Ask anyone."

"So you were best friends."

The girl frowned—it made her look tough, and made little cakey lines in her foundation and powder. "Didn't I just say that?"

Audrey smiled. For some reason she welcomed the girl's biting attitude and defensiveness. It gave her something to crash into and beat down. It was a welcome distraction. "No, you said you spent a lot of time together."

"I'm not going to hang out with someone I don't like."

"That makes you different from most girls, then," Audrey replied.

Lucy went still, and Audrey knew it had been the right thing to say. As much as she desperately wanted to be like all the other girls, Lucy Villeneuve wanted to be special.

"So was Tala the kind of friend who always had a tampon if you needed one? Did she have your back? Did she hold your hair while you made yourself puke?"

Heavily lined eyes widened. Audrey's gaze didn't waver. She wasn't going to give away how she knew the kid had purging issues.

"Tala never had tampons—she didn't need them." She gave Audrey an assessing glance. "You know she wasn't really a girl, right?"

Audrey fought a sigh. So much for the enlightened youth. But Neve had said the girl had a tampon in her bag. "I know she was transgender, if that's what you mean."

Lucy made that face again. "I'm sorry, but if you don't have a vag, you're not a girl."

"But you refer to Tala as 'she,' so obviously you thought of her as a girl."

"Okay, so she wasn't a girl where it counted. She acted like it was this horrible thing. Do you know what I'd give to be able to pee standing up? Or not have a period every month? God, she went on about how much she envied Kendra and me. She could have my cramps if she wanted them." She frowned a little. "She used to rub my back for me when they got bad."

"Sounds like a good friend."

"She could be. She could also be a total nut job if her hormones got messed up. Sometimes she was such a bitch to Luke. I don't know why he put up with it. Not like he was getting sex out of her. Although, apparently she gave him a couple of blow jobs." She said this as though Audrey should find it interesting. "I wonder if Luke ever gave her one?"

"Why?" She didn't bother to explain that Tala's hormone therapy probably made that impossible.

Lucy looked surprised—as though she'd forgotten Audrey could speak. "Just nosy, I guess. It used to drive Kendra cray-cray wondering about it."

Okay, time to steer the conversation elsewhere. "Did the four of you spend a lot of time together?"

"Yeah. Mostly because Tala and Luke couldn't stand to be apart, and Kendra couldn't stand the idea of them being alone together."

"What about you?"

She shrugged. "I don't think any of them cared what I wanted. I was just there to hang out. It was better than being at home. Plus, I couldn't let Kendra go through that alone. I'd try to get her to go out with other guys, but she'd only do it when Luke was around. She thought he'd get jealous."

"Did he?"

"Are you kidding? He never noticed. One time Ken practically fucked a guy right on top of him. Oh. Is it okay if I swear?"

"You can say whatever you like." She folded her hands in front of her. "Do you guys see Luke much now?"

She shook her head. "Everything changed when Tala disappeared. Luke didn't want to see anyone, and Kendra's been a mess."

"What about you?"

"I just want everything to be like it was." Her eyes filled with wetness before a little gray tear streaked down her cheek, leaving a trail of eyeliner in its wake. "But it's not going to be, is it?"

Audrey handed her a tissue. She felt genuine sympathy for the girl, because she knew firsthand the kind of effect such violence could have on a friendship and the people around it. "No. I'm afraid it's not."

"Okay, I'm telling you this because I think it will help your investigation, and because it in no way puts me in moral or professional conflict."

Neve looked up when Audrey walked into Gracie's late Tuesday afternoon. "Telling me what?"

Audrey sat down with her. "Tala did not normally carry tampons in her purse."

"How did you find that out?"

"I asked Lucy Villeneuve."

"So there's a chance she had another girl with her that night."

"It could have been from another day, but sure."

Neve shot her a narrow look. "I notice you bypassed the bar and came right over here. He's watching you like a kicked puppy, you know."

Audrey didn't have to look to know Jake was behind the bar. She felt his presence with every nerve in her body, the secretive jerk. "I wanted to talk to you first."

Neve frowned. "You okay?"

She was not going to talk about it with him right there. She wasn't going to talk about it at all—at least not with anyone other than Jake. "Yeah, just a little frazzled. With Grace Ridge and the school, and then Bailey wanting to talk to me—"

"Bailey wants to talk to you? About what?"

Balls. "I don't know. I had a voice mail from her lawyer. I thought you might know."

Neve shook her head. "Something about the trial, maybe. She told her father she wants to live with her mother when she gets out."

Audrey nodded. "I understand that. If I could have gone somewhere else I would have. How did Gideon take it?"

"He's heartbroken and trying not to be. He loves that kid."

"That's why he's a good dad."

"Yeah, well, it would be great if Bailey's mother was a good mom."

"I don't know her. She wasn't from around here, was she?"

"He doesn't talk about her if he doesn't have to. The man's had some shit luck with women."

"Until now," Audrey reminded her with a smile.

Neve grinned. "Right. Listen, thanks for the information. I won't bring it up when I interview the girls—at least not in a way that brings you into it."

"I appreciate that. I do take privilege seriously, but I want you to find out who killed that girl."

"Nothing else you want to share, then?"

Audrey rolled her eyes. "Neve, no one is going to come to me on the first visit and admit to murder."

"I suppose that would be asking too much."

"And too easy. How's it going with the phone?"

"Oh, my God." She took a drink of cola. "There's so much drama on that thing. The only sensible friend she had seemed to be Alisha."

"Lish is a good kid."

Neve nodded. "And she's a Tripp so she knows better than to put anything in writing."

"Damn right," came a voice from beside them. Audrey started. She hadn't heard him approach. He was like a damn spider. When she lifted her head, he was watching her.

"Got a minute?"

Inside, she sighed. She ought to have known he wasn't going to let her just waltz in without a hello, even though he'd left that morning without a good-bye.

"Sure." Then to Neve, he said, "If you want help with the phone stuff, let me know."

"That's not a conflict of interest for you?"

"I don't think so. Plus, I'm fairly fluent in teen passive aggression."

"I'll take you up on that. I've got some interviews to do, but you want to get together later?"

"I'll call you."

"Great. Gideon wants to have you guys over for dinner some night, so we can discuss that too." Then she took a twenty out of her purse and handed it to Jake. "Thanks for lunch—and for letting me use this place as an office. See you guys later."

Then she was gone, leaving the two of them. There was only

one other person in the place, and that was Bertie Neeley. He sat at the bar with a beer, reading a book. He paid absolutely no attention to them. An intellectual alcoholic. Audrey supposed he wasn't the first, but how well could a person read when loaded?

Jake slid into the chair across from her. "I'm sorry about this morning," he said, and it was obvious he meant it. He looked like hell, and that wasn't an easy thing for him to achieve—at least not in her opinion.

"Are you having second thoughts about the wedding?" she asked. "Is that what's going on?"

"What?" He frowned. "Of course not. How can you even ask me that?"

"Because you're being weird and you're keeping something from me." She would not ask who Ashley was. She *wouldn't*. He would tell her. She had to believe that, because if she couldn't trust Jake then she couldn't trust anyone.

"It's nothing."

She leaned forward and grabbed both of his hands in hers. "Do not give me that bullshit, Jake. That might have worked for Gracie and Mathius, but it is *not* going to work for us. You and I don't have secrets, remember?"

He actually looked away. From *her*. When his gaze finally came back, it was full of uncertainty. She almost recoiled from the sight of it. His fingers tightened around hers. "I didn't go supply shopping today. I went to a doctor. Dr. Ashley."

Ashley was a fucking doctor. Okay, that was more of a relief than it ought to have been. "What kind of doctor?"

"He's an oncologist."

It was like a punch to the chest. "What?"

"This is why I didn't want to say anything. After your mother's surgery, and your father's heart attack, I didn't want you to worry about me too."

"Jake, just tell me why you went to an oncologist."

"Last week in the shower I found a lump."

"Where?"

He tilted his head with a slightly exasperated look. "Where do you think?"

Audrey's heart was beating a mile a minute. "And?"

"He wants to do an ultrasound before anything invasive. I'm going Thursday to have it done."

She inhaled a deep breath. She knew there was no reason to panic, but it clawed at her insides all the same. This was Jake. He was her life. If anything happened to him . . .

"Does it run in your family?"

He shook his head. "Nah. Cancer doesn't like our bunch. Look, it's probably nothing."

"But you're worried."

"Of course I'm worried. I just got you back. I was kind of hoping for a happily-ever-after for us."

In her mind, she could imagine Gracie, with her white hair and sharp eyes. *You got steel in your spine, my dar. You make sure you keep it.*

Right. She drew another calming breath. "You and I are dying in our sleep—together, sixty years from now. This is probably nothing, but if it is, it's got a great recovery rate."

"Yeah. I know."

Of course he did. He'd probably read everything he could find on it. "That paperwork you were doing last night?"

He actually flushed. "My will."

"You asshole."

His hazel eyes widened as he laughed in surprise. "I couldn't sleep. I was worried—it was something I could control."

"You should have woken me up. You should have talked to me about it. Jesus, Jake, I didn't know what was going on."

"I'm sorry."

"I know. Just, don't do that to me. Don't treat me like I'm fragile."

"I don't think you're fragile. I just didn't think there was any point of both of us worrying."

"Both of us worrying *is* the point. We're in this together."

Something changed in his gaze that made her realize she wasn't the only one with insecurities. Somehow, that only made her love him more. He wasn't infallible.

"I'm coming with you to the ultrasound."

He looked like he wanted to argue, but he didn't. "Okay."

Audrey leaned across the table and kissed him. "Good."

The sound of an accelerating engine and rubber on asphalt made both of them turn their heads. When it was followed by screeching tires and raised voices, they both rose to their feet and started for the door.

When they stepped out onto the front porch of the tavern, the sun was still high in the sky and there was a car stopped in the middle of the road. It was Lincoln's girlfriend's car—and both Lincoln and Marnie were in the ditch. Jake and Audrey shared a glance before running toward them.

Lincoln looked up when his brother shouted at him. Marnie was on her cell phone. Both of them were pale and looked shocked.

"Call Neve," Lincoln ordered. "We're on with 911 now."

Jake already had his phone out as Audrey looked down. T here on the grass was Luke Pelletier. She could tell only because she recognized the sneakers. He was battered and bloody beyond recognition.

"They tossed him from the car," Lincoln told her, an expression of disbelief on his face. "I think he's dead."

CHAPTER TEN

Neve hadn't quite reached the Granger house when Jake called. She did a U-turn in the middle of the road, flicked on the siren and lights, and headed back to Gracie's. What little traffic there was on the road quickly got out of her way—and then followed after her.

By the time Neve arrived on the scene, there were already three cars pulled over on the side of the road, and a small crowd had gathered. Jake and a couple other people she recognized as first responders and part of the volunteer fire department were in the ditch with the kid, the grass up around their knees. They'd take care of Luke until the ambulance from Eastrock arrived.

Audrey met her as she got out of her car. "I called Linda. She's at work, but going to meet them at the hospital. Lincoln and Marnie were behind the car that dumped him—not close enough to see the driver. Black Volkswagen with Maine plates. The last three digits." She handed Neve a receipt from Gracie's with numbers written on the back. Neve put it in her pocket to run later.

"The car didn't stop?"

"No." This came from Marnie, who stood behind her car,

out of the way of those in the ditch. "They threw him out like a bag of garbage. That's what we thought it was at first. T hen Lincoln realized it was a person." She shook her head, her perfectly highlighted blond hair swinging about her shoulders. She was an attractive woman a few years older than Lincoln, and she'd had a good influence on him. "Assholes."

"I'll need to get a statement from both of you," Neve told her. "Hang around for a bit once the ambulance has come and gone, okay?"

Marnie nodded and Neve left her to drop down into the ditch. It was only three to four feet below the road—part of a hayfield that belonged to an old farm. Luke Pelletier was on his back, looking like he'd been trampled by a moose.

"Has he been moved?" She asked.

Jake glanced up at her. He was crouched beside the boy, his fingers on Luke's wrist, monitoring his pulse. "No. We're not sure how badly he's hurt. His pulse is steady but weak."

Neve squatted beside him. She was careful not to touch anything as she took out her phone and photographed the teen. "Is that a boot print on his face?" she asked.

Jake nodded. "Looks like the Doc Martens logo on his cheek."

She took a photo of it. Blood was great for trapping evidence—like ink and glue rolled into one. "What size would you say that was?"

"Men's eleven."

She glanced at him. "What size do you take?" And then at his feet. "When you're not wearing flip-flops?"

"Eleven and a half to twelve, depending."

So she was looking for someone probably a little smaller than him—not that shoe size was that great an indicator. But she could be relatively certain it hadn't been a woman to kick Luke in the face.

Luke's eyelids fluttered. Neve leaned closer. "Luke? It's Detective Graham. The ambulance is on its way." She could hear the siren now. "You're going to be okay."

He didn't respond.

"Luke?" Neve glanced up to see Alisha standing on the edge of the road with Audrey holding her back. The girl looked right at her. "What happened?"

Before Neve could answer, Lincoln appeared and took the girl aside—where she couldn't see the boy.

The ambulance arrived a moment later, and the EMTs had Luke secured on his way to Downeast Hospital in a matter of minutes. Neve stuck around to take statements. Audrey and Jake both told her how they'd heard the car from inside Gracie's, and then Marnie and Lincoln told her how they'd started following the car when it pulled out of the Falls road.

Neve chewed on that. It was no coincidence that Luke Pelletier had been dumped from a car coming from the same road where Tala Lewis's body had been found.

"A black Volkswagen," Alisha repeated, her nostrils flaring. She looked right at Neve, and for a second, Neve was reminded of old Gracie Tripp, who used to scare the crap out of her when she was a kid. "Josh Lewis drives a black Volkswagen SUV."

Neve merely nodded. She'd run the partial number Lincoln had gotten against Josh's plates. "I'll look into it."

The girl looked like she wanted to say more. Hell, she looked like she wanted to set something on fire. Her uncle Jake took her aside and told her to go home. Neve stopped her just as she was about to get into her car.

"Don't do anything stupid," Neve said for her ears alone.

Alisha's eyes widened. "Like what?"

"Like going after Josh Lewis. You let me do that." Alisha opened her mouth to speak, but Neve cut her off. "You go home now, and stay there. Promise me. And I will personally call you once I've talked to Luke and let you know how he's doing, okay?"

The girl nodded. "Okay."

"Good girl."

"You don't have to patronize me."

"I wasn't. We should all be so lucky to have friends as loyal and stupid as you." It was said with a smile, one that Alisha returned. "Now, get."

With statements taken, Jake, Audrey, Lincoln, and Marnie went back to Gracie's while Neve got into her car and got on her laptop to check DMV records. Sure enough, the Lewis family owned a black Volkswagen with the numbers Lincoln had given her.

Pretty stupid of Josh to do this in broad daylight, but then again, why not? Not like there was a lot of traffic around usually. It had been luck that Lincoln had happened along. Maybe the kid didn't care if he got caught. Maybe he'd say that Luke jumped from the car and he kept going. Whatever his excuse, it didn't change anything.

She pulled out of the gravel lot and headed east toward the Lewis house. When she parked in the drive, there was only one other car there—Mrs. Lewis's Subaru. Neve climbed the steps to the house and rang the bell. A few minutes later, Mrs. Lewis opened it.

She looked surprised. "Detective Graham. What is it? Did you catch Tala's killer?"

"I'm afraid I'm here looking for your son, Josh. Is he home?"

The tiny Filipina woman frowned. "No. He's just home from college and is out with some friends. Why?"

"Is he driving your Volkswagen?"

"Yes. What is going on?"

Neve gestured for her to go into the house. "I need you to call him, Mrs. Lewis, and tell him to come home."

"But he's with his friends. Will you please tell me what this is about?"

Neve followed her into the kitchen. "It's about Luke Pelletier being beaten and tossed from a moving car, Mrs. Lewis. Now, please call your son and have him come home or I'll put out an APB on his car."

Mrs. Lewis pressed her hand to her chest. "Oh, my God," she said, but she also picked up the phone and started dialing. Neve listened as she told her son she needed him to come home right away. Obviously he put up a fuss, because she had to raise her voice. "I said come home right *now*, Joshua!"

Neve was waiting when Josh Lewis walked into the house. He was a good-looking kid—tall and athletic. He looked at her and his jaw lifted defiantly. She took one look at his bruised and torn

knuckles and shook her head. "You're in a lot of trouble, Josh."
Then she looked at his feet. He was wearing sneakers. "Let's start
by telling me who left his boot print on Luke's face."

Did u hear about Luke?

Alisha sighed as she read Kendra's text. She didn't know how
to respond. If she said yes, Kendra would wonder why she
hadn't told her, and Alisha didn't have an answer for that except she hadn't fucking wanted to. It was bad enough, Lucy
giving her a hard time for being friends with Luke; she didn't
need Kendra down her back either.

Yeah. It happened in front of Gracie's. She didn't mention that
she'd been there, or that she was waiting for Neve to call her.
And she didn't mention that she was sitting in front of her laptop with Twitter and Facebook and Instagram up just in case
someone posted something.

Has he called u? Kendra asked.

Had he called Kendra? It shouldn't matter, but it did. No,
there was no way Luke was calling anyone. He looked like her
uncle Jake had after that biker guy beat him up last fall. God,
that had been scary.

No. U? Still, she held her breath a little.

No. Let u know when I hear something.

She was not going to agree to the same. *Thanx.* She tossed
the phone on her bed only to pounce on it when it finally rang.

"Hello?"

"Fuck texting." It was Kendra. "Luke's sister just told me
Detective Graham arrested Josh Lewis."

Alisha sighed. "That's why I haven't heard from her."

"What?"

Shit. "Nothing. Did your cousin say if she arrested anyone else?"

"Don't know, but I just saw on Twitter that there's a cop car at Nick Taylor's house."

"I'm not surprised." Nick was one of Josh's best friends.

"You think they'll get in a lot of trouble?"

"I hope so. Luke was really badly hurt."

"Amie said it wasn't that bad."

Amie was a fucking idiot. "Kendra, one of them kicked him in the face."

"How do you know that?"

She really needed to learn to think before she spoke. Lying took so much frigging energy, and she didn't have it in her to do it anymore. "I got there just before the ambulance. I saw him."

"What?" Kendra practically shrieked. "Why didn't you say anything?"

"Because I didn't want to say something I shouldn't."

"If anyone deserves to know what's happened to him, isn't it me?"

Alisha couldn't help herself. "Why?"

"Because I'm . . . I *was* his girlfriend."

"Yeah, but you're not anymore." If she could, she'd have taken the words back.

"Right. And you want to be, is that it? Lucy told me you had a thing for him, but I didn't believe her. I guess I was wrong. Careful, Lish. His last girlfriend ended up dead." She hung up.

Alisha stared at the phone in her hand and shook her head. If she didn't know better, she'd think Kendra had just threatened her.

Neve kept her promise and called Alisha from the hospital early that evening. She apologized for making her wait so long and tried to make amends by telling her that Linda said she could come by the hospital the next day if she wanted. Luke was going to be there for a few days.

The Pelletier family wanted to press charges, and Neve didn't blame them. It didn't matter at that moment if Luke was Tala's killer or not. She hated it when people took the law into their own hands. There was a lot of that sentiment in Edgeport: this weird throwback to the Dark Ages when an eye for an eye reigned supreme.

Not on her damn watch.

The Lewises were upset, understandably. Their daughter had been murdered and now their son was locked up for assault. Josh maintained his defiant attitude, saying that Luke had killed his sister and deserved what he got. He refused to name his accomplice, but Neve didn't think it was going to be too hard to find him.

No, what had her pissed and wishing she could lock people up for being shit-disturbers was Josh's reason for the beating.

"I heard what he said about her," the boy told her. "What he said about Tala."

When he didn't immediately offer it up, Neve arched a brow. "Which was?"

The young man's babyish face hardened. "He said he could never love a freak like her and that she deserved to die. He said he was glad she was gone."

"Who told you that?" Neve had asked.

He looked away, jaw tight.

"Josh, you are in a lot of trouble right now, my friend. You need to tell me what got you so riled up, or things are just going to get worse. You think your college is going to appreciate a criminal record on one of their students? What do you think this is doing to your parents?"

It was the parental card that did the trick. Josh looked down at the floor. "Kendra."

"Kendra Granger?"

He nodded.

Neve frowned. Kendra was supposed to have a thing for Luke, so why make trouble for him with Josh? "She told you Luke said those things?"

"Yeah. She said he was already over Tala—that he'd been fooling around with Alisha Tripp behind her back."

Ah. Neve rubbed the back of her neck. God save her from jealous teenage girls. "And you took her at her word."

"Kendra was the first friend Tala made when we moved to this fucking stink hole. Why would she lie?"

Neve just shook her head in response. Why would Kendra talk about wanting to kill that same friend? Because some teenage girls have an awful lot in common with psychopaths.

Which was why she was standing on the Grangers' front step waiting for someone to answer when she could have been home enjoying a cold beer and a nice thick steak grilled to perfection by her gorgeous man. Her underarms were sticky, and she hoped she didn't have BO. She needed a shower and still had bits of hay stuck to her socks.

Kyle answered the door. "Detective Graham." He grinned. "Couldn't stay away, huh?"

A smirk was as good as she could muster. "Is Kendra home?"

"Yeah, sure." He stood back and let her in. "Kendra!"

Neve didn't even wince. She was used to bellowing boys, thanks to her brothers and their friends.

Mrs. Granger appeared in the hall. "Kyle, there's no need to shout. Oh. Hello, Neve. What can we do for you?"

"I need to speak to Kendra, Elle."

"Can't it wait? This business with Luke Pelletier has her very upset."

"That's why I want to talk to her."

Tiny lines of concern fanned out from the woman's blue eyes. As a kid Neve had imagined rich white women looking exactly like Elle Granger.

Kendra came downstairs in leggings and an oversized top. She looked as though she'd been crying. Her pretty face was red and blotchy and her eyes swollen.

Neve smiled at her. "Hi, Kendra. Got a minute?"

It was that hesitation, that look of "oh shit" that the kid sent her mother that told Neve what she needed to know. Kendra Granger was a girl who realized she'd fucked up, and now she was trying to think of a way out of it.

"Come into the living room," Elle said. "I'll make tea."

"That won't be necessary," Neve told her. "I won't take any more of your time than necessary. Kendra, did you tell Josh Lewis that Luke said his sister deserved to die?"

Elle's perfectly lipsticked mouth dropped open. "What?"

Kendra's eyes were wide. "No," she said in a small voice.

"So, he's lying then? You didn't tell him that Luke had been cheating on Tala with Alisha Tripp?"

The girl frowned. Shifted her weight from one foot to the other. "I didn't say he was. I said I thought he was."

"*Was* Luke cheating on Tala with Alisha?"

She shrugged.

"Oh, Kendra," her mother said on a long-suffering sigh. "Why would you do that?"

It was a good question. Neve waited for the answer.

"Because I was upset that Luke and Alisha are spending so much time together. I didn't mean for Luke to get hurt. I was just mad."

"Did you tell him Luke said Tala deserved to die?"

"You already asked that," Elle said.

Neve kept her attention focused on Kendra. "Did you?"

She nodded, a tear rolling down her cheek.

"Oh, you are *so* busted," Kyle crowed.

Neve looked at him, then down at his feet. When she was a kid her mother would have smacked her for wearing shoes in the house. There was a rusty smear on the side of the glossy leather on his right foot, and some on the laces. "Are those Doc Martens?"

His expression turned wary. "Yeah."

"Size eleven?"

"Yeah."

She cocked her head. "Is that blood on your laces?"

Elle braced a hand against the staircase. "Oh, my God."

"Are you and Josh friends?" Neve continued when Kyle didn't answer her previous question—not that she needed him to. She knew blood when she saw it.

He swallowed. "Yeah." And then, "Okay, I was with him. He said Luke killed his sister—and he fucked around on mine."

Kendra sank down onto the stairs, pale and scared-looking. Elle looked as though she needed a drink. "Kyle. What did you do?"

"He helped beat another boy severely, Mrs. Granger. He left his boot print on Luke Pelletier's face. And he did it because your daughter lied." She glanced at Kendra. "That pretty much sum it up?"

The girl nodded. She looked like she might throw up.

"So, now I have to arrest your brother for assault. Do you understand what that means? He's going to jail."

Tears were flowing down the girl's cheeks now. Elle was talking, but Neve ignored her. She kept her attention fixed on Kendra. "Did you and Lucy ever talk about wanting to kill Tala in front of Luke?"

"Now just one second!" Elle cried. Kendra's tears were coming harder now. "My daughter may have made a terrible mistake, but she is not a killer."

Neve looked her in the eye as she took Kyle by the arm. "Does Mr. Granger own any hunting knives?"

The woman's face darkened with fury. "Get out."

Shrugging, Neve drew Kyle toward the door. "You're under arrest, Kyle. Do you know your rights?"

"I'm calling our lawyer now!" Elle remarked, stomping down the hall.

Neve turned to Kendra, still sitting on the stairs. "Did you say you wanted to kill Tala?"

"We were joking," she sobbed. "We wouldn't have really done it. I was just being jealous. It was just a joke."

"I get the feeling it's not so funny now," Neve retorted, dragging a protesting Kyle out the door. Once she talked to Lucy and other kids from the class, she'd be back, but she'd had her fill of the Grangers' lies and the fact that everyone involved seemed to want to make Tala's murder about them, and not about the girl who was actually dead.

CHAPTER ELEVEN

Audrey had a full pot of coffee made when Neve and Vickie arrived at the house Wednesday morning. Since the school had called and asked if she'd switch to afternoon appointments that day instead of morning, she didn't have anywhere she needed to be for a couple of hours.

Neve had Tala's laptop, her phone, and a stack of papers with her for the three of them to look at. They sat in the dining room, with its tall windows and original wainscoting. It was one of Audrey's favorite rooms. When Gracie was alive the family always ate in that room. Quite a few times, she ate there with them.

"I've flagged several things," Neve told her. "But feel free to go through feeds and screen shots. Anything you can offer or that jumps out is great."

"No promises," Audrey said. "But sometimes a fresh pair of eyes is good."

They sat down at the table with tea and biscuits and got to work.

Neve dumped sugar in her mug. "Techs are working on recovering deleted texts from Tala's phone. We should have them today."

"I'm assuming they use software to recover them?" Audrey asked.

"Either that or they sacrifice a goat," Vickie quipped. "Regardless, it works. What about this? On February sixteenth Tala tweeted, 'People say they accept you as you are, but they never do.' Probably a dig at Luke?"

"I remember that from when she first disappeared," Neve commented. "Did he respond?"

Vickie shook her head. "No."

"Not to Tala," Audrey said, looking up from her laptop. "But on his own page he said, 'Wish things were different. Wish I was different,' and then, 'Don't feel much like talking, Twitterverse. Out of here for a few days.' Then Kendra asked him what was wrong and he didn't reply. He didn't post again until almost a week had gone by. 'I miss u. I'm sorry. Come home.' He posted it once a week for the first four weeks she was missing."

"Yeah, her phone was full of texts from him begging her to get in touch. Some of them more agitated than others. Nothing that makes him look good for the murder, though," Vickie said.

"Might just mean he was smart enough not to say anything publicly," Neve reminded her.

"What about the girls?" Audrey asked. "What were Lucy and Kendra tweeting while they thought Tala was missing?"

"There were a lot of 'please come home' and 'we miss you' posts. Then some about hoping she was in New York following her dream. Kendra stopped posting before Lucy did. Lucy was still tweeting at Tala a week before we found her. Not even once a week, but she was still posting."

Audrey looked through the screen shots Neve had provided. "December sixteenth, Kendra posted, 'The people you're supposed to trust most r the ones you can't turn your back on.'"

"Yeah, that's around the time Tala and Luke got together," Neve supplied.

Audrey flipped through the pages. "Kendra had a lot of passive aggression where Tala and Luke were concerned." She turned back to her laptop. "And she spent a lot more time asking how he was after they broke up than she did Tala."

"Yeah, but she would have seen Tala in person—at least for a couple of days. She might have asked her then."

Arching a brow, Audrey glanced at her. "Defending the girl whose shit-disturbing efforts put one boy in the hospital and got two more arrested?"

"I didn't say she was smart—or necessarily nice."

"I'm just glad we didn't have this kind of social media when we were teenagers." Audrey shook her head. "Can you imagine?"

Neve chuckled. "Imagine the shit Maggie would have been posting."

"Or the stuff people would have said about you," Vickie offered, glancing at Audrey. "*To* you, even."

Audrey's smile faded. She hadn't thought of that. For one second she'd forgotten that she'd been a pariah. Social media would have torn her apart back then. It tried to on occasion now. "You're right. Kids these days are aware of that. We're not going to find any clues in tweets. We should be looking at the people who haven't said anything. Who has been uncharacteristically quiet online?"

"Not sure, other than Luke," Neve replied.

"What about Randy Dyer?"

"He doesn't have any social media accounts except for Twitter. He's not on there very often."

"Maybe he has half a brain after all."

Neve's phone dinged. She flipped her finger across the screen. "They're sending me Tala's deleted texts."

Audrey pushed her laptop aside and reached for a biscuit. She had no idea how long this kind of thing took and she was starving. Plus, eating gave her something to do while they waited.

A few moments later, Neve opened the files. "Not too many." She read off a phone number. "Who is that?" she asked Vickie.

"That's Kendra."

"Okay, the day before she was killed, Tala got this text from Kendra: 'I can't believe u did this to Luke.' And then, 'U might not have been born a girl, but you're a bitch enough.'"

Audrey swallowed. "That's harsh—and typical of seventeen-year-old girls."

"Here's one from Lucy," she continued after verifying the number again. "'How could you have done this to Luke and Kendra? What the fuck is wrong with you?' And then a few minutes later, 'Do you want to break Ken's heart?'"

Audrey frowned. "Is she talking about the two of them dating? Because that happened months before the murder."

"Here's another from Lucy: 'You lying backstabbing bitch.'"

"Whoa," Vickie said. "What's that about?"

Neve's eyes widened. "Maybe about this. Check this number." She read it off before continuing. "'Cum'—spelled *c-u-m*—'over tonight. At house alone.' Tala replied, 'I shouldn't. It's not right.' The person replies, 'No one will know. Our sercet'—must have meant 'secret'—'I just need to be inside you again. I miss you.' Tala wrote back, 'I want it too. C u soon.'"

The women exchanged glances. "What the hell?" Audrey said. "*Again?* I thought Tala hadn't had sex."

"Everyone did," Neve replied. "Or at least that's what Tala wanted them to think." Then to Vickie, "Any luck on that number?"

"It's not one we have on file." She pulled out her cell phone. "Should I call it?"

"Block your number," Neve told her.

They all sat in silence as Vickie put her phone on speaker, dialed, then waited as it rang.

"Hey, it's Kyle. Leave a message. If I care I'll call you back." Vickie ended the call.

The workings of some teen lives, Audrey reminded herself, were more interesting than any soap opera. "If Tala was seeing Kyle, that definitely gives him motive to go after Luke. And for Luke to be pissed."

"Did Luke know?" Vickie wondered out loud.

"I think so," Neve replied, her face tense. "Listen to this: 'I know what you did. And I know why. I'll make you wish you'd never met him. You'll wish you'd never dumped me. You'll regret it, I promise.'"

It was at that moment that Audrey realized they weren't alone. Alisha stood in the doorway, her pretty face pale and hurt. How much had she heard?

"What are you doing here?" Audrey asked. "You okay?"

She shook her head. "Mom said I could stay home and go visit Luke in the hospital. He didn't say that. He wouldn't hurt Tala. Never."

Audrey nodded. "Okay." At that moment she didn't want to say anything to upset the girl further, especially since she had a car she could jump into. "Everyone says shit when they're mad. That's probably all there was to it. Did he ever say anything to you about Tala cheating?"

She shook her head. "A little while ago he asked me why I thought people cheated, but he never said anything about Tala. She never said anything to me about Kyle either."

"Alisha," Neve began calmly—but sternly. "It's very important that you don't tell anyone what you just heard."

"I know. I won't say anything."

"It might also be a good idea if you don't go see Luke."

The girl's expression turned to a glare. "Why? Because you think he's dangerous? He's in fucking traction."

"Lish," Audrey said, trying to calm her down.

"No. I'm going to see him. You know, maybe you guys should stop looking so hard at the guy who actually loved Tala and wasn't afraid to be seen with her in public and instead look at the one who pretended to hardly notice her while using her as a booty call. How about that, Detective?" She pivoted on her heel and left the room. The screen door slammed behind her.

"I think I've been schooled," Neve remarked wryly.

"She's not wrong," Audrey commented, with a bit of pride.

"No, she's not." Neve stood up. "Which is why we're going to visit Kyle while I still know where he is. I'm thinking Josh Lewis might be interested in the fact that his best friend was doing his sister behind his back."

"You don't think he knew?" Vickie asked.

Neve shot her a narrow glance. "You don't have brothers, do you?" When the trooper shook her head, Neve smiled. "I do. And If Josh had known about Kyle and Tala, Luke Pelletier wouldn't be the one in traction right now. Let's go."

* * *

Alisha put the car in park at the bottom of the road and sat there for a second. Uncle Jake had told her never to drive angry, and she had promised him she wouldn't, so she took a couple of calming breaths. Rationally she knew it was Neve's job to look at everyone as a suspect; she just wished people would stop looking so hard at Luke.

He wasn't guilty. She knew it in her heart that there was no way he could hurt anyone, let alone someone he cared about. She'd been raised in a family that would kill to protect what was theirs—and it was a sentiment in which she firmly believed. But it was nice to know there was someone in the world who was honestly so good he couldn't imagine a circumstance in which he could end another person's life.

So, even if everyone else believed the worst of Luke, she

believed in him. But she had also believed in Tala, and now she knew that her friend had been fooling around with Kyle Granger behind Luke's back. Did Luke know?

It was so disappointing. And it pissed her off. She could maybe understand it if Tala had gone to Kyle after Luke had rejected her, but it sounded like it had been going on before that. How could you be with a stoner guy-whore like Kyle when you had Luke? She just couldn't wrap her mind around it.

And then Kyle helped Josh beat the snot out of Luke. Asshole. At least Neve had arrested both of them. Maybe she knew what she was doing after all. At least a little bit.

Finally, she put the car in drive and headed toward the hospital. Her mother had let her go see Luke only because the classes she would miss were ones she had really high grades in. She had to be at school by the end of lunch so she wouldn't miss the entire day.

Luke's mother met her at his room. She was a nice woman who reminded her a bit of Audrey's mom. She went to get a coffee so Alisha and Luke could visit.

He looked like shit. Good thing both of his eyes were swollen practically shut so he couldn't see the tears in hers. She hated crying in front of people.

"Lish?" He said.

"Hey, Luke."

"Sit down so I can see you." His voice had that low, drawn-out quality that she usually only heard in people who were drunk or really stoned.

She plunked down in the chair by his bed, catching a glimpse of blue under one puffy eyelid. "Are you in pain?" She asked.

He made a noise that might have been a laugh, but it turned into a moan. "Fuck, yeah."

"Neve arrested Josh. Kyle too."

"Kyle." He practically spat the name. "Fucking asshole. Did you know about him and Tala?"

"No!" How could he even ask her that?

"Didn't think so. You're not like other girls." Another one of those pained laughs. "Thought Tala wasn't either. I was wrong."

"Tala just wanted to be accepted."

"I tried."

"I know."

"Kendra lied. Told Josh I said shit I didn't say."

"Kendra's a bitch."

"Just jealous."

"Don't defend her, Luke."

His eyelashes fluttered as though he was trying to open his eyes further, but the swollen lids didn't budge. "Be careful."

She frowned. "Me? Why?"

"She's still jealous of Tala, and she's dead. I don't want her to go crazy on you."

"She already knows we're friends."

"You're more than a friend. You know that, right?"

Alisha's heart skipped a beat. It might have skipped two. "No. I didn't."

"Now you do. So promise me you'll be careful. Don't trust Kendra."

She didn't to begin with. "I won't." Then, on a wave of braveness she didn't know she had, she put her hand on top of his. He moved his fingers so he could lace them with hers, her heart pounding a crazy rhythm. If this was how Audrey and Jake felt about each other all the time, no wonder both of them were pretty much crazy.

"I'm not going back to school," he told her. "Mom's decided it's not safe. She's going to see if they'll send work home and let me take my exams privately."

"That's pretty hard-core."

"She's scared."

She didn't tell him that she was too—or that she was mad. Mad enough that every part of her that was pure Tripp wanted to do something dark and vengeful. But she also knew she had to be smart about it. "I'll tutor you," she offered.

His thumb rubbed against the side of her hand. It made her entire palm tingle. "Yeah? I'd like that."

When his mother returned, they were still sitting there, holding hands. Alisha went to pull hers away, but Luke wouldn't let her. "Mom, Lish said she'd help me with school stuff."

Linda's shoulders sagged. "Alisha, you have no idea what a help that would be." Then, to her son, "Neve Graham arrested Josh."

"Kyle Granger too," Luke said.

"Really?" His mother looked to Alisha for confirmation. "Is that true?"

Alisha nodded.

"Thank God. I hope the little bastards rot."

"Mom..." Luke began. "...Don't."

Alisha looked at him. His expression went slack and the fingers around hers loosened their grip.

"Pain medication," his mother said. "He'll be out for a while. You can stay if you like." She was looking at their entwined hands.

Blushing, Alisha pulled her hand free of Luke's. Her fingers felt cold. "Thanks, but I promised Mum I'd go to school. Would it be okay if I came back later?"

His mother smiled, making apples of her cheeks. "I think he'd like that."

Alisha returned the smile with an awkward one of her own. "See you later, then." She left the room with tingling fingers, a tight chest, and a fluttering feeling in her stomach.

She still had plenty of time before she had to return to class, so instead of going to school, she went to the library. Luke's warning to be wary of Kendra rang fresh in her head as she searched for books for the project she was working on for history class. If Kendra was cracked enough to get the boy she liked beaten up, what would she do to the girl he liked?

She wasn't worried for herself. Not really. But it did make her wonder if Kendra was capable of hurting Tala—or manipulating someone else to do it like she manipulated Josh. She and Lucy were supposed to have been Tala's best friends. They were among the last people to see her alive. If anyone knew what happened the night she was killed, it was the two of them. They had to know *something*. Alisha hadn't been as close to Tala and she knew about the sex thing, and other personal stuff she didn't want to think about now that Luke had held her hand. God, she was *such* an idiot.

Before meeting Audrey she really wouldn't have suspected her classmates of being capable of murder, but then Bailey proved her wrong. Bailey, who had been her best friend and so sweet and kind, had been driven to a place where she snapped. If Bailey could get there, Kendra certainly could.

Holding the two books she'd found on the Stonewall riots, she went downstairs to where the public computers were. T here were only three—not like Eastrock was a booming metropolis. One was available, so she sat down and went online. It only took a few minutes to make the fake Twitter account. She felt absolutely no guilt about using Tala's school e-mail to set it up. Of course she knew the password—it was *Luke4ever!*. She'd been there one day when Tala logged in and thought it was cute.

Now, she was starting to wonder if she'd known Tala at all.

Before she could change her mind, she composed her first tweet as @TroothGrrl. *@Kenndrahh69 @LuceeVeeMD Your BFF is dead & u don't know *anything*? Come on. Everyone knows u know something. #JusticeForTala.* She clicked to post, her heart pounding even harder than it had with Luke. Could she get in trouble if anyone figured out it was her? No. She hadn't done anything wrong.

Yet.

But she was beginning to realize she was a lot more like her family than she wanted to admit. Tala had been her friend, and even if she'd lied or kept secrets, that was still true. And then there was Luke, who she liked more than she was willing to admit to anyone, even herself. She wanted to help him. Wanted to prove he wasn't a killer. Uncle Jake told her to be certain she was willing to face the consequences for her actions. That was how she would know if she was doing the right thing.

Was she willing to face the fallout for trying to find Tala's killer and clear Luke's name? Yes, she was. No matter what they were.

CHAPTER TWELVE

When Neve had said that "we" were going to visit Josh Lewis and Kyle Granger, Audrey had thought she meant Vickie, not her. Regardless, she found herself a short time later in an interview room with Neve, staring across a table at Kyle Granger's face. He didn't look like a boy who had just beaten another practically to death. In fact, he didn't look like a boy at all. He looked like a young man. He was probably only a couple of years older than Luke Pelletier, but Audrey understood why Tala would have been attracted to him. Luke still had a bit of a babyish look while Kyle didn't.

"I already told you everything about the fight," Kyle said to Neve.

"That wasn't a fight, it was a beating," Neve reminded him. "And I'm not here to discuss it. I'm here to discuss your relationship with Tala Lewis."

He shrugged. "Josh is my best friend. I've known Tala since they moved here."

"How long had you and she been seeing each other?"

"We weren't," he replied with a frown.

Neve tilted her head. "So you were just hooking up for sex?"

"No!"

"We found a text from you on her phone, Kyle. In it you said that you wanted to see her and 'be inside' her again. So, were you seeing each other, or was it just sex?"

To his credit, Kyle didn't look embarrassed, but he did look worried. His slacker-cool veneer had slipped, revealing the boy beneath. "You didn't tell Josh, did you?"

"I assume, then, he didn't know about you and his sister?"

"No. He was really protective of her. He wouldn't have wanted her dating someone older. He thought there was less chance of her getting hurt with someone her own age." He glanced at Audrey. "I guess he was wrong. Who are you?"

Audrey gave him a half smile. "I'm Dr. Harte."

"The shrink."

"Psychologist, actually."

Kyle glanced at Neve. "So, what? You think I'm nuts?"

"No. Dr. Harte is here because she's very good at telling whether someone is hiding something."

He frowned. "Like what?"

"Well," Audrey began, "the fact that you were sleeping with your best friend's sister, for a start."

"I would never hurt Tala. I liked her."

Audrey maintained the smile. "But only enough to sneak around with her, not openly date her."

His frown deepened as he leaned closer. Neither Neve nor Audrey moved. He was no danger to either one of them. "T hat was what she wanted. She didn't want Josh to know about us. She didn't want her friends to know either."

"Why not?" Neve asked. "When I was that age I would've bragged to my friends about dating a college boy."

"Because she already had a boyfriend." Kyle flushed. "He was the one that couldn't accept her as she was, not me. But I was the one she wanted to keep secret."

"That must've been upsetting for you," Audrey surmised.

He leaned back in his chair. "Yeah, it was." His fingernail scraped at something on the top of the table. Audrey didn't want to know what it was. "It was like she was ashamed of me or something."

Tala's guilty little secret. The girl probably was ashamed of the sexual feelings Kyle awakened in her.

"When was the last time you saw Tala?" Neve asked.

"The weekend before she disappeared. Josh and I were home on spring break. She showed up at a party we were at, but Randy Dyer was there and she didn't want to stay. I told Josh I wasn't feeling well and that I'd take her home."

"So, Luke Pelletier wasn't at this party?"

"No. We don't usually allow high school kids."

Audrey couldn't help the slight smirk that twisted her lips. "You mean you don't normally allow high school boys, right? High school girls are always welcome." She'd been to a few of those kinds of parties after being released from Stillwater. Being a convicted murderer kind of put the kibosh on getting hit on, though Maggie never seemed to have any trouble getting laid. But then, Maggie had made it obvious that she was looking. Audrey hadn't.

He lifted his chin. "Yeah, they are."

Neve tapped her finger on the table. "Did you and Tala have sex that night?"

"What's that got to do with anything?"

"It just helps us establish what happened leading up to her death. Did you have sex with her that night?"

"Yeah. We did."

"Did she ever talk to you about Luke?"

He shook his head. "We didn't talk about him. And before you ask, we didn't talk about the girl I was seeing either."

"Did anyone else know you were taking Tala home that night?"

"She told my sister. Kendra knew what a prick Randy was being, so she understood why Tala didn't want to be there."

"But she didn't know that you and Tala were seeing each other?"

"Not that I know of. Kendra would've been pissed. She would've come at me about it."

Audrey had been silent through this exchange, but she wondered if maybe Kendra had figured out what was going on between her best friend and her brother. Had Kendra told Luke in the hopes of breaking him and Tala up?

"Maybe she went at Luke about it instead," Neve suggested, as though she'd read Audrey's mind.

Kyle shook his head. "Ken's not like that."

"Really?" Neve asked. "Because she admitted lying to you and Josh about Luke."

His face paled, but his expression was resolute. "I don't believe that."

"You were there," Neve reminded him.

"Your sister was jealous because of Tala's relationship with Luke," Audrey informed him. "She wanted to get back at him. She just didn't think the two of you would take it so far."

For the first time since they'd walked in, Kyle Granger looked as though he'd regretted what he'd done. "Are you being serious? You're not just saying that?"

"She admitted it." Neve gave him an assessing look. "The Pelletiers are pressing charges against you and Josh. The two of you are in a lot of trouble. Is there anything you want to tell me that might make things easier for you?"

Kyle didn't hesitate. "Okay, Tala did say something about Luke once. The night of the party, when I took her home, I asked her why she hadn't called her boyfriend to come get her. I was being a douche. She said that Luke would've been mad that she'd gone to the party, and that sometimes she was afraid of him when he got mad."

Neve nodded. "Okay. One more thing, where were you the night Tala was killed?"

"Back at school. I was with Josh when his parents called. I kept expecting her to show up at our dorm. When she was still gone the next day I knew something bad had happened." Poor kid looked like he might cry. Audrey actually felt for him. He might be, as he'd said in his own words, a bit of a douche, but he seemed to have been the one person who'd been able to accept Tala exactly as she was.

"Thank you, Kyle." Neve rose to her feet. "That's all for now."

He looked up at her, an almost desperate expression on his

face. "It wasn't my fault, was it? He didn't kill her because he found out about me, did he?"

As Audrey watched, Neve's expression turned to one of startling compassion. "I don't yet know why Tala was murdered, but unless you were the one to end her life I can honestly tell you that you are not responsible for the actions of anyone else." It might not be complete absolution, but it was pretty damn close, Audrey thought.

Apparently, Kyle thought so too, because he actually smiled. "Thanks. You know, if Pelletier did it, I don't mind facing charges."

"And if he's innocent?"

His smile faded. "He still deserved it for breaking her heart."

Audrey and Neve watched as he was led from the room by a guard. "You know," Audrey began. "I can't help but kind of respect the little bastard."

"Yeah," Neve agreed with a sigh. "Me too."

Kenndrahh69 @TroothGrrl Who are u?

TroothGrrl @Kendrahh69 Someone who wants to know the truth.

LuceeVeeMD @TroothGrrl @Kendrahh69 What truth?

TroothGrrl @Kendrahh69 @LuceeVeeMD The truth about what happened to Tala. #JusticeForTala

LuceeVeeMD @TroothGrrl @Kendrahh69 WTF? Why are you asking us? We don't know.

Kendrahh69 @TroothGrrl She was our friend. We loved her. @LuceeVeeMD

TroothGrrl @Kendrahh69 @LuceeVeeMD Which is why no one believes that you don't know something. Why keep it secret? Unless you have something to hide?

"Who the fuck is this bitch?" Kendra demanded as she sat down beside Alisha in the cafeteria at lunch.

Alisha looked up from her pizza. Kendra rarely swore, but it was becoming more of a habit lately. The sight of the girl responsible for Luke lying in that hospital bed made her want to drop a few F-bombs herself. "What bitch?" she asked—as if she didn't know. She'd spent more time at the library earlier than she'd meant to.

"Truth Girl," Kendra replied.

"You mean 'troooooth grrrrrrrrrrrrl.'" Lucy chuckled as she joined them, pizza, fries, and diet soda on her tray. "Stupid name."

Inside Alisha bristled, even though she'd wanted to get a reaction from them. "Never heard of her."

Kendra shot her a disbelieving look. "You didn't see what she said to us on Twitter?"

Alisha shook her head. "I haven't checked my feed yet."

Lucy's eyes narrowed. "Where were you this morning, anyway? You missed English."

She opened her mouth, trying to think of a reply, but Kendra beat her to it. "She was at the hospital. Weren't you? T hey don't like cell phones there. How's Luke?"

It was an innocent enough question, but Alisha was wary. Before she'd seen Luke she probably would have told them where she'd been, but now that he'd told her that he liked her, everything had changed. She felt protective—possessive, even. And she was wary of both their reactions. Still, she wasn't about to be intimidated, despite Luke's warnings that she not trust Kendra. "He's good, considering what your brother and Josh did to him."

Kendra's face turned white. "I feel so bad about that."

She looked guilty, Alisha thought. Good. "Yeah? Why? You have something to do with it?"

Lucy swatted her on the arm. "Shut up."

But Alisha kept her gaze focused on Kendra, whose eyes were filling with tears. "It was an accident. A mistake. I would never hurt Luke, you know that."

Alisha didn't know shit. "Well, he *is* hurt. Pretty fucking bad too." She had no sympathy as a tear trickled down Kendra's pale cheek. "He said you lied to Josh."

Lucy snorted. "If anyone's lying, it's Luke. Fucking Truth Girl should be asking him what happened that night."

"Why?"

Lucy turned her bright gaze toward her. It felt like being stuck with a pin. "He was the one she was fucking around on, not us. We were her friends. He was the jealous asshole."

"Luce," Kendra said, chastising her. "That's not fair."

"Oh, wake the fuck up, Kendra! We all know Tala was screwing your brother. That's why she broke up with Luke— not because he couldn't get it up, but because she was already getting it from Kyle. Luke found out about them and killed her. It's simple."

"Shut your damn mouth," Alisha ordered. "You don't know shit."

Kendra was staring at Lucy. "You knew about Tala and Kyle and never told me?"

Lucy shrugged. "I thought you knew and didn't want to talk about it."

"No, I didn't know!" Kendra was pissed. "Jesus, you're supposed to be my best friend."

Lucy's gaze narrowed. "Yeah? I'm your bestie again now that Tala's dead? You had no fucking time for me when she was alive."

"That's not true!"

"Sure it is. You were so jealous of her and so horny to break her and Luke up that you spent every moment with her, and fucked off on me."

Alisha shook her head. "I really don't want to be part of this."

"You already are," Lucy informed her. "Why do you think she's so interested in you now? It's because she knows Luke likes you. She's fucking obsessed with him, even though he popped her cherry and then dumped her."

Kendra flushed from the neckline of her shirt to her forehead. "Shut up, Lucy. You don't know shit."

"Oh no?" Lucy said, challenging her. "Tell Alisha what you told me. Tell her how Luke broke up with you like two days after having sex with you."

Alisha stared at Kendra. "Is that true?"

Kendra nodded, tears trickling down her cheeks. "I heard he did it to his last girlfriend too."

"He's like a virgin collector," Lucy said. "Fucks and leaves."

Alisha's appetite vanished. Suddenly, all she wanted was to be as far away from them as possible. "I have to go." She grabbed her backpack and leapt up from the table. She moved as fast as her legs would carry her, her stomach churning with dread.

Then she thought of Luke's beaten face, and how he'd pleaded with her not to trust Kendra.

Ducking around a corner, Alisha waited two breaths before peeking around it to where she'd left the girls. They were sitting closer together, talking quietly. She watched in disbelief as Kendra—not a tear in sight—grinned at Lucy and high-fived her.

It had all been a big show—designed to make Alisha turn her back on Luke. And she'd almost fallen for it. God, how stupid did they think she was? They were the stupid ones if they thought all their manipulation would ever convince Luke to get back together with Kendra. And just how far was Kendra willing to go to eliminate the competition?

Alisha checked her phone. She had fifteen minutes before class. Instead of going to her locker, she headed to the library. There was no one around, so she logged in with Tala's information and went straight to Twitter.

TroothGrrl: Best Actress goes to @Kendrahh69 for her display of waterworks in the caf at lunch. Funny, she was all smiles 2 secs later w/ @LuceeVeeMD.

And then, because she was really pissed:

TroothGrrl: Hey @TrippyLish, hope you didn't fall for @Kendrahh69's fake tears.

She logged off that account and left the library. A few minutes later at her locker, she logged in on her phone and tweeted *@Kendrahh69 @LuceeVeeMD WTF?*

When the bell rang, she went to class, took her seat, and waited for Kendra and Lucy to walk in. When they did, they didn't even look at her. Alisha bit back a smile. They thought they could fuck with her head? She was a Tripp. She'd show them how head-fucking was done.

CHAPTER THIRTEEN

You don't need to come with me," Jake told her as they got ready to leave for his ultrasound on Thursday. "It's no big deal."

"I'm coming." She grabbed her purse. "You think Gracie would have let your grandfather do this alone?"

He actually chuckled. "Not a chance."

"Well, then get your skinny ass in the truck and let's go."

Neither one of them was overly worried about the outcome of the tests. Audrey was pretty certain it was just going to be a cyst or something equally benign, but there was still that whisper of "what if?" in the back of her mind. Jake had it too—she could tell. She supposed they both had a sense of the macabre—not that anyone could blame them. They had lost a lot of time together because of pride and hurt. They had a shared fear that something would happen to cut short the time they had left.

It made her all the more aware of her mother's struggle with cervical cancer. It didn't run in the Pelletier family, and Jess hadn't had any issues, but that didn't mean Audrey wouldn't. It had been too long since her last exam, and so she'd made an appointment with her gynecologist for later that month just to be on the safe side.

"How's the crew making out on the girls' dorm?" He asked as they drove.

"Pretty good. They should be done by the end of June." The benefit of having an old farm as the basis for the facility was that there were plenty of outbuildings to remodel. Audrey had decided that the main house would serve as dining hall, recreation area, and classrooms, with a couple of the upstairs bedrooms reserved for teens who might not feel safe with a roommate.

"Angeline planning another visit soon?"

"July, when she makes a trip up to the Cambridge office." She sighed.

He shot her a glance. "You losing your love for the place?"

Audrey shook her head. "Hell, no. I'm anxious to get it done. I want it open and working. But sometimes it feels like we'll never get it all done."

"You will."

"I couldn't have done half of this without you." He was not only her main emotional support, but he'd invested a lot of money in the place. So had Angeline. Even with the extra funding they'd managed to obtain, she was humbled by the amount both of them had sunk into her dream.

"Guess you'd better stick around then," he joked. "You still going to love me if I have to lose a nut?"

"I'll knit you a falsie."

"Use something soft. You know how delicate I am."

She smiled. "Yeah, right." It was funny: because he was fairly quiet and lean, people always assumed he wasn't strong. Wasn't tough. The man was fast as a snake and deceptively strong. He'd been the only person—other than her father—who thought her choice of fight over flight was a positive trait.

When he reached across the seat for her hand, she met him halfway. Their fingers twined together like vines.

"Did you remember to wear shoes?" she asked, glancing down at his feet.

Jake laughed. "Yes, mum."

"You've forgotten before." He hated shoes and wore them as little as possible. Audrey was not a fan of flip-flops or anything that got between her toes, but they were Jake's footwear of choice if he had to wear something. That day, however, he was wearing a pair of gray slip-on sneakers she'd gotten him at Target. They were half a size too big, just to meet his psychological need for room.

When they got to the hospital, they had to wait about twenty minutes before he was called in. Since they had no idea how long it might take, Audrey decided to check in on Luke—partly for Alisha and partly out of family duty. Her mother would never let her hear the end of it if she knew Audrey had been at the hospital and hadn't looked in on her cousin.

And partly because she needed to see if she got any kind of dangerous vibes off the kid. So far she hadn't, but she'd been wrong before, and this time and she wasn't prepared to risk Alisha's emotional or physical well-being.

She took the elevator up to Luke's floor and made her way to the room number her mother had given her. As she walked down the quiet corridor, she saw a familiar form walking toward her, her head bowed, sobbing into her hands.

"Kendra?"

The girl stopped and looked up, hastily wiping at her swollen eyes. "Dr. Harte. Hi."

Despite the fact that the girl's lies had gotten Luke hurt—and that that she'd been trying to manipulate Alisha—Audrey felt compassion for Kendra. She was a hot mess, obsessed with a boy who no longer wanted her and desperate for attention. In a way, she reminded Audrey a bit of Maggie, and of herself. At seventeen she'd been so in love with Jake she couldn't see straight. She'd considered not going to college to be near him. And then he slept with Maggie—the one thing he knew would make sure she left.

As much as she loved him, there was a part of her that would never forgive him for that, that would always feel the sting of that betrayal, no matter how noble the reason. He'd known how to play her and he'd done it with precision purpose.

"Are you okay?" It was a stupid question, because obviously the girl wasn't, but it was the least intrusive one she could think of.

Kendra shook her head, her long brown hair drifting around her shoulders. "Luke won't see me."

Had the kid really thought he would after all she'd done? "He's probably tired and in a lot of pain."

Her eyeliner was half an inch below her eyes, smudged and wet. "He saw Alisha."

As much as Audrey liked working with teens, she knew better than to think of them as unaware. So Kendra's defiance and tone when she said Alisha's name sparked a feeling of protectiveness. She kept her tone low and neutral, however. "Alisha didn't try to get him in trouble with Josh."

The tears fell again—harder this time. "I didn't mean to! I was just so mad."

Audrey was totally unprepared when the girl threw herself at her. The next thing she knew, she was being held in a viselike grip around the ribs, and getting mascara stains on her shoulder. She gave Kendra's back an awkward pat. "Once he's better you can apologize and try to make it up to him, if you want. Right now, he's hurt and angry and not in a place where he can hear it."

The girl nodded and Audrey lamented not wearing black. She tried not to grimace. "Dry your eyes now, and go on back to school. Do you want me to tell Luke you're sorry?"

Kendra's head whipped up. "Would you?"

Jesus, the little thing was a mess. "Yes. Why don't you go splash some water on your face and fix your makeup? It will make you feel better."

"I will." Kendra hugged her again. "Thank you."

Audrey watched her walk away, then continued down the corridor. Linda watched her from the door of Luke's room.

"Thought I heard her carrying on to someone. Sorry it was you."

She smiled. "It's all right."

Her cousin's face hardened. "No, it's really not. She ought to be ashamed of herself after what her actions did to Luke."

Audrey wasn't about to argue with an upset mother, especially not one who was family. "How's he doing?"

"Good. Better than expected, but it's going to take a while for him to heal."

"It will, but he's young and that helps." When Jake had gotten beaten up last fall it had been so hard to watch him recover, but now there was no indication anything had ever happened to him. The same could be said about her own injuries when she got into a fight with Matt Jones almost a year ago.

"It's so hard watching your child in pain."

That was something Audrey could not relate to, and to be honest, she had no desire to. She saw what her sister and brother-in-law went through with the girls, and she'd seen how devastating a miscarriage had been for them. It wasn't an experience she was prepared to face.

Plus, there was all that poop.

"He's sleeping right now, or I'd have you come in and talk to him." Linda's brow furrowed in concern. "I worry what kind of effect this is all going to have on him."

"I can only imagine how hard it's been. You know, I can recommend some good therapists if you think he might benefit from one."

Linda nodded. "Thank you. And thank God he has friends like Alisha and Lucy. Both of those girls have been there for him, especially Alisha."

Pride blossomed in Audrey's stomach. "She's a great kid. Very loyal to those she cares about."

"Yes, well, I think Luke cares about her too." There was a wealth of meaning in her tone. "I appreciate Yancy allowing the friendship to continue despite all the rumors. More than a few mothers have gone out of their way to tell me they don't want my son near their daughters."

"They just want to protect. They don't care if the rumors are true."

Linda nodded. "I suppose I can't fault them for wanting to keep their children safe, but when it's my child they're calling a monster...well, I understand now what your mother went through." A heartbeat. "Oh. Audrey, that came out so damn wrong. I'm sorry."

Audrey had no regrets about what she'd done except for the pain it had caused her family. She didn't like thinking about what her mother had gone through. "It's okay, Linda. I imagine it's very hard, but the difference between Luke and me is that I actually did it." She wasn't totally convinced of Luke's innocence, but again, they were family. She wasn't going to say that to his mother.

Her cousin grabbed her hand and squeezed hard. "Thank you for believing in him. Can I...may I ask a favor?"

Audrey wasn't sure, but there was no way she could refuse to listen. "Okay?"

"You're a smart woman. You helped the police find killers before."

"I think the killers found me." She wasn't joking. Since coming home she'd found herself stumbling upon a variety of terrible secrets and the people who kept them.

"Will you help my son? Help prove Luke is innocent?"

Seeing the dark circles under her eyes and the strain in the lines of her pretty face—so much like Audrey's mother's—

Audrey could not refuse her. "I can't make any promises, but I'll do what I can." So much for telling her father she'd stay out of it.

They talked for a little while longer, until Jake texted that he was done. His tests had gone way faster than Audrey expected. She said good-bye to Linda and gave her a hug and then walked toward the elevator. As she walked past a waiting room she heard a familiar voice: "Can you believe his fucking mother wouldn't let me see him? I'm his alibi for the night Tala disappeared. You'd think she'd be nicer to me, the fucking bitch."

Audrey put her back to the wall near the doorway and listened.

"Yeah, I was going to stay until she left and try to see him again, but I think she spends all her time here... No, Alisha hasn't been here yet. I bet fucking Linda will let her in to see him... That shrink the school hired was here... She's the only person who's been nice to me about all of this. You know I didn't make Josh and Kyle beat Luke up. All I want is to apologize to him... Would you really...? Thanks so much, Luce. You're the best... I'd better get going. Mom doesn't know I cut class to come here. I'll see you in a bit."

Quickly, Audrey backed down the corridor, then started walking again. She met Kendra just as she came out of the visiting room.

"Hey," Audrey said in greeting. "Still here."

"Yeah." Kendra smiled sheepishly. "I needed a minute to calm down. I'm going to school now. Did you see Luke?"

"No. He was sleeping. Can I offer you some advice?" Audrey hit the button for the elevator.

Kendra looked hesitant. "Okay."

"Give Luke and his mother a little time before you try to visit again. Right now she's really worried about him, and incredibly protective."

The elevator doors opened and they both stepped in. "But I would never hurt Luke."

"In her mind you already have." Audrey tried to put it as gently as she could. "Obviously I can't tell you what to do, and you have to do what you think is right, but I think they both need a little time."

Kendra was still silently mulling that over when they arrived on the ground floor.

"See you, Kendra. Have a good day."

"You too," the girl replied absently. "Hey, Dr. Harte? T hanks."

Audrey smiled. She felt absolutely no guilt about trying to worm her way into Kendra's confidence. No shame in manipulating a teenage girl. After all, she had been one once, and she knew how devious they could be.

She found Jake standing in the waiting area, looking restless. "Well?" she asked as she approached.

He looked tired. "We wait for the doc to call with the results." He took her hand. "How's Luke?"

"Didn't see him. He was sleeping. Talked to Linda, though. She asked me to help catch Tala's killer."

"And you said?"

"That I'd do what I can, not that it's very much."

"Oh, give it some time. You'll do something that brings whoever did it right to our doorstep."

"You don't look worried about it."

"I'm not. Son of a bitch comes after you, he deserves what he gets." He squeezed her fingers. "Let's go get some lunch."

Audrey squeezed back as they walked outside, but part of her couldn't help but wonder if there was seriously something wrong with her for thinking just how convenient it would be if the killer did come knocking.

She just hoped it wasn't actually Luke.

Randy Dyer answered the door in sweatpants and a T-shirt. He looked as though he had just gotten out of bed even though it was almost two in the afternoon. He also looked hungover.

"Hello, Randy." Neve greeted him with a bright smile. "Got a minute?"

"You know, I don't gotta talk to you anymore. They dropped the charges, so fuck off."

Her smile turned into a baring of teeth as she shoved her foot in the door frame so he couldn't close the door. "Tommy Boggs says he saw Jimmy Dodsworth's truck on Park Road the night Tala went missing. Jimmy says you were with him. He also said you took off on your own for a while."

The door swung open again. "Tommy's an asshole."

"I won't argue with you, but that doesn't change the fact that you left out your whereabouts when I asked you about that night. You knew I'd ask, Randy. Now you just look suspicious."

"I told you I didn't kill the faggot."

"You know, Randy, I'm beginning to think you're a bit of an asshole too."

"Fuck off." He started to close the door again.

"If that door touches my foot I'm going to arrest you for assaulting a police officer," Neve said quickly. "Now, get your bigoted ass out here and talk to me."

She'd never seen anyone look so sullen. She'd obviously been spending too much time with Audrey, because—seriously—she wanted to pistol-whip the expression off his face. "What do you want to know?" he asked.

"Did you see Tala at the Falls?"

"No, but I did take off for a little while, so she might have come by. Tommy likes it when high school girls show up at parties."

Back to referring to Tala as a girl. "Where did you go?"

He looked away, the muscle in his jaw tensing.

"You're making this harder than it needs to be, Randy. I'm just trying to find a killer."

He sighed. "I was banging this chick."

Neve frowned. That hardly seemed to be something he'd want to keep to himself, a fine young man like Randy, who wasn't insecure about his sexuality at all. "What, is she someone else's girlfriend?"

"No."

Her shoulders sagged. "Is she underage?"

Now he looked at his feet. "I don't know."

"Who was it?" When he said nothing, she added, "Just spit

it out. I can start asking around. Shouldn't take too long. T here are probably at least three girls in this town stupid enough to get with you. But then I might get a lot of fathers upset— including yours."

Randy lifted his chin to glare at her. "Lucy Villeneuve."

Huh. That actually came as a surprise. Lucy didn't really seem to be a fan of Randy's. Maybe he was right to be insecure. "Well, you're in luck, Romeo. She's seventeen and that makes her legal." When he visibly relaxed, she added, "Might want to make certain of that next time before you get your dick out."

A sneer tugged at his lips. "You really don't like me, do you?"

"Not even a bit. So Lucy was back there. Was Kendra with her?"

"Kyle's sister? Yeah, she was there. Tommy kept trying to get with her, but she told him off."

"What time was this?"

"How the fuck should I know? Around eight or nine. I brought Lucy back around ten. The two of them hung out until probably eleven and then they left. Kendra got all drunk and sloppy and was talking about Luke Pelletier and how much she loved him or some shit. Tommy made another play and she started crying and told Lucy she wanted to go home."

If Kendra had been at the Falls with Lucy, she couldn't have been with Luke—as she'd told Neve she had been back in February when they first looked into Tala's disappearance. At the time there hadn't been a lot of talk about alibis because the thought was Tala had run off or had been abducted. So why lie, unless Kendra knew something about what had really happened? Was she covering for Luke? Or using Luke to cover her own ass?

"Is there anything else you need to tell me?" she asked. "Because I don't want to come back here any more than you want me to."

Randy thought for a moment, then shook his head. "Nope. No, wait..." His eyes widened. "Right before they left, Lucy told Kendra that she was worried about Tala—she'd called but hadn't gotten an answer. Kendra got this hateful look on her face and said that Tala could die for all she cared."

Neve stared at him. "You're *just* remembering this?"

He shrugged. "I was pretty drunk. And hey, it sounded like something bitchy girls say about each other. I didn't care."

"You're a real piece of work, Randy." Neve turned on her heel and walked down the steps. "You should go back inside and change that T-shirt. I think it's got puke on it."

"You're fucking welcome, Detective!" he called after her.

Neve raised her hand in a wave. He didn't even notice that she'd given him the finger.

Her phone rang. She fished it out of her pocket and glanced at the screen as she opened the car door. She recognized the name as belonging to a reporter for a local news station. She tapped the screen to send it to voice mail. She'd deal with the woman later. Better not to leave it too long, though. The reporters had already started talking to anyone in town willing to be on TV. Jesus, one night they'd had Bertie Neeley on there asking him his opinion on the murder. Bertie did the town proud by staring drunkenly at the camera as he asked, "Which one?"

She needed to verify Dyer's story about the party. If Luke was the killer, or if Kendra was, she was going to need to make sure she had as much evidence as possible. The courts hated prosecuting juveniles because it was such a slippery area. She was going to need an expert in kids and murder to put it all together.

She was going to need Audrey.

CHAPTER FOURTEEN

A lot of kids came into the office wanting to talk about Tala. It had been a week since her body had been found, and the shock of it had given way to the realization that she was never coming back—and that someone they knew might have ended her life.

"I can totally believe Luke did it," one guy in a buckskin and work boots said.

"Luke would never hurt Tala," said another as tears slid down her round, freckled face. "Why would anyone want to hurt her?"

There was one student, however, for whom Audrey took extra time, and who offered insight into Tala and her life. On the appointment calendar, it said their name was Shannyn, but when Audrey looked up to say hello, her first thought was that the person in the doorway did not identify as female.

"Hi," she said. "You can close the door if you like."

The teenager did just that before crossing the floor and sitting on the love seat. They wore loose jeans and a black T-shirt that hid whatever slight curves might lie beneath. Their blond hair was shaggy and reminded Audrey of something a surfer might sport.

"Shannyn?" she asked. When the teen winced, Audrey knew her assumption had been correct. "Is there a name you prefer to be called?"

The kid looked a little surprised, which made Audrey's heart hurt. In this day and age, how hard was it to try to respect a person's identity? It might be awkward to come out and ask, but she'd always found that better than assuming and then being wrong. Her job was to make people comfortable enough to open up, not shut them down.

"Hank," they replied. "I identify as male."

She smiled. "Welcome, Hank. Do you mind if I ask what brings you here today?"

"My mother wanted me to come. I've been kinda sinking into a depression ever since they found Tala's body."

"I've heard that from a few people. Were you and Tala close?"

Hank nodded. "Sort of. We didn't hang out a lot in groups, but once in a while I'd go to her place or she'd come to mine. It was nice to have someone else who was transitioning to talk to."

"I imagine it was good for both of you. How did you meet?"

"She just sat down one day with me at lunch. She told me I looked lonely, and that she knew how that felt. It took me a second to realize what she meant. I mean, Tala could really pass, y'know?"

Audrey nodded. If Neve hadn't told her, she never would have guessed that Tala hadn't been born physically female. "So, the two of you bonded?"

"We did. She said she could talk to me about things she couldn't talk to Kendra and Lucy—or even Alisha—about."

"Such as?"

"The fact that she was seeing Kyle in secret, and how guilty she felt about it. I think she really liked Kyle but felt like Luke was the guy she ought to like, you know? Luke's popular, but not too much, and he's nice and smart."

Not too smart, Audrey thought, if he sent threatening notes to his girlfriend.

"Plus, I think Tala kind of liked driving Kendra crazy."

"Oh?"

"Yeah. She knew how much Kendra hated the fact that she was dating Luke. She kinda got off on rubbing it in whenever Kendra was being a bitch to her—which was a lot."

Girls. "You must miss having someone to talk to like that."

Hank swallowed. "I do. I mean, I have the online community that Tala introduced me to, but it's not the same."

"What's the group?"

"INTO—Intersex, Nonbinary and Trans Online. It's kinda like Facebook, but safer."

Audrey nodded. Neve must already know about it. She had Tala's laptop. "The Internet can feel like a dangerous place." How many social media–induced suicides had she come across in her research? So much bullying and threats—and not always from their peers, but from adults as well. People were just shit sometimes.

"Yeah—not like here is much better. Until Tala showed up I was the only trans person at school—that I know of. And that's just it. There might be more, but they're afraid to come out. Jesus, being trans is probably what got Tala killed."

"Maybe try not to think of it like that," Audrey cautioned.

"The responsibility for her death falls on the person who killed her, not who she was." She didn't mention that maybe Tala had been killed for another reason. Tala's murder had been very personal. Unless they were serial crimes, most murders were over something specific. She hadn't killed Clint just because he was rumored to be a child molester. She'd killed him because he'd raped her best friend. And she didn't think Tala had been killed because she'd been trans—it wasn't that well known a detail. No, she was certain Tala had been killed because of something much more personal, but what?

"I've been having dreams the last few nights that someone is trying to kill me," Hank confided. "I wake up screaming. That's why my mother made this appointment. It's getting so I'm afraid to be alone."

Audrey wanted to hug him, but that would have been so unprofessional. "What would make you feel safer?"

"I don't know. Knowing I could fight them off, maybe? I've just started on hormones and I don't have the same strength as a cis guy."

"My father taught me to fight," Audrey confided. "Then, when I was older I took some kickboxing and Krav Maga classes. Isn't there a martial arts studio in town?"

Hank straightened. "Yeah, on Main."

"Maybe they have a class you'd be interested in taking? The exercise will be good for easing your anxiety, help you sleep better, and the training might make you feel safer, or at least better equipped to protect yourself. And it will build muscle tone."

He brightened at the prospect. "You're right."

"I also want to ask if I'm right in assuming you don't have a regular therapist?"

"No. I'm supposed to with the transitioning and all, but I haven't found one yet."

Audrey gave him her card. "This is so you can reach out if you want—at least until you get something regular going. I'd like to see if I can find a few suggestions for you. Is it all right if I call your mother and give her the names?"

"Yeah. That would be great, thanks."

The change in his demeanor—that brightening of spirit—was a not-so-subtle reminder to Audrey that she loved her job. It wasn't all about forensics, it was about helping kids.

She and Hank talked awhile longer, until their time was up. Audrey made another appointment for him the following week and watched him leave the office with a lighter burden than when he'd come in. She was pretty damn proud of herself at that moment.

She was still basking in it when her phone rang. It was Neve. "What's up?"

"Do you have Linc's cell number? The one I have doesn't work anymore."

"Oh, yeah. He and Marnie got new phones."

"Jesus, he's gone domestic."

Audrey laughed. "It's a bizarre thing to witness." She gave Neve the number. "Can I be nosy and ask why you need it?"

"Are you alone?"

"Yep."

"ME found traces of GHB in Tala's tox screen. We're lucky

winter was as long and cold as it was because normal decomp would have destroyed any evidence. I want to know if anyone local is hooked up. I figure Linc would know more than our database."

"That's a sad commentary."

"Yeah, well, we just have the ones who have gotten caught. He might know some that haven't."

"You think he'll give you names?"

"He will."

Audrey didn't want to know why she was so confident. "T he drug certainly would have made her easier to kill."

"Don't I know it. Thanks for the number. Talk to you later."

She hung up. As she made notes on her appointment with Hank, she couldn't help but be distracted by thoughts of Tala. Had someone drugged her intending to assault her and then killed her when they discovered she wasn't physically female? Or had someone planned her death and drugged her to make it easier to do the killing?

Clint's being drunk had made him easier to kill. The alcohol thinned his blood, making him bleed out faster. It also slowed his reaction time, making it easier for a young girl to bring down a man bigger and stronger than she was.

Tala hadn't been that big, so who was she bigger and stronger than?

Another girl, of course.

TroothGrrl wasn't the only person calling out Kendra and Lucy. Other people had started demanding to know what happened to Tala—and what the two of them knew about it. Unfortunately, these people weren't just sticking to Kendra and Lucy, they were making demands of the state police and the town of Edgeport itself. News coverage of the murder had spread across not only the state but the entire country.

And of course, the fact that Tala had been transgender only made it more scandalous. Sometimes Alisha just hated people.

She went to the hospital after school. Luke's mother was asleep in the chair next to his bed when she walked in. Luke's left eye opened—the right was still swollen shut.

"Hey," he said with a sleepy, mangled smile.

Alisha smiled back. Even beaten stupid he made her heart skip a beat. "Hi."

His mother stirred, then woke. She blinked and pushed herself upright in the chair, wincing as she straightened her neck. "Alisha. Hi."

"Is it okay that I came by?" She asked.

"Of course, sweetie. You two can visit while I run down to the cafeteria for a coffee and something to eat." Rising to her feet, Linda smiled at the two of them and then grabbed her purse and left the room.

"Has she even gone home?" Alisha asked.

"Yeah, but after Kendra tried to visit today she won't leave my side unless someone else is here."

She moved closer. "What happened when Kendra showed up?"

"Before I could say I didn't want to see her, Mom lost it. I've never heard her talk to anyone like that. Ken was in tears when she left."

There was part of Alisha that was pleased by that news, and she didn't like it. "I guess she probably wanted to apologize."

"You know what she can do with her apology."

Yeah, that made her happy too. "Can I ask you question?"

Luke reached out and touched her hand. "Sure."

"Did you text Tala that you'd make her sorry she hooked up with Kyle?"

"Oh, fuck," he groaned. "Yeah, I did. But I didn't mean it like that." His fingers grasped at hers as she turned to go. "Seriously, Lish. I meant I'd be a better boyfriend and make her regret ever seeing anything in that loser. It was just before we tried...you know." He might have blushed, but she couldn't tell under all the bruising.

Maybe she was dumb where he was concerned, but she believed him. He looked her in the eye and she couldn't see any hint of a lie. But then, she hadn't known her best friend was a fucking killer either.

"I guess that doesn't look good, does it?" he asked.

She shook her head. "I told Neve you didn't mean it as a threat."

"Thanks, but I doubt she took your word for it." He sighed. "She'll probably come question me."

"I'm surprised she hasn't already."

"Apparently she tried, but Mom and the doctors told her no. She probably figures I'm not going anywhere soon."

"Neve's not stupid. She'll figure out you didn't do it. You have an alibi for that night."

His thumb stroked the side of her hand. "Yeah," he said, but his tone was hesitant. Alisha didn't push it. "Mom wants to press charges against Kyle and Josh."

"You should."

He shrugged—or at least she thought that was what it was. He didn't really move a whole lot. "I think Tala's family has suffered enough. And I don't blame Kyle. He obviously had a thing for Tala. I should have just walked away from her and let the two of them be together. Obviously he's more accepting than I am."

"She had a way of making people want to be with her."

"Yeah, she did." His gaze met hers. "So do you. You make me want to be better."

Alisha laughed. "Liar."

"No, I mean it."

She shifted uncomfortably. "Okay. Thanks."

Luke laughed and then winced. "Ow. I think I just popped a stitch."

"Really?" Alisha reached for the call button.

"Wait. I think I'm okay. Can you just check my stomach?"

She peeled back the sheets. "Um, you're only wearing a gown."

"Just lift the left side. What? You're getting shy on me now?"

He was right. It wasn't like it was a sexual situation. He might actually need medical attention. Besides, he held the sheets against his groin, so it wasn't like he was going to flash her. Slowly, she lifted the edge of the gown.

"Oh, my God," she whispered hoarsely.

"That bad?"

She'd never seen bruising like it. His ribs were wrapped like

Uncle Jake's had been last fall, but the damage looked so much worse. The idea of what kind of force they'd had to use against him made her throat tight and her eyes burn.

"Hey, don't cry."

"I'm not going to fucking cry." She sniffed. "I don't cry in front of people."

"I'm not just any people, am I?"

She shook her head, blinking back the hot moisture that had formed behind her lashes. Then she inspected the bandages that covered the places where he'd had to be stitched up. "I don't see any fresh blood."

"Good. Okay, cover me back up before Mom walks in and thinks you're trying to molest me."

Alisha rolled her eyes. "Right, because I couldn't resist you."

He smirked—but it was cute. "You can't. Admit it. I am your Kryptonite."

"I think they must have kicked you in the head."

"They did."

Heat rushed up her cheeks. "Shit. I'm sorry."

"Hey, it's okay."

"No, it was stupid of me."

"Kiss me and I'll forgive you."

That seemed like a fair trade. Smiling, she leaned forward, lowering her head. Gently, she pressed her mouth to his.

"Well, isn't *this* cozy."

Alisha jumped back, heart thumping against her ribs. Standing just inside the doorway was Lucy, and she looked pissed. A sneer twisted her lips as she walked into the room.

"Just what the fuck do the two of you think you're doing?"

Alisha's temper flared. "None of *your* fucking business."

Lucy hesitated. Alisha took that opportunity to advance on her instead of being stalked as prey. "Nothing that Luke and I do has anything to do with you."

"How can you do this to Kendra? I thought you were her friend."

"I'm not doing anything to Kendra. And I'm not sure I want to be friends with someone who got a guy she's supposed to like almost beaten to death."

"But you've got no trouble going after her ex-boyfriend."

"Ex is right," Luke said. Alisha glanced at him. He'd pushed himself up against the pillows. It must have hurt like hell because he was sweating and his breath was sharp and shallow. "Kendra and I have been broken up for a long time. I'm sorry if she can't accept that, but she's the one who broke up with me."

"You know she didn't mean it," Lucy told him.

"Whatever. It's done."

She turned back to Alisha. "You're a real piece of work, you know that? We just found out Tala is dead. She hasn't even been fucking buried yet. The two of you going to go to her funeral as a couple?"

"Yes," Alisha and Luke chorused. Alisha flashed a smile in his direction.

"Whatever," Lucy said in disgust. "Maybe when he kills you, everyone will see what he's really like."

Alisha straightened. "Get out."

"If you really think I'm a killer, why do you want me to get back together with your best friend?" Luke asked. "I'd think you'd care about her more than that."

Lucy glared at him. Her silence made it obvious that she had no argument against that logic. "Fuck you both," she said finally, and stomped out of the room.

Slumping in relief, Alisha turned to face Luke. "Well, that was..."

"Look out!" Luke cried.

Alisha whipped around just in time to catch Kendra as she launched herself at her. Nails raked her neck as fingers grabbed her hair and pulled hard enough to rip out the roots. Alisha shoved an arm up in an attempt to protect herself, and then she did what Jake had taught her to do. Her feet instinctively went into a fighter's stance and she caught the other girl in the jaw with a right hook, which was followed by a left cross when Kendra staggered backward. That wasn't enough, however. Kendra immediately came at her again.

Alisha's neck burned, and she could feel blood running down her chest from where Kendra's nails had clawed her. Her head snapped back when Kendra slapped her, and then Alisha let her right fist fly again.

Snap.

Kendra cried out as she fell to the floor, hands clutching at her nose. Blood seeped between her fingers. Lucy ran to her. She shot Alisha a look of pure hatred. "You bitch!"

"What is going on here?" Luke's mother demanded as she walked into the room. As soon as she saw Kendra, she ran back out into the hall and yelled for security. Lucy pulled Kendra to her feet.

"We have to go," she said to her friend, but it was too late. Security got to them just as they reached the door and escorted them away.

Alisha was stunned. She couldn't believe what had just happened. She'd gotten into a fight—over a boy. God, how *high school*. She'd sworn she'd never do anything so stupid. She'd sworn she'd never do a lot of things, several of which had changed when she started hanging out with Luke. That should have scared her, but it didn't.

A nurse came and cleaned up her neck, then applied a few Steri-Strips and a gauze pad over the scratches. Two of them were quite deep, but she'd had a tetanus shot just two years ago after stepping on a nail, so she was good.

Linda hugged her when the nurse left. "You poor thing. I'm so sorry."

"It's not your fault," Alisha told her.

Linda looked at her son. "I don't know what you ever saw in that girl."

"She used to be nice," he said. Then, to Alisha, he added, "I'm sorry too. And it is *my* fault."

She was suddenly too tired to argue, but she shook her head—it hurt her neck.

Alisha left a few minutes later. There didn't seem to be a reason to hang around—and it felt awkward after what had happened. She walked out into the parking lot and looked around to make sure there was no sign of Kendra or Lucy before heading toward the car. Her right hand throbbed and her neck burned and she was beginning to wonder what was wrong with her that she seemed to attract fucking crazies.

She hit the unlock button on the remote as she approached the car. She took one look at the driver's-side window and stopped dead in her tracks. Someone—gee, she had a fifty-fifty chance of guessing who—had left her a note. It was written in a dark red lipstick, like Kendra often wore, and it was short and to the point. Alisha took out her phone and snapped a picture of it.

DIE BITCH.

CHAPTER FIFTEEN

There was a camp not far from the Falls, just outside the state park, so that part of Randy's story was at least true. Neve went to the Granger house to ask Kendra about it—and to discuss the call she'd gotten from Linda Pelletier earlier demanding a restraining order against the girl. Elle Granger had retaliated with talk of filing charges against Alisha, who had apparently broken her daughter's nose, and then told Neve she was not stepping foot in her house without a warrant.

It wasn't the first door to ever be closed in her face, but it pissed her off all the same. She was just getting into her car when she got a call from Audrey, asking her to come by because of something to do with Alisha.

When Neve arrived at the house on Tripp's Cove Road, she found Alisha with a red mark on her cheek and a bandage on her neck.

"Kendra Granger attacked her," Audrey said.

Yancy, Alisha's mother, was there as well, standing beside her daughter's chair. "The Grangers obviously think they can assault people and get away with it."

"Mom," Alisha protested.

"From what I hear, Alisha did a good job of defending herself. Kendra Granger's nose is broken."

"Broken?" Alisha's head came up. Her eyes were wide as they turned to her mother. "I didn't mean to hurt her. I just wanted her off me."

Yancy's mouth tightened. She turned her attention to Neve. "What are you going to do about this?"

"Your best bet is a restraining order. Linda Pelletier asked for one against Kendra as well."

"Linda told Kendra Luke didn't want to see her," Alisha offered. "She kept coming to the hospital anyway, waiting for Linda to leave the room so she could sneak up."

"The girl's definitely been exhibiting obsessive behavior where Luke is concerned," Audrey offered. Then, to Yancy, she said, "I think a restraining order is the way to go. Certainly, it will be a faster way to keep Lish safe."

"I don't need to be kept safe," Alisha countered. "I just don't want to have to watch my back when I see Luke."

Neve shook her head. "I told you staying away from him was your best option." The girl simply stared at her. "Okay. Elle wouldn't let me see Kendra to take a statement, so I'll get one from you. I'll give you a written receipt of the complaint. Then I'll tell the Grangers Kendra needs to stay away from you. If that doesn't work, you'll need to go to the courthouse in Machias and get Protection from Harassment forms from the clerk. If you need help or have questions, I'll do what I can. Now, tell me what happened."

She wrote down Alisha's version of events.

"Show her what was on the car," Yancy urged, nudging her daughter's arm.

Alisha seemed reluctant as she picked up her phone and unlocked it. Neve understood far too well what it was like to be a teenager and not want to cause trouble, but she wondered if something else was keeping Alisha from wanting to talk. When the girl offered her the phone, she took it.

"Is that lipstick?" she asked.

Alisha nodded. "Same color Kendra wears a lot."

"Did you see her do this?"

Alisha shook her head. "No. I found the car like that when I left the hospital."

"Why is Kendra so hung up on you?"

The girl looked away. "She thinks I'm what's keeping her from getting Luke back."

"They always want to blame who they think is the other woman," Neve commented. "Never the man—or themselves. She ever act this way with Tala?"

"Not that I know of."

"It could be," Audrey began, "that Kendra saw Tala as a temporary rival for Luke's affections. When they broke up, she thought she had a chance to get him back, and now she sees Alisha as a threat to that goal. It would explain her erratic behavior."

"Or," Alisha added, "she killed Tala to get rid of her and now she's completely losing her fucking grip."

Yancy swatted the girl in the shoulder. "Language."

Neve turned to Audrey, who was giving her that look that

meant she'd thought the same thing. "Let's just stick with what we know, okay? Conjecture never does well in court."

"Really?" Alisha challenged. "Because you have no problem believing Luke threatened Tala."

"I saw the text." Neve tried to not sound argumentative.

"And now you've seen the threat Kendra left for me."

"Yes," she allowed. "I have. And the reason I haven't arrested Luke is that I don't have any concrete evidence against him. And evidence is what I need to put the right person in jail."

Alisha didn't have a response to this, and for that, Neve was glad. Arguing with teenagers was not her strong point. Eventually she reverted to her father and just started shouting orders. Her mother was so much better at this kind of thing.

"So you'll take care of the Kendra problem?" Yancy asked. T here was something in her eyes that made the hair on the back of Neve's neck stand up. She and Lincoln and Jake all shared this kind of flinty glint to their eyes that seemed to say, *'Cause if you won't, I sure as hell will.*

"I'll talk to both girls and their parents," she promised. Then to Alisha, she said, "I'll tell them to stay away from Luke too, but that said, I want you to stay away from them. If you see them, walk away. Don't give either one of them reason to engage."

"We have classes together."

"Avoid them within reason."

"You could take a few days off school," Yancy suggested.

Alisha shot her mother a dark look. "I'm not hiding."

Yancy actually smiled. "Didn't think you would, little Gracie."

Her daughter blushed. Apparently, that was high praise.

Neve's only memories of Gracie Tripp were silvery-white hair, an intimidating gaze, and the fact that she always scooped the biggest cones of ice cream. Her father hadn't trusted the old gal. Said she was "Bonnie without Clyde" after her husband died.

Audrey walked Neve out. "Did you get in touch with Lincoln?" She asked.

Neve nodded, shrugging out of her blazer. It was a warm day and she was done with feeling sticky. She was going to go home and have a beer. "I did. He didn't know anyone off the top of his head, but he's going to ask around."

"Listen, a drug like that would make it easier for a girl to be the killer."

Neve arched a brow. "Yeah, Nancy Drew. I thought of that."

"Fuck off. I'm just trying to be helpful." It was said with a smile.

Neve jerked her chin toward the front door. "What's going on with Alisha and Luke?"

"Not sure. And I'm not sure I like it, either."

"I'm pretty sure it wouldn't matter if you did."

"You're not wrong. She's a Tripp through and through."

"Have you ever suspected...?"

"No." Audrey pointed a rigid finger at her. "And don't you, either. After all she's been through, the last thing Alisha would do is kill someone over a boy."

"I'm glad you clarified that. Otherwise I might mistakenly think she'd never kill anyone period."

She was given a droll look in response. "You know what I mean. Looking at her is grasping at straws. She had no motive."

"I can't see that anyone had a strong motive at all," Neve confessed. "It's like that case we were discussing—the Virginia one."

"The Neese girl?"

"Yeah. Those girls said they killed her because they didn't like her anymore. How lame is that?"

"It's a better reason than some I've heard."

"I suppose. Still, no one seemed to really dislike Tala. I mean, there were those who didn't get her or understand her gender identity, but I can't find anyone who hated her."

"Except maybe Kendra."

"But she's such a twit."

Now Audrey was the one with spastic brow. "Go watch some YouTube videos on the Neese case and then we'll talk about unlikely killers. I once made the mistake of underestimating a girl and Alisha almost paid dearly for it."

That was true. Neve had been there to rescue Alisha and bring her abductor to justice, but Audrey had actually gotten shot. "I'd better get going. I told Gideon I'd be home after I stopped by here. Apparently a reporter actually came by the house today."

"That's ballsy. I hope you catch a break in the case soon."

"Mm," Neve replied. "If for no other reason than to keep Bertie Neeley off the news." With that quip, she walked down the steps and got into her car. Gideon had a beer and dinner ready for her when she got home, gorgeous man that he was. Later, when he was watching sports on TV, she sat down with her laptop and took Audrey's suggestion of watching YouTube videos regarding the Neese case.

When she was done, she set the laptop aside with an uneasy feeling in her stomach.

She needed to have a good long conversation with Lucy and Kendra.

Audrey was at the school when Jake called.

"It's a cyst," he said.

"That's it?"

"Yeah. I'm going next week to get it removed."

She closed her eyes. You never realized just how much you were trying not to worry until there was nothing to worry about. "That's really good news. I made an appointment with my gyno for my annual as well."

"As far as I know cysts aren't sexually transmitted."

"I needed to make the appointment anyway. It's been a while since I had one, and since my mother's cancer, it's something I should be more diligent about."

"I'm not going to argue. And hey, great news about the waiting list."

Audrey preened, even though he wasn't there to witness it. "I know, right? I just hope we can get Grace Ridge open in time to get them all in." And really, as happy as she was that there were kids ready to come to her facility, the fact that there were so many was a little disheartening. There simply weren't the facilities around to handle all the need. Maybe if she made this gig with the school a semiregular thing…

"It will be open. For what we're paying Gideon and his crew, they better have it fucking ready."

Gideon was a contractor, and he'd given them the best bid on the work. Plus, he employed local people, and Audrey—and Jake—trusted his work.

"Well, it's not going to benefit me to worry about it, so I'll just focus on what I can." She glanced up and saw Micheline standing in the doorway. "I've got to go. Call you later."

She hung up and slipped her phone into her bag. "Hey, Micheline. What's up?"

The counselor stepped into the office. "Good morning, Audrey. Do you have a minute?"

Audrey gestured to the love seat. "Sure."

Micheline sat down and crossed her legs. "I wanted to talk to you about Tala. It's probably nothing, but I know you're good friends with Neve and I thought you might be able to tell me if it's worth sharing with her."

"What is it?"

"You know, now that I think of it, it's probably nothing, but..." She pursed her lips. "You know how you get vibes from people?"

Audrey nodded. "Yeah, sure."

"Well, I feel terrible saying this, but I always felt there was something a little sneaky about Tala. Like she could be manipulative."

"Okay. How so?"

"Oh, I don't know, but whenever I talked to her I felt like she was trying to play me in some way."

"Maybe you were just picking up on the fact that she had a secret. There was so much about herself that Tala tried to keep protected that it may have come across as something more sinister."

Micheline considered this. "Yes, that may be. But it always struck me as strange how the four of them were always together—Luke, Tala, Kendra, and Lucy. The girls being friends after each dating him was one thing, but then wanting him to hang out with them was another."

Audrey started. "Wait. Are you saying that Lucy also dated Luke?"

Micheline seemed surprised she hadn't known. "Freshman year Lucy and Luke were one of the more popular couples. I suppose since she broke up with him, maybe she didn't mind him dating her friend, but you know how girls can be about boys."

Yes, she did. "Why did she break up with him?"

"Well, rumor had it that he was cheating on her, although at that age, cheating can be anything from hanging out to actual sex."

Luke sure did get around, Audrey thought. He was nice enough, and seemed to be good to Alisha, but she really didn't like the idea of her soon-to-be niece getting involved with a guy who couldn't keep it in his pants. Color her messed up, but loyalty was more important to her than the idea of the kid being a killer.

"So Luke dated Lucy, she dumped him, then he dated Kendra, dumped her because of Tala, and then Tala broke up with him. And Tala had someone on the side as well."

Micheline's eyes widened. "Really? Good God, you know,

this place is worse than any teen TV show. All the machinations and backstabbing. I can't keep up with it all."

Audrey regarded her with a new sense of respect. "But you hear about a lot of it."

She nodded. "If it goes on here, yes. But I'm going to assume Tala's side deal was someone who doesn't go to the school…" She snapped her fingers. "Kyle Granger. Now it makes sense that he jumped Luke with Josh."

Audrey was impressed. "How did you get there?"

"Well, I wouldn't feel right breaking confidence, but let's just say that when he was a student here, Kyle and I had several conversations about the fluidity of gender and sexuality. He may be a bit of a goof-off, but he wouldn't blink an eye at Tala being transgender."

"Yeah, he's very enlightened in this area."

"Anyway, Luke, Lucy, Kendra, and Tala were always together. I used to call them 'the sultan and his harem'—not out loud, of course."

"No." The whole thing did seem a little odd to Audrey. She supposed the four of them could have made the friendship work, but she didn't like having Maggie around boys she liked—she didn't trust her not to make a move. And it didn't matter if it was a boy she didn't like anymore; she still wouldn't want Maggie to be with him. Maybe Lucy had been okay with Luke being with Kendra and then Tala, but it was obvious that Kendra hadn't been okay with it—at least not where Tala was concerned. According to Alisha, Kendra had wanted Luke back. And still did. Lucy didn't seem to have a problem with that either.

"They were like this little island—no one else would go near them but rarely."

"So it would be odd, in your opinion, for Tala to go off on her own that night and at least one of the other three not know about it."

Micheline appeared surprised by the question. "Yes. Is that what the three of them are saying, that they don't know where Tala was?"

Audrey nodded. "Apparently her breakup with Luke shook up the group dynamic."

"I can understand that *he* wouldn't know, but Lucy and Kendra?" She shook her head. "I don't believe that for a minute. Those girls knew one another's schedules, locker combinations—everything. If they're saying they don't know where Tala was, I'd think they were lying—or that Tala lied to them."

Audrey looked at her for a moment, letting her words sink in. "You know, Micheline, I think you should definitely talk to Neve."

CHAPTER SIXTEEN

Whereas Eleanor Granger wanted to slam the door in her face when Neve came calling, Janine Villeneuve was downright hospitable that afternoon. Earlier, she'd gone by the school to talk to Micheline at Audrey's urging, and now she needed to have a few words with Lucy, because there had been a lot of weirdness going on in their incestuous little group, and Neve was tired of it. She was getting pressure from her bosses to solve the case and wrap things up, and the Lewises wanted to bury their daughter.

Poor people. They'd moved to Edgeport to keep Tala safe and it ended up being the place where she died.

"Detective Graham," Janine said in greeting. She was a tall woman with reddish hair and green eyes. Very striking. "I assume you're here to talk to Lucy about what happened at the hospital?"

"That's part of it," Neve admitted. "Is she home?"

"Just barely. Come on in. Lucy!" And then she said, "Have a seat, Detective."

Neve seated herself on the sofa closest to the door. She always felt bad about going into people's houses and not taking her shoes off, but it wasn't as though she really could. What if she had to chase someone or leave in a hurry? At least it wasn't raining.

Lucy came down the stairs in yoga pants and a long T-shirt and plunked herself down in a chair opposite Neve. "Alisha started it," she said.

Neve tilted her head. "That's not how I heard it."

The girl made a scoffing noise. "Yeah, from Alisha."

"And from Luke."

"Like they're going to tell the truth."

"Linda Pelletier and Yancy Tripp both approached me about filing restraining orders against you and Kendra."

"Fuck off. Really?"

"Lucy!" Her mother chastised her as she came into the room with glasses of water. "You do not speak to Detective Graham that way! I'm so sorry." She set one of the glasses on the table in front of Neve.

Neve nodded. She wasn't going to drink the water, but she appreciated the gesture. Janine had always been one of the few people in the area who had known her a long time but still treated her job with deference. It was kind of nice—and weird. "Lucy, I'm here to tell you that you need to stay away from Alisha and Luke, or things will go very badly for you."

"I have to see her at school."

"I know you have classes together, and that's fine, but don't speak to her. Don't even look at her. I'm going to be telling the Grangers the same thing."

"Alisha broke Kendra's nose!"

"And Kendra left some pretty deep fingernail tracks in Alisha's neck. She needed stitches, you know."

"Oh, my God," Janine said as she sat down in the chair beside her daughter. "Lucy, why didn't you break it up?"

"I tried to," her daughter retorted. "Kendra was insane, and Alisha is way stronger than she looks."

Alisha was a Tripp—fighting was in her blood. "I know Kendra was upset about seeing them together, but she can't attack every girl Luke dates."

"She hasn't."

"She never got physical with Tala over him? Maybe said some mean things?"

Lucy shook her head. "No."

"What about you? Did she ever get nasty with you?"

The girl frowned. "Why would you ask me that? She's my best friend."

"Because you and Luke used to date."

Snort. "In grade *nine*. And then I found out he played seven minutes in heaven with Jennifer Stokes. Not like we were serious."

Neve didn't believe her, but it didn't matter. "Kendra never gave you a hard time about it?"

Lucy shrugged. "Maybe she's made a couple of digs, but not for a long time. She knows I have no interest in dating a guy our age."

"Your taste runs older?"

The girl went still. Her mother noticed. "Oh, Lucy." She sighed. "This isn't something you're going to talk about in front of me, is it?"

Lucy shook her head.

"Lucy's not in any trouble, Janine." Neve clarified. "And she's certainly not under arrest, so it's okay for you to leave us alone. I just want to talk."

Janine nodded, but to her daughter, she said, "You call if you need me." That was fair enough. Neve couldn't ask for more.

When they were alone, she turned her attention back to Lucy—who looked so young and fragile with her hair in a ponytail and her eye makeup worn off. "Older guys like Randy Dyer?"

Wide eyes rolled. "I knew hooking up with him was a mistake. It only happened once."

"When?"

"Is that really important?"

"Yeah, it is."

"The night Tala disappeared."

"You and Kendra went to a party back Park Road?"

"Yeah. Tala was supposed to come but she never showed. I figured her mother told her she couldn't go."

"I thought you hadn't spoken to Tala that night?"

"No, we talked about it earlier. We knew about the party for a few days. Everyone did."

"And you were with Randy the entire evening?"

"Unfortunately. More of it than I wanted. As soon as I could get away from him I went home. You know, older guys are supposed to know more, but he was a disappointment."

Neve wasn't surprised. "What was Kendra doing while you were with Randy?"

"Talking about Luke with whoever would listen. A friend of Randy's tried to get with her, but she didn't want any of it. She got sloppy drunk instead. I used her as an excuse to leave— said I had to get her home."

"Would you say she was obsessed with Luke?"

"Uh, yeah. If by obsessed you mean never shuts the fuck up about him." She sighed. "Look, I'm really hoping this thing with Alisha puts an end to her mooning over him, because I'm getting really tired of hearing it. He's not that great. She should just let Lish have him and move the fuck on. Sorry."

Neve gave her a little smile. "Don't worry about it. That day in class when Kendra said she'd like it if Tala died, did you believe her?"

A frown creased the girl's smooth brow. "No. Not really. She just wanted to shock Luke, I think. All she wanted—wants— is for him to realize they're meant to be together." This was delivered in a very mock-dramatic tone.

"How upset was Kendra that things were getting serious with Luke and Tala?"

"More than she should have been. I knew he wouldn't be able to actually go through with it. Luke's pretty vanilla."

"He certainly seems to have gotten around."

Lucy shrugged. "We didn't really have anything in common. Neither did he and Kendra. At least Alisha likes some of the same stuff he does."

"You sound very calm. Alisha told me you were pretty upset with her at the hospital."

"I was upset for Kendra. I knew she'd lose it. And Alisha was supposed to be her friend. She was supposed to be Tala's friend. You don't go after your friend's boyfriend—ex or otherwise."

"But Kendra went after yours."

"I told you, I didn't care. I wasn't in love with Luke like she was. Is."

And what if Alisha was in love with Luke? Neve didn't ask. "How far do you think Kendra would be willing to go to get Luke back?"

The girl stared at her for a second before she burst out laughing. "Seriously?"

Neve was *this* close to slapping her in the head. "Yes, seriously."

The smile faded. "Kendra's on antianxiety medication. She hates the sight of blood. There's no way she could kill someone. You know, Luke's the one who has a knife collection. Just because he got his ass kicked doesn't mean he's innocent."

A knife collection? That was interesting. "She had no trouble attacking Alisha, or seeing her blood."

Lucy frowned. "That was different. She was mad."

"Whoever killed Tala was very, very mad."

The frown grew. Then Lucy opened her mouth...

"Mom!"

LuceeVeeMD @TroothGrrl I know who you are, bitch.

Phone clutched in her hand, Alisha stared at the message in her Twitter feed, her heart pounding. Had Lucy actually figured her out? It didn't matter. She wasn't afraid of either of them, and she'd proved that at the hospital when Kendra came at her.

She'd gotten some backlash for her @TroothGrrl posts—

mostly from girls at school who wanted to be in with Kendra and Lucy. For some reason the two of them were considered popular, even though they were such hot messes.

What was interesting, however, was the number of tweets from other people urging the girls to come clean with what they knew. Some went so far as to accuse the girls of being involved in Tala's murder, without actually coming right out and saying it point-blank.

Others still blamed Luke, and those were the ones who really pissed her off. She had to force herself not to respond to them as TroothGrrl, or from her own account. In fact, she hadn't tweeted much of anything as herself. Every moment she had the chance to sneak off to a public computer and post under her secret account, she did just that.

One person stood out from the others—@HeadSick2017. They wanted to know how everyone could be so quiet. Someone had to know something. But they also talked about the murder in a way that Alisha envied—as an outsider.

@HeadSick2017 About 30% of murders are committed by someone the victim knew.

@HeadSick2017 Murder is the second-highest cause of death among teenagers.

@HeadSick2017 75% of teen murderers know their victim. Almost half of those victims are friends.

@HeadSick2017 Who killed Tala Lewis? Someone violent, angry, and impulsive. Someone who knew her well.

@HeadSick2017 Tala probably trusted her killer. She probably went willingly with them.

@HeadSick2017 7 transgender women were murdered in the first 6 weeks of 2017.

Some of those tweets had been sent directly to TroothGrrl, others independently made under #JusticeForTala. It was the "violent, angry, and impulsive" that jumped out at Alisha. T hat sounded just like Kendra.

HeadSick2017 also indicated that the killer might have poor reading skills and lack an ability to empathize. That they might have grown up with some sort of abuse.

That was when she knew that HeadSick2017 was Audrey. And she was willing to bet that Audrey knew she was Trooth-Grrl. She wasn't going to say anything, though. Plausible de-niability and all that. She was just glad to not be alone in her quest to find the real killer. It meant a lot to her that Audrey felt the same way, though she knew that a part of her soon-to-be-aunt was concerned about Luke.

Thank God her mother was more of an innocent-until-proven-guilty type of person. Though maybe that was just because Luke was hospitalized and not much of a threat.

Because he was still stuck in the hospital, Alisha had promised Luke that she would bring him fried clams from Fat Frank's after school. She was just picking up her order when someone stepped up beside her.

"That's a lot of food for just one person," Kyle Granger said. "Is some of that for your murderer boyfriend?"

His sneer combined with the thought of what he'd done to Luke made Alisha want to ram a plastic fork into his eye-ball.

"Who it's for is none of your business." She picked up the paper bag and turned to leave.

Kyle blocked her. "Better be careful. You might be next."

"You know, your sister warned me of the same thing, but the only people I've seen get violent are you, Josh, and Kendra. What is it with your family, Kyle? What is it with you?" Her voice had risen and they were attracting an audience. Alisha didn't care.

Kyle did. "Shut up."

"No. You beat up someone Tala cared about like you have the right, but when she was alive you wouldn't be seen with her. She was good enough to screw so long as no one knew about it, right?"

His face turned red as a few people snickered. "She was the one who didn't want people to know about us."

She gave him a scathing once-over. "Gee, I wonder why?"

"Bitch."

"That's original. You know, maybe you killed her, Kyle, because you were her guilty secret. She wasn't ashamed to be seen with Luke, was she?"

"Aw, snap!" said someone in the line to pick up food.

Kyle straightened. He was several inches taller than her and at least fifty pounds heavier, but Alisha had two plastic forks in her fist and was not afraid to use them.

A hand clapped down on Kyle's shoulder. It was Randy Dyer, of all people. "Back off, man."

Kyle tried to shrug him off, but Randy was older, a little bigger, and a lot stronger.

"Seriously," Randy continued. "Jake and Linc Tripp are her uncles. This will go badly for you in so many ways." His words seemed to sink in, because Kyle's body relaxed a bit, and he took a step back.

"Whatever," he said, finally escaping Randy's grip. Then, to Alisha, he said, "You and Pelletier deserve each other."

"Yeah, I don't take that as an insult," Alisha told him, holding his gaze—and her forks.

Slowly, Kyle backed away, then turned on his heel and stomped out. A faint chorus of wisecracks and jeers followed him.

Alisha glanced up at Randy. "Thanks." Not that she had needed his help, but she'd been raised to be polite.

He nodded. "Be careful. I wouldn't trust him not to hit a girl."

She bit her tongue to keep from saying, *Like you wouldn't?* "Right. I will be." She shifted her grip on her food and started to walk away.

"Hey," Randy said. "Maybe you could tell your uncle about this?"

She frowned. "Which one?"

"Jake."

She shrugged. "Yeah, sure thing." When Randy's shoulders lowered, she shook her head and continued on her way. People used to be afraid of her grandmother. Now they were afraid of Uncle Jake.

Maybe someday, they'd be afraid of *her*.

*　　*　　*

"You are not talking to my daughter."

Neve was pretty sure Elle Granger silently added *bitch* to that statement. "Mrs. Granger, I need you to understand that while Kendra is fully within her right to not speak to me, not doing so makes her look as though she has something to hide."

Elle's cheeks flushed hot and angry. "My daughter has done nothing wrong."

"Your daughter attacked a girl because she kissed her ex-boyfriend. Alisha Tripp has substantial injuries."

"That little slit broke Kendra's nose!"

Neve cringed. She'd always hated that word, "slit." It was so degrading. Worse than "slut," or even the C-word. "Self-defense. Yancy Tripp and Linda Pelletier have asked me to advise Kendra to stay away from Alisha and Luke, or she may be served a restraining order."

"They're telling Kendra to stay away? I asked you to do that for Kendra first."

Neve shook her head with a look of mock regret. "Yes, but in order to do it, I needed a statement from Kendra and you wouldn't let me speak to her."

She thought Elle might actually explode, she was so angry. "What do you have against my family? Is it because we're white?"

Neve's mouth dropped open. "You did *not* just ask me that."

"My husband has friends in state government—"

"Finish that sentence and I will arrest your ass for threatening an officer of the law. And attempting to obstruct justice." Did she have crazy eye going on? She felt like it. "This has nothing to do with race and everything to do with a girl's murder—your daughter's friend, remember? Now, I need to talk to Kendra. I suggest you go get her."

Elle didn't budge.

"*Now*," Neve ordered. "Unless you want to take a drive."

The woman looked as though she could cheerfully strangle her. Kendra obviously got her temper from her mother. When Elle finally turned on her heel and walked off to get her daughter, Neve breathed a sigh of relief. Still, she kept her hand near her gun just in case.

Kendra appeared a few minutes later. She looked like hell, with her nose bandaged and black bruising under both eyes. Alisha sure had done a good job of breaking her nose.

"What do you want?" she asked. Swelling made her voice super nasal.

"I want to talk to you about the night Tala died."

"I already told you everything."

"No. You told me you were with Luke that night, but Lucy just told me that the two of you were at a party."

Kendra blinked. "She's wrong."

"Is Randy Dyer wrong too?"

The girl looked away. Under other circumstances, Neve might have some sympathy for her, but not at that moment. "You need to stop lying to me, Kendra. It's going to get you in a lot of trouble. Were you at the party or were you with Luke?"

"I was at the party," came the mumbled reply.

"Did Luke ask you to lie for him?"

She shook her head. "No."

It was odd because Luke had told her that he'd been at home

that night, but that his parents had been out. Kendra had claimed that she went to the house and hung out with him—something that would have upset his parents. If Kendra hadn't been with him, had Luke actually been at home? Why hadn't he taken advantage of Kendra's lie?

"Have you ever seen Luke's knife collection?"

The girl started to frown, then made a small, painful noise. "Yeah. His father got him some kind of freaky dagger for his birthday."

"Does he own any hunting knives?"

"That's not what he's into. He likes ancient and fantasy-type stuff. He hates hunting."

"Why did you attack Alisha at the hospital?"

Kendra studied her toes. "Because she was kissing Luke."

"And that made you angry."

"Yeah."

Looking at her, the languid way she moved and the slow hitch to her speech, Neve had to wonder just how medicated the kid was. "You need to stay away from both of them. I mean it. If you go near Luke or Alisha you will be in a lot of trouble. Do you understand?"

She nodded. "It doesn't matter anyway. What's the point?"

Well, that was positive. "It matters because they were your friends."

"Bullshit. If Alisha was my friend she wouldn't have gone after Luke."

"Sometimes things just happen. You could have tried talking to her rather than going for her throat."

Narrow shoulders lifted in a halfhearted shrug. "It wouldn't have made a difference. Everyone I thought was my friend has betrayed me. Luke with Tala and Alisha. Tala with my brother. Alisha with Luke."

"What about Lucy? Has she betrayed you?"

"Lucy's the only real friend I have. Do you have any other questions? I'm tired."

She looked about ready to collapse right there. "I need you to tell me you understand that you cannot go near Alisha or Luke. If you see them at school you can't talk to them, and you need to be as far from them as you can be."

"Yeah, I get it. Whatever. Like Luke is going to be back at school anytime soon."

That was said a little too gleefully for Neve's liking, but the girl was obviously seriously fucked up where the boy was concerned. "No trips to the hospital to try to see him either." That seemed to burst her bubble. Jesus, had nothing Neve had just said to her made it to her brain?

The girl's chin lifted. Her black eyes looked terrible in her pale face. The bandage gave her a slightly inhuman appearance.

"Luke loves his knives," she said, swaying a little. "He likes to throw them. And stab things. He showed us. He was really good at it, but I wasn't. Do you know how much strength it takes to stab a person repeatedly?"

"Yes," Neve said. "I do. Go take a nap, Kendra. We're done." Jesus, the kid was a piece of work. One minute she was trying to protect Luke and the next she threw him under the proverbial bus.

Thankfully, she didn't have to deal with Elle again when she left. As she walked to her car, Neve pulled her phone from her pocket and speed-dialed a work number.

"Yeah," she said when someone answered. "I'm going to need a search warrant."

CHAPTER SEVENTEEN

It was early Friday, and Neve was having a crap day. In fact, her day was about to get super shitty. She was getting tired of Edgeport, the surrounding towns, and the collective small mind between the three. Or maybe she was just tired of always seeing the asshole side of people. Regardless, she wasn't looking forward to the look on Linda Pelletier's face when she saw the search warrant in Neve's hand.

"What the hell is that for?" Linda demanded when she saw it.

"Specifically Luke's room and any outlying buildings or vehicles."

The woman shook with rage. "I can't believe you're doing this."

"It's my job," Neve reminded her.

"Your job sucks."

She nodded. "Sometimes it does. Will you tell me where his room is?"

"You're the detective," the woman said with a sneer. "Find it yourself."

Neve sighed as she walked away. "Let's make this quick, Vickie."

The two of them walked up the stairs and easily found Luke's room—it was the only one that obviously belonged to a teenage boy. There were band posters and fantasy art on the walls—no half-naked women, though. For a kid who was rumored to be such a heartbreaker, he didn't have much exploitative material. Vickie found only one titty magazine under his mattress and a couple of sites in his browser history.

"He did a lot of searches for articles on being transgender," Vickie informed her as Neve searched the bedside table. "And some searches on Tala's name plus New York."

That made Neve pause. That was the only evidence they'd found that anyone actually believed Tala had simply run away. Would Luke be smart enough to conduct such a search if he'd been the one to kill Tala? Maybe her instincts were off, because even though she'd warned Alisha to be careful around the boy, she couldn't bring herself to actually see him as an offender. At the moment, he screamed "victim." Josh Lewis had told her the reason they stopped beating him was that he didn't really fight back.

At first Neve thought maybe Luke let them hit him because he felt guilty, but she didn't think it was because he killed anyone. He felt guilty for another reason. Maybe it was the sex thing, or maybe it was something else.

"Take a photo of that search history. We'll get the guys to look into it."

"Looks like he was looking at pre- and post-op photos of trans girls too."

"Before or after Tala disappeared?"

"About a month before."

Probably wanted to know what to expect. Still, even if he seemed like a decent kid, there was still that text he'd sent say-

ing Tala would regret being with Kyle. That she'd be sorry. T
here was no doubt he was pissed off about the infidelity.

Neve opened the closet door. On the floor was a small chest
that had a bit of a medieval aesthetic to it.

"I think I found the knife collection," she said.

The trunk wasn't locked, so she pressed the latches and
popped it open.

"Oh, shit," Vickie said.

Neve sighed. On top of the rest of the daggers and blades
was a hunting knife. The blade was bloody, and the tip had
been broken off.

"You think that's it?" Vickie asked.

"Of course it is," Neve replied. "Right there on top, just
waiting for us to find it."

"You think it was planted?"

"I think that nothing—and no one—involved with this case
is what it seems. Everyone's hiding something."

"Like this knife."

"This wasn't hidden," Neve said, giving her a look that
spoke of slight disapproval. "This was planted. I don't know if
it's Luke's or not, but I know he didn't just leave it here."

"What are you going to do?"

Another sigh. "What I have to do. I'm going to have the
knife tested." She picked it up with two gloved fingers and
placed it in an evidence bag. "And if the blood is Tala's, I'm going to arrest Luke Pelletier for murder."

* * *

On Friday, Kendra tweeted: *I wasn't always a good friend 2 u, but u were 2 me. Miss you, Tala. Rest in Peace.*

TroothGrrl replied *@Kendrahh69 A real friend would want her killer caught.* It was smarmy, and she felt bad after she posted it, but not bad enough to try to delete it. She was still upset that Neve had been at Luke's. And when he told her that his mother said they found a knife with blood on it, she'd almost lost it.

In fact, she was so upset that she skipped class. She was in a stall in one of the upstairs girls' bathrooms, with her phone on silent, texting with Luke. Or, at least she had been. He hadn't responded to the text she sent five minutes earlier, which worried her. Maybe he was asleep, but she kept imagining something terrible happening—like Neve dragging him off to prison.

She sent a note to her mother explaining that she'd skipped and why, and hoped that her mother would call in for her so she wouldn't get sent to the office. And then she checked again for anything from Luke.

Nothing.

Suddenly, someone banged on the stall door. "I know you're in there. Get your traitorous ass out here."

Lucy.

Alisha slid the latch and slowly opened the door, prepared to use it as a shield if the other girl took a swing. "Did you miss the part about you staying the fuck away from me?"

"I plan to, but first you're going to lay off Kendra and me."

"I don't know what you're talking about."

"Yeah, right. TroothGrrl. You think we didn't know it was you?

So pathetic. We had a laugh over it at first, but now you're just pissing us off. You and that HeadSick person. A friend of yours?"

Alisha shook her head. "I still don't know what you're talking about. I have better things to do than tweet at you and Kendra—like spend time with Luke."

Lucy's eyes darkened. "You're a fucking cunt, you know that?"

"And I'm recording this conversation for the cops, so keep talking, bitch."

That actually made Lucy take a step back. "Whatever. Leave us alone."

"I told you, it's not me."

"Yeah, right." Lucy's phone buzzed in her purse. As she checked her messages, a big grin spread across her face. "Looks like you'll get your justice for Tala after all, TroothGrrl. My cousin works at the hospital. She just texted me that the cops are there right now. Arresting Luke for Tala's murder."

Alisha didn't know what happened. One minute she was fine, and the next she was on Lucy. Her knees hit hard against the tiled floor as she took the girl down. Her fingers, like claws, dug into Lucy's scalp as she picked the girl's head up and was about to smash it back down.

"Alisha, stop!"

The familiar voice cut through her rage. She hesitated, still holding Lucy's head as the girl swore and struggled. Audrey stood just inside the door with a worried expression on her face. Not afraid. Not disgusted. Just worried. That was why she loved Audrey so much.

"Let her go, sweetie. You don't want this kind of trouble."

Alisha had to force her fingers to loosen. She moved off Lucy, who hurriedly got to her feet, her hair sticking out like a demented ginger halo around her face. There were strands of it between Alisha's fingers. "You fucking bitch," she snarled. "You'll pay for that."

"I'm pretty sure you started it," Audrey said, giving her a cool look. "Didn't Detective Graham tell you to stay away from Alisha?"

Lucy glared but didn't say another word. She stomped out of the bathroom.

Audrey didn't look at her, and for a second, Alisha wondered if she was in trouble, and then she saw where Audrey's attention had gone; Lucy had dropped her cell phone.

Crouching down, Audrey grabbed the phone and looked at it. It must have still been unlocked, because she did something with it before offering her hand to Alisha. "Come on. You're coming to my office with me. I think you're done for the day."

"Neve arrested Luke," Alisha said dumbly, as if that was all that mattered. It *was* all that mattered.

"I know, sweetie. That's why I came looking for you when your mother told me you skipped class. Now, come on. That's a good girl."

Class was still in, so at least there weren't people roaming the halls. Alisha would hate to be seen with Audrey's arm around her like she was some kind of invalid.

"What are you going to do with that?" she asked, nodding at the phone in Audrey's hand.

"I'm going to turn it in to lost and found, of course." She gave Alisha's shoulders a squeeze. "After we take a look at it."

Jake came home early from Gracie's that night. Yancy called in backup for the front desk at the resort, and even Lincoln made time to come to the house and be there for Alisha. The poor kid was so upset, no one knew what to do with her. Alisha wasn't normally emotional, so seeing her cry was tough on everyone.

"I don't know what to do to make this better," Yancy said, her eyes filling with tears.

Lincoln stood beside the sink, arms over his chest. His haircut made him look older—more like the eldest. He was silent.

Jake put his arm around his niece, who sat at the table, wiping her eyes. "It's okay," Alisha said. "I'm okay."

"If his parents can't afford it, I'll pay for his lawyer," Jake offered.

Audrey shot him a warning look, but he ignored it. The kid better not be guilty if he invested actual money in him. That would not go well.

A car pulled into the drive. "It's Neve," Audrey said. Jesus, it was not a good time for her to show up.

Suddenly, Alisha viciously wiped both of her eyes, stood up, and went to the door. The adults exchanged glances but let her go. From the dining room entry, Audrey watched as the girl opened the door.

"Hello, Alisha," Neve said. "How are you holding up?"

"I'm all right," was the flat reply. "Thanks for coming by."

Audrey started. *Thanks for coming by?* "Did you ask Neve to come here?" she asked.

Alisha turned her head to look at her. The kid looked thirty rather than almost seventeen. "Yeah, I did. There's something I need to tell her—all of you."

For a second, Audrey lost her breath. She actually considered praying. If Alisha told them that she had killed Tala, she didn't know what she'd do. Jake would immediately start talking lawyers, and Yancy would cry and Lincoln would brood, but she…she would blame herself. Alisha might be a Tripp, but Audrey was the only one the kid knew who had actually killed someone.

Christ, she needed a drink, but the thought of rum made her stomach churn—traitorous bastard.

They all adjourned to the dining room. Yancy had made tea, so she put the pot on the table along with strainers and milk and sugar.

"Did you actually take Luke to jail?" Alisha asked.

Neve poured herself a cup. "No. He's under police guard at the hospital for now. The blood on the knife we found matched Tala's."

"He didn't do it."

"We found the murder weapon in his knife case."

"It's not his. He doesn't collect hunting knives, and even if he did, he wouldn't keep it there. It's too obvious."

Neve nodded. "I thought that too. Listen, Alisha, I can't really discuss this with you. I'm only telling you this much because you're you. For now, Luke is being held on suspicion of murder."

"Neve, he didn't do it. You have to believe me."

"I want to, hon. I really do, but he doesn't have an alibi for the night Tala disappeared. Kendra was lying when she said she was with him."

"Yeah, I know she was lying." Alisha was becoming agitated. Audrey wanted to go to her, but she stayed where she was. The entire family seemed to have silently taken a vow to allow her to handle whatever it was she was doing on her own.

Crossing her legs, Neve frowned slightly as she leaned back in her chair. "You know she lied? Do you know where Luke was that night? Why didn't you say anything before this?"

"Because we swore we'd keep it a secret," was Alisha's reply. "I promised I wouldn't tell."

Audrey's stomach rolled. Either she was becoming over-nervous, or she'd eaten something that hadn't agreed with her. Since that rarely happened, she had to assume the nausea was because she loved that kid so damn much, and she was terrified she couldn't help her.

Neve kept her gaze on Alisha. All attention was focused on Alisha. "But you're going to tell now?"

She nodded. "If it keeps Luke from going to jail, then yeah."

"Okay, so tell me where he was."

"He was with me."

"Where?" Yancy demanded. "You were at home that night."

Alisha glanced at her mother. "I was. Luke came over."

"You didn't tell me he came by."

"Yeah, I know." The look Alisha gave her mother begged for

silence. "I didn't tell you, because we were going to pretend it never happened."

"Pretend what never happened?" Audrey asked, but she already knew the answer.

Alisha looked down at the floor before lifting her chin and meeting Neve's gaze. "Luke came to my place while Mum was at work. He was upset about Tala breaking up with him, and about her hooking up with Kyle. He needed someone to talk to, so we talked."

Neve tilted her head. "You don't pretend talking never happened. Did the two of you have sex?"

"Oh, fuck around," Lincoln groaned, obviously not ready to think of his niece as ready for that sort of behavior.

Alisha's cheeks flushed, but she nodded. She didn't look at any of them. "We didn't mean for it to happen, it just did."

"It's okay, Lish," Jake said, ignoring the glare his sister cast in his direction. "You didn't do anything wrong."

Neve was still focused on the girl sitting across from her. "Alisha, I need to ask you this—you're not lying to me hoping to protect Luke, are you?"

"My daughter doesn't lie," Yancy informed her, coldly.

Neve glanced up, unaffected. "Your family is incredibly loyal to those they love. I want to make certain Alisha's loyalty isn't misplaced."

Good save, Audrey thought.

"It's true," Alisha affirmed. She took out her cell phone and flipped through her photos, finally finding one that she showed to Neve. Whatever it was had Neve nodding.

"Okay," the detective said. "I still have to investigate the knife. Are you willing to make a statement?"

Alisha nodded.

Neve looked to Yancy again. "I can come by the house tomorrow."

"I'll be at work," Yancy replied.

"It's okay," Alisha said. "I'd rather not have all of you around. Maybe Audrey could be there, though?"

All gazes swung toward her. Audrey had a list of things she needed to do the next day, but family came first. "Sure. You just tell me when."

A few minutes later, Audrey walked Neve to the door. "What did she show you?"

"A photo of Luke in a bed I assume to have been hers," Neve answered in a low voice. "Look, you know her better than I do..."

"I don't think she's making it up." Audrey was honest. "But, is she capable of putting herself on the line for a boy she likes? Fuck yeah."

"Well, we'll see how Luke reacts when I ask him about it." With that, Neve said she'd see her the next day and left.

Audrey shut the door and turned to rejoin the others in the dining room. They were clustered around Alisha like a trio of awkward mother hens. The girl looked up, her gaze locking with Audrey's.

If she's a liar, Audrey thought, *she's a damned good one.*

CHAPTER EIGHTEEN

Jake was beside himself. Audrey had never seen him in such a mood. Pacing the hardwood floor in their bedroom, he was anxious and angry, and it was all because his teenage niece had sex with a boy.

"You were having sex at that age," Audrey reminded him. She did not remind him of who he was having sex with.

"I know, and I hate to say it, but I'm more afraid for Alisha because she's a girl. I saw what having a baby young did to Yancy—and that's the good-case scenario. What if some jerk gives her a disease?"

Audrey thought of the guy who had given her crabs in her early twenties and almost shuddered. "We make sure she's on the pill, uses condoms, and doesn't sleep with assholes."

He shot her a droll look. "You know it's not that easy."

"No, it's not, but it's out of our hands. She's growing up, and she's going to do what she thinks is best for her."

Jake shook his head. "I don't feel like she's ready for it."

"Doesn't matter. You and Yancy did a great job raising her; now all you can do is hope she uses all the tools you gave her."

Another look—this time narrow. "You're not helping."

She shrugged. "I don't know what you want me to say. She's a good kid. She'll be all right. I'll talk to her tomorrow before Neve comes by. Does that make you feel better?"

He stopped pacing and considered it. The tension in his jaw eased. "Yeah. I think it does."

Audrey smiled softly. What Jake wouldn't admit—mostly because he hadn't realized it yet—was that he was feeling separation anxiety. Lish might be his niece, but he'd helped raise her, and he loved her like she was his own. She always confided things to him that she would never tell her mother, and now she'd kept a secret from him. He was probably feeling a little lost.

"Come to bed," she said. "I'm getting to the point where I'm so tired I could puke."

"You've been taking on too much lately," he said, peeling back the blankets. "You're making yourself sick."

"I'm done at the school this week, so then it will be back to normal crazy."

They both lay down at the same time. Jake tucked his arm under his pillow and looked at her. "Your father's impressed that you haven't inserted yourself into this murder investigation."

She rolled her eyes. "If he doesn't think I'm in it, fine, but Alisha puts us right smack-dab in it." She sighed. "I really hope Luke didn't do it."

He pulled her close. "Me too. I'd hate to have another guy killed in prison."

Even though she knew it was wrong, Audrey laughed.

*   *   *

Alisha was on the couch reading a book when Audrey arrived on Saturday. She wore gym shorts and a T-shirt with her hair back in a messy ponytail.

"How are you doing?" Audrey asked.

She shrugged. "Mum grounded me. I'm not allowed to go see Luke." She held up her phone. "She didn't say anything about calling or texting, though."

Sneaky. "She just wants to keep you away from the investigation."

"Yeah, I know. Not stupid."

Audrey sighed. "If having sex with a guy makes you this much of a bitch, maybe you should consider becoming a nun. You've been incredibly hard to live with, you know that?"

Alisha looked surprised. "Seriously? The guy I like is suspected of murder, and you think I should be more concerned about people's feelings?"

"I think you should have more respect for the people who are trying to help, and try not to be a dick."

The girl opened her mouth—probably to make a smart-ass retort, but then she thought better of it. "Sorry."

"Your uncle was literally pacing last night because he's worried about you."

A shrug lifted Alisha's shoulders. "I don't see what the big deal is."

Audrey smiled slightly. "No. You wouldn't, because teen self-centeredness is what makes you decide to fly off on your own. Without it you'd be too scared to leave the house."

"You don't know everything, you know."

"No, I don't. And if that's true, think of how much less you know than me. Now, are we going to continue this pissing contest, or are we going to talk?"

Alisha tossed her book aside and put her feet up on the coffee table. "What do you want to know?"

"Condoms. Did he use one?"

"Yes."

"And you're on the pill?"

"Yeah."

"Okay."

"That's it?"

Now it was Audrey's turn to shrug. "The rest of it's none of my business."

"You don't want to know if he was nice to me, or if I enjoyed it?"

Audrey met her gaze. "You want to hear about my first time?"

"No."

"Well, then..." She gave her a pointed look. "What I really want to know before Neve gets here is that you're being one hundred percent honest."

"I can't believe you, of all people, are so worried about me lying to the cops."

"I'm not worried about it. I'm worried that you're not ready to face the consequences of it if you are. And I want to make sure Luke is worth those consequences."

The girl leaned back against the cushions. "You ever feel like you know someone right down to their bones?"

Oh, hell. "The only person I've ever felt that way about is Jake."

"That's how I feel about Luke. You probably think that's stupid."

"Not at all. You know Luke has a reputation for bouncing from girl to girl."

She nodded. "If he bounces, then he's not who I think he is, but I don't think he's going to bounce—not from me."

Audrey wasn't about to argue with her. The kid knew her own mind, seemed to know the risks, and was willing to take them anyway. Who was she to tell her to be careful or not to do something?

"Okay." She nodded. "Is there anything I can do?"

"Trust me."

"I can do that."

"And keep posting as HeadSick, because I have to stop."

Audrey was more pleased than surprised that Alisha knew it was her. "Okay, TroothGrrl."

"Who do you think did it?"

"I don't know, but I think Kendra and Lucy know more than they're saying. And I think other people know more too; they're just not coming forward, or they don't realize they have information."

"But you don't think it's Luke?"

Audrey shook her head. "I suppose it could be, but I like to think you wouldn't get involved with a guy dumb enough to hide a murder weapon in his closet."

"I know, right? It had to be planted." Her jaw tightened. "I wish I knew who did it."

"I'm glad you don't," Audrey said with a faint smile.

When Neve arrived, Audrey made tea—which Neve didn't drink. She never ate or drank anything offered to her when she was on duty. She took Alisha's statement with a blank expression that Audrey tried to duplicate. It was difficult to listen to the girl talk about her first sexual experience and how guilty both she and Luke felt about it later—so guilty they decided to pretend it never happened. Alisha hadn't wanted to hurt Tala—or Kendra. And Luke apparently didn't want Tala to know, because then she'd know for certain why he hadn't been able to be with her. He felt horrible for it. Audrey respected that, but she still didn't like the fact that he'd broken more than his fair share of hearts in his brief life.

A life that would be that much briefer if he hurt Alisha.

When Alisha was done, Neve closed her notebook and thanked her.

"So you'll let Luke go now?" Alisha asked.

"I still have to follow up on the evidence we found at his house," Neve replied.

It was obvious that answer wasn't what Alisha wanted hear. "But I'm his alibi."

"For the night Tala disappeared, yeah. But we don't know for sure if that's when she was killed. The medical examiner gave us a window, and while that night falls within it, there's a cushion of time around it. Just because Luke was here doesn't mean he didn't kill Tala. I'm sorry, Alisha, but I have to do my job."

"You didn't do your job when Josh and Kyle beat him up, did you? I don't see them handcuffed to a hospital bed."

Audrey shot her a warning look. "Lish, none of this is Neve's fault."

The girl looked like she might implode. "Whatever. I'm going to take a nap. You two let yourselves out." She stomped off.

"That went well," Neve quipped.

"She's really nuts over him."

"Yeah, I figured that much out."

"Can you talk about the knife?"

Now she picked up the tea she had ignored and took a drink. "Jesus, Audrey, it's such an obvious plant, but how am I supposed to prove it?"

"How do you know it's a plant?"

"They left the blood on the blade, but cleaned the handle. Who does that? No one. You either clean the whole thing or you don't."

"They could have worn gloves."

"No, I mean they literally cleaned the handle. We found traces of a solvent-based cleaner on it. That's why it's so weird, because they hadn't used the cleaner on the blade."

"So someone wanted to make sure their prints and DNA weren't on the hunting knife, but kept Tala's blood."

"Yep. The piece missing from the tip matches what they took out of one of her wounds. It's definitely our murder weapon, but I find it hard to believe Luke would be so sloppy in cleaning it, or that he'd leave something dirty and bloody on top of the collection he's so proud of."

"Yeah, it doesn't add up. Any suspicions?"

Neve met her gaze. "Probably the same as yours, but that I

can't say. I'm still trying to find out about the GHB, and need to run Luke's blood against what we found on that glove." She took another drink of tea. "The press is breathing down my neck and my superiors are getting antsy. I need to solve this. Soon."

"Anything I can do?"

"Keep doing that Twitter thing."

"What?" And here she'd thought she was being so clever.

"All those stats? What teenager's going to post that shit? It reeked of you."

"Well, shit."

"It's not an insult; I read them and immediately heard your voice. I didn't know for certain until you just confirmed it."

"Wow, and I thought I was supposed to be the one good at mind games."

"Oh, honey," Neve said with a smile. "You have no idea what you're up against." They both chuckled. Then Neve checked her phone. "I better go. I have a million things to do and I promised Gideon I'd try to make it a short day."

"Good luck with that."

Alisha returned just as Neve was about to leave. "I owe you an apology," she said.

Instead of shrugging it off, Neve nodded. "Okay, give me what you've got."

"I'm sorry for my attitude and the way I've spoken to you. I'm scared for Luke and it's making me a bitch."

The detective smiled. "We've all been there, honey. Thank you for the apology, though. I haven't gotten many of those lately. I want you to know I'm doing my best to find Tala's killer."

"Thanks."

When Neve was gone, Audrey decided it was time for her to go too. She could use a nap, but she needed to check on a few things at Grace Ridge, get groceries, and try to get a visit in with her parents while Jake was at work at Gracie's. They'd also promised each other an evening together since life had been so hectic and was only going to get busier as summer hit.

"Think your mother would let you help your old auntie get groceries?"

"Probably, but do I *want* to help an old woman get groceries?" It was said with a smile.

"I'll buy you ice cream." It was the most effective bribe to use against her—and her uncle Jake.

"You're on. Let me check with Mum first."

Audrey watched her pick up the landline and call the resort. She was a good kid, growing up into a good woman who knew her own mind and wasn't about to let anyone stand in her way. It sounded so great on paper, but in life it was a constant battle of wills that again made Audrey glad she wasn't a mother. She just didn't have the energy for it.

Yancy said Alisha could go. As they walked down the bungalow's few front steps, a car drove back the road. Whoever was in the passenger side waved exaggeratedly.

"Is that Lucy?" Audrey asked.

Alisha sighed. "Yeah." A few seconds later, the car came by in the opposite direction. Kendra was driving—and laughing.

"Do those girls not understand what it means to keep a reasonable distance away from someone?" Audrey put her phone away—she'd taken a picture as they passed.

"They don't think they're going to get into trouble," Alisha informed her as they got into Audrey's car. "They've already gotten away with murder."

Monday found Audrey back at the school for the second week of her term there. She only had appointments booked for the morning so she could spend time at Grace Ridge later that day. She had a couple of follow-ups—one of which was with Hank. She saw that Kendra Granger was booked to be her final appointment of the day, and didn't expect the girl to show at all.

She was surprised when she staggered in around noon.

"Hey, Dr. Harte," the girl said.

Audrey frowned. Kendra was paler than usual. Normally the girl took exceptionally good care of herself, but her makeup was smudged and her dark hair was stuck to her forehead by sweat.

"Hi, Kendra. Come in." She didn't detect body odor when the girl walked by, so that was at least something. But she sat on the love seat, hugging her hoodie around her like she was cold.

"I didn't think you'd see me," Kendra said, playing with the piping on the arm of the sofa. "I thought you'd tell me to fuck off because of Alisha."

"That wouldn't be very professional of me."

"I guess not. It's what I'd do if I were you, though."

Audrey managed a smile. "Well, then I guess you're lucky you're not me. How are you today, Kendra?"

"I'm okay. Is the AC on in here? It's cold."

It actually was on the warm side of comfortable. "There's a blanket behind you if you want to use it."

"Thanks." Slowly, she took it from the back of the sofa and clumsily draped it around herself. Her coordination was crap. The girl had to be stoned.

"Is there anything you want to talk about?"

The girl blinked. "They arrested Luke for Tala's murder. You probably already know that."

Audrey nodded. "Yes."

"I'm not sure how I feel about it." This was said in an almost singsong voice. "I'm not sure I feel much of anything." She laughed.

"Kendra, what did you take?"

"Take?" Another slow blink. "Are you accusing me of stealing something?"

"No. What drugs did you take before coming here?"

Her expression turned to baffled indignation—a look Audrey had seen on her drunken father's face many times during her life. "I didn't take anything. I'm sober as a judge." The giggle that followed totally ruined any chance that statement had of being believed.

"I wish the judge I was in front of had been in the same state you are right now." She wouldn't have been sent to Stillwater.

Kendra leaned her head against the back of the couch and

looked up at the ceiling. Her eyes moved rapidly from side to side as a smile curved her lips. "These tiles are cool."

Audrey reached for her phone. The girl was sweating profusely now but continued to huddle within the blanket. This wasn't right, and it wasn't just a little high. She needed to get some help before this turned nasty.

Kendra hiccuped, and then she was choking. Audrey jumped out of her chair and went to the girl, lifting her head.

Vomit splashed onto the carpet. It just missed Audrey's shoes.

"Oh, shit," Kendra whispered. She was like a rag doll beneath Audrey's hands. A shaking rag doll.

Audrey called 911 and requested an ambulance for a possible drug overdose. Then, making sure Kendra was in a position so she wouldn't choke if she puked again, she opened the door of her office and calmly asked for a little help. Micheline was the first to rush over. She took one look at Kendra and swore.

"My reaction exactly," Audrey said. "Can you contact her parents?" She had a number for Elle, but not for Mr. Granger.

Micheline said she would.

Kendra's eyes rolled upward to meet Audrey's gaze. "I hurt Tala," she said. "I hurt her really bad."

Audrey's heart kicked. "What did you do, Kendra?"

But she was staring at her own vomit now, her breathing slower than it had been. This, Audrey knew, was not a good sign. When she puked again, Audrey held her hair and wiped her mouth with a tissue. The girl's eyes were closed.

"Come on, Kendra." Audrey patted her cheek. "Stay awake."

When the ambulance arrived, Kendra had passed out despite Audrey's attempts to keep her lucid. The EMTs loaded her onto a gurney and wheeled her through the office. Audrey went with them. Someone needed to be with the girl. The bell had rung, so there were kids in the corridor as they hurried toward the closest exit.

"Kendra? Ken!" It was Lucy. She ran up to Audrey, her face pale. "What did you do to her?"

Audrey shot her an exasperated glance. "Seriously? Get out of the way, Lucy, and let these people do their job."

"I want to go with her."

"You can't. You don't have permission to leave school property. I'll go."

Lucy looked like she wanted to argue. Hell, she looked like she wanted to take a swing. Audrey stared her down. "I don't have time for this, and neither does Kendra. Do you know what she took?"

The girl shook her head, staring after the gurney that carried her friend away. "I don't. Will you take care of her?"

"I will. You should call your mother and get permission to go to the hospital if you want to be there for her."

"Yeah. Right."

Then Audrey chased after the EMTs. As she climbed into the ambulance with Kendra, all she could think about was what the girl had said in the office.

"*I hurt Tala.*" As far as confessions went, it wasn't much, but happy, lighthearted people didn't get stoned before a counseling appointment. That was a cry for help from someone burdened—someone who didn't know what else to do.

As the ambulance tore down the street, Audrey dialed Neve's number. "Meet me at the hospital," she said when Neve answered. "Kendra Granger just OD'ed on me, and I think it had to do with Tala."

"She's seizing!" one of the EMTs exclaimed as Kendra began to thrash beneath her restraints. Audrey pressed herself into a corner to get out of their way and watched as they tried to quiet the girl. The other EMT said something about respiratory depression and having to get her breathing under control. Apparently her blood pressure was out of whack as well. Audrey wasn't a medical doctor, but she knew the symptoms of an overdose, and she knew that Kendra's chances of survival depended on the two people trying really hard to keep her alive.

Audrey hoped they succeeded, because the last thing her community needed was another dead teenager.

CHAPTER NINETEEN

When Neve arrived at the hospital after getting the call about Kendra Granger, the first person she ran into was Audrey.

"What are you doing here?"

Audrey shook her head. "She OD'ed with me."

"Jesus, woman. It's like this case wants you neck deep in it."

"It's a gift," came the dry reply. "Of course, the doctors won't tell me anything."

"Elle here yet?"

"No."

"Good." Neve adjusted her jacket. "Let's see what the doctors will tell me."

It took just a few seconds to find a nurse, and then several minutes before she managed to snag a doctor. Downeast wasn't a huge hospital, and the emergency room saw considerably less action than the ones Neve had seen in New York.

"Have you done a tox screen?" she asked the doctor.

"We're waiting on the results now."

Neve nodded. "Check her for GHB. And I need those results as soon as you have them."

"What are you doing here?"

It was Elle, of course.

Neve turned as the doctor backed up. "I'm here because I'm police, and because I suspect your daughter overdosed."

"Ridiculous. Kendra doesn't do drugs."

The woman was a twit. "Then she was drugged, and I should definitely be involved. I assume you want to talk to her doctor, so I'll leave you to it." Neve walked away in search of one of the people who knew everything that went on in the emergency ward—a nurse.

She had briefly dated Ed Delaney when she first moved back to Edgeport. It had been fun but hadn't lasted long. Ed was looking to indulge his "brown sugar" fantasy and it turned out Neve wasn't quite black enough for him. Whatever. She stayed friendly with him because it was always good to have a connection at the local hospital.

"GHB?" he asked after she filled him in. "That would explain why the girl's still out. Scary shit. I'll give you a call as soon as I know anything."

Then Neve went back to Audrey and took her statement. "Was this a professional appointment?"

Audrey nodded. "I didn't think she'd show up. I knew as soon as I saw her that she was high."

"Can you tell me what the two of you talked about?"

"It wasn't much—she wasn't very coherent." Audrey frowned. "Neve, she told me she hurt Tala. That she hurt her 'really bad.'"

Neve paused her writing. "I thought you weren't going to repeat things you're told in confidence."

"That kind of goes out the window when the person's a danger to themselves or others. I think Kendra might be both."

"You know, the symptoms she showed have all the signs of a GHB overdose."

"The date rape drug?"

"One of them. There are, unfortunately, several. We found traces of it in Tala's remains."

"If the same person drugged the two girls, it wasn't Luke."

"Yeah, I know. Was Lucy around when all this happened at the school?"

"She was, but there was no faking how scared she was."

"Kendra might have OD'ed on her own."

"She told me she didn't know what she'd taken."

"So maybe she got it from someone." Neve shook her head. "What kind of stupid kid takes drugs they can't identify?"

Audrey looked at her. "Seriously? We knew people who did it all the time. Kids are invincible, remember?"

"Kids are fucking idiots," Neve muttered. "I haven't heard of GHB being a trend around here, have you?"

"No. Has Lincoln found anything for you?"

"Not yet. I'll check in with him later. Right now, I think I should go upstairs and talk to Luke."

"You think he was set up?"

"I'm not sure he's entirely innocent, but I don't think he's dumb enough to leave the knife for us to find like that. Plus, Alisha said he wouldn't want to harm the rest of his collection."

"And he was with her the night Tala disappeared."

"I wish we had a more conclusive time of death." Neve

pursed her lips. "C'mon, Audrey. Put that juicy brain of yours to work. What am I missing?"

"This wasn't a hate crime. I mean, hate might have been a motivation, but it was much more personal. It was someone Tala knew. It's also someone with access to Luke's house, who knew about his collection."

"Someone who doesn't care if he takes the fall."

"Someone who wants to punish him." Audrey turned to her. "Sounds like Kendra."

"And then she OD's for sympathy—or to throw suspicion off herself."

"She's shown a tendency toward violence."

Neve made a face. "The girl's a fucking mess—between you and me. Come with me to Luke's room. You can make Linda chill while I talk to Luke."

"You're using me for my family connection." It was said with more amusement than anything else.

"I also want you looking for any clues in the way Luke acts or what he says." Neve's phone buzzed in her pocket. She checked the text. "It's from Vickie. Luke's blood type doesn't match the secondary sample we found on the glove at the scene."

"But you confirmed the first was Tala's?"

"Yes. And Mrs. Lewis confirmed the glove was hers as well."

"It was a plain glove. Was it marked in some way?"

"Mrs. Lewis had a matching pair. She sewed little purple felt dots in the inside of Tala's so they wouldn't get mixed up."

"God love super-organized mothers."

"I know, right? Mine was like that with the boys, but no so much with me."

"I guess she never had to worry about mistaking your stuff for theirs." Audrey's smile faded. "Here comes Elle. Let's go before she says something that makes me want to punch her."

The two of them headed toward the elevator and stepped in just as Elle reached the waiting area. She shot them both daggers with her red-rimmed eyes.

"She's such a bitch I can't even feel sorry for her," Audrey remarked as the doors closed.

"She asked me if I was going after her kids because they were white."

"Fuck off."

"God's truth. I thought I was going to stroke out." A thought struck her as the elevator rose. "Audrey, could that poor girl have been killed over a damn boy?"

"Yes."

"At least Bailey had a good reason."

"Speaking of Bailey..."

Neve shook her head. "Gideon's talking about moving if she gets out. She doesn't want to come back here."

She could feel Audrey's gaze boring into her. "What does that mean for you?"

"I've been thinking about leaving myself."

"Really?"

"I'm putting in an application with the FBI."

Audrey's silence was proof of her surprise. The woman never stayed quiet for long. "Good for you."

They got off the elevator on Luke Pelletier's floor and walked down the corridor shoulder to shoulder. Neve nodded at the cop by the door. Linda looked up from the chair where she was sitting when they walked in. Her expression brightened when she saw Audrey, then darkened when she saw Neve.

"What's going on?" She asked.

"Good afternoon, Linda," Neve said. "I need to talk to Luke. I thought you both might feel more comfortable with Audrey here."

Linda looked suspicious. "Haven't you done enough?"

Really, this being perceived as the perpetual bad guy was getting tiring. "Linda, I believe someone put that knife in Luke's things. And I believe it was someone he knows. I also need to verify his whereabouts for the night Tala disappeared."

Linda didn't seem to know how to react to that—if she should be relieved or angry. "Fine, but I'm staying in the room."

"Of course." Neve approached the boy handcuffed to the hospital bed. "How are you feeling, Luke? You're looking better."

"I'm okay," he replied. "Is it true Kendra OD'ed?"

She really shouldn't be surprised he'd already heard. "Who told you that?"

"It's all over Twitter."

"I guess it's true, then. Luke, who has had access to your bedroom since February?"

He frowned. "You mean, who's been in it?"

"Yeah. Other than you and your family."

"My friend Scott. Alisha. Lucy and Kendra. Those are the only people who have ever come over to the house."

"Have you ever left any of them alone in your room?"

"Sure. Not for long, but yeah."

Neve nodded. Three out of those four were girls who had also known Tala and had been sexually intimate with Luke. Didn't narrow it down much, although why would Alisha give him an alibi only to set him up?

"Luke, I spoke to Alisha. She told me where you were the night Tala disappeared."

The kid's eyes widened. "She did?"

Suddenly, his mother was right there. "What does that mean? Luke?"

Neve turned to Linda. "Alisha says Luke was with her that night." Her focus shifted to Luke. "Is that true?"

He nodded. "We were at her place. She said . . . we agreed to keep it a secret."

"Apparently she figured it was worth telling if it helped keep you out of jail."

"You should have been dating that sweet girl all along," Linda told him. "She's been a good and loyal friend to you, and never once has she tried playing head games like those other three."

"Three?" Neve asked.

"Kendra, Lucy, and Tala. All three of them were so much drama. So demanding and jealous. One night at our house Tala pitched a fit because Kendra called while she was there. She told Luke he had to choose."

Neve stared at her. For a woman known for her skills as a gossip, Linda sure had been withholding. "When did this happen?"

Linda frowned. "Late January?"

"It was February fourth," Luke reminded her. "My birthday."

"Tala was upset that Kendra called on your birthday?"

She thought the boy blushed, but it was hard to tell with the bruising on his face. "She had wanted that night to be the night we...you know." He swallowed. "She said Kendra ruined the mood."

His mother's mouth dropped open. "Tell me you didn't answer your phone while you and Tala were..."

"Mom! No. I'm not an asshole. I wouldn't have answered at all. It was after dinner—when you and Dad went to the movie."

Linda glanced at Neve. "I thought they deserved a little time alone."

"Anyway, Kendra called. Tala got mad and I told her there wasn't a choice—that I chose her."

"Smart man," Audrey commented from behind Neve.

"Not that smart," Luke said, his tone dry as sand. "Tala told Kendra what I said the next day."

"Girls," the three women in the room chorused.

"Yeah," Luke agreed. "It was at Big Al's Pizza. There was a big fight and Lucy tried to break it up, but then she started yelling at Tala. That's when Alisha arrived—we were all meeting for my birthday. She and I sat at another table. She was nice and calm. She thought it was stupid that they were fighting too."

"And that's when your feelings for her started to change," Audrey interjected.

Luke nodded. "Yeah. She's not like the other girls."

"She certainly is not," his mother agreed. "And that's why you are going to apologize to her for using her like that."

"It wasn't like that!" he protested. "When we heard about Tala...well, we figured it would make us both look bad. And Alisha didn't want to be a rebound girl. She told me to figure it out, and that she'd be around. I haven't looked at another girl since. I haven't wanted another girl. If Tala hadn't disappeared, Lish and I would be dating."

"None of this has been about Tala." Audrey spoke up, coming to stand beside Neve. "It's all been about Luke."

Neve turned her head. "It had nothing to do with Tala."

Audrey's face was pale. "It could have just as easily been Alisha. It might still be."

"Wait a second," came a voice from the doorway. It was Alisha—and she didn't look happy to be the topic of conversation. "Are you saying someone might try to kill me because I slept with Luke?"

Audrey went to her. "Did you tell anyone else what really happened between you and Luke that night?"

She shook her head. "No."

Neve looked at Luke. "Did you?"

"No."

Neve and Audrey then shared a glance. Neve knew exactly

what she was thinking, what she was afraid of. And Neve wondered if she could use it to her advantage.

She turned her attention to Alisha. "How do you feel about being bait?"

"No," Audrey said. "No frigging way, Neve!"

Alisha folded her arms over her chest. Luke, his mother, and Neve were watching her while Audrey glared at Neve. "Bait for the killer, you mean?"

Neve nodded.

Audrey clapped Neve on the shoulder. "I said no."

"I want to do it," Alisha said. "I'm going to."

The woman she already thought of as her aunt looked heartbroken—and afraid. "Haven't you been close to enough danger this last year?"

"Haven't you?" she countered. "I want to help."

Neve folded her arms over her chest. "All we have to do is get word out that you and Luke were together that night."

"Wait," Luke said. "I don't want people talking about Lish like that."

"Like what?" Neve challenged.

"Like they still talk about girls who have had sex," he replied.

"I don't care about that," Alisha told him. "People are going to say whatever they want anyway. Someone already asked me if you and I killed Tala together."

"Who the hell was that?" Audrey demanded.

She shook her head. She wasn't getting into that now. "It

doesn't matter." Then to Neve, she said, "Do you really think this will work?"

"I do."

Alisha walked over and put her hand on Luke's arm—the one without the handcuff. "If it proves you're innocent, I have to do it."

"I don't like it," he said. "I'll worry about you."

"Don't," she told him. "Neve's got my back. I won't go anywhere alone, and I know how to use a gun."

"No guns," Neve amended. "Stay away from the damn guns. I'll make sure you've got someone watching you at all times."

"How can you do that when she's at school?" Audrey asked.

Neve looked like she was debating whether to answer. "We've got someone who we use at the school from time to time."

"A cop?"

Neve nodded. "The point is, I can make sure Alisha is safe, and she's not stupid. She knows how to protect herself."

At least someone had faith in her. Of course, it was the person wanting to use her for her own gain. "I'm going to do this," she told them. "Whether you all want me to or not." She looked at each of them, daring them to stop her.

Surprisingly, it was Linda who spoke. "Alisha, I love you for wanting to help my son, but are you sure you know how dangerous this might be? Someone murdered Tala and they hadn't even...shared the same intimacy as you and Luke."

Alisha smiled at her as she blushed. "Tala didn't see it coming. I will."

"Jesus," Audrey swore under her breath.

Alisha turned to her. "You have to promise not to tell Mum or Uncle Jake."

Sometimes there was something unnerving about staring into Audrey's mismatched eyes. It was like looking at two different people in one head. This was one of those times.

"You're putting me in a tough spot, kid."

She knew that. She also knew Audrey was the only person who understood how she felt about Luke. "Please."

"All right. How do you plan to do it?"

Alisha smiled at her. "Oh, I have a friend on Twitter that I think will help me."

Audrey arched a brow, but she didn't say no, so Alisha knew that she had won.

Before leaving the hospital, Neve went back downstairs to check on Kendra. Elle wasn't in the waiting area anymore, but Lucy, Kyle, and Josh were.

"Any word?" Neve asked as she approached. She expected attitude from at least Kyle, but they all looked so scared and young. None of them offered any lip.

"Not yet," Kyle said.

Neve's phone rang, so she went a short distance away to answer. "Hello?"

"Hey, it's Ed. I only have a minute, but I wanted to tell you that your girl tested positive for GHB as well as lorazepam. I think she's been using for a while, because the amount should have brought down an elephant."

"Thanks, Ed. I owe you." She hung up before he could respond. Turning and pocketing her phone, she walked back toward the young people in the waiting area.

"I know the three of you are worried about Kendra, but I need to ask you a question. Do you have any idea where she might have gotten her hands on GHB?"

The three of them looked startled. Lucy stared at her, but Josh looked at Kyle first.

"Isn't that a drug rapists use?" Lucy asked.

"Sometimes," Neve replied. "It's a sedative."

"That's what she took?" Kyle asked.

Neve nodded. "A lot of it, apparently, over an extended period of time. Have you seen her with anything at home?"

He shook his head. "She's got some prescriptions, but I've never seen her do any other kind of drugs."

"What about you?" Neve asked Lucy.

The girl shrugged. "We've smoked pot, that's it. She's started smoking more since Tala disappeared."

Ed hadn't mentioned finding THC in the girl's system, however. Neve turned to Josh, who rubbed the back of his neck. "I found Kendra and Tala all done up on something one night, but I don't know what it was."

"And none of you have heard of anyone selling GHB in the area?"

Three heads shook.

"Is my sister going to be okay?" Kyle asked. His voice sounded almost meek. It seemed strange coming out of him.

"I don't know," she replied, honestly. "I hope so. Has she been depressed lately?"

Lucy snorted. "Yeah." *Like, haven't you been paying attention?* she seemed to ask. "But not suicidal, if that's what you're asking. If she killed herself she'd definitely never get Luke back."

Kyle scowled. "Like he's good enough for her."

Neve took that as her cue to leave. She was walking to her car, and shrugging out of her jacket because it was too damn hot, when her phone rang again. She had to grope around to find the right pocket. "Neve Graham."

"It's Lincoln."

"Hey. Please tell me your buddy came through."

"He did, although reluctantly. He said he only knew of a couple of people buying GHB in the area."

"Is that how he put it? Like he knew people who had bought it, but not that he had sold it?"

"Yeah."

Asshat. "Okay, who?"

He didn't know names, but he said he'd sold some to a frat boy over spring break. A kid with brown hair and blue eyes. T hat was all he remembered."

That was more than enough. "Think he'd recognize the kid if you showed him a picture?"

"Probably, but I'm not sure he'll talk again."

"Tell him I've got no interest in nailing him for drugs. He can be classified as a confidential informant." That meant compensation.

"Really?"

"Linc, I'm after a fucking killer. Yes, really. I'm going to text you the photo now. Call me when you've gotten an answer." She hung up and sent him a photo of Kyle Granger she'd snapped when she arrested the kid for beating up Luke. Then she got into the car and headed toward her office in Machias. She had paperwork to do, and she wanted to sit down with Vickie for a face-to-face.

She was just going through the door when her phone dinged. It was a text from Lincoln—with no punctuation: *He says thats him.*

Neve smiled grimly as her thumb tapped the keypad. It rang twice before a familiar voice answered.

"Yeah," she said. "It's Neve. I need another search warrant."

CHAPTER TWENTY

When was your last period?"

Audrey sat on the exam table, in the ugly little johnny shirt the PA had given her. "About a month ago. I should start soon."

"About a month?"

"I've never been terribly regular. Stress goes right to my ovaries." She smiled when she said it. The PA didn't return it. "Okay, we'll put down a month. If you remember a date, let me know."

"Sure." *And if you happen to find a personality, you let me know.* She'd peed in their little plastic bottle, been weighed, and all that crap—she was up a couple of pounds—and was now just waiting to see the doctor so she could poke around Audrey's insides without even buying her a drink first. It was the icing on the cake of an already shitty day.

She hated Pap tests. They literally made her grit her teeth. Now, there was the extra awesomeness of having cervical cancer in the family. She tried to curb her anxiety by looking around at the various posters on the walls, but there were just too many that kind of freaked her out.

Yancy had made an appointment for Alisha, apparently. She

was totally paranoid about the girl getting pregnant, or worse, and Audrey didn't blame her. Yancy had been fifteen when she got pregnant with Alisha. Audrey didn't know who the guy was, but apparently he'd been much, much older. It was around that time that Yancy went to live with Gracie—where Jake had been since he was much younger. Their mother wasn't much in the mother department, and figured Brody Tripp's family could have his annoying offspring. The only one she ever seemed to like was Lincoln, and he'd be the first one to say her love wasn't something to wish for.

Alisha didn't seem to think the appointment was necessary, but apparently Yancy put her foot down. Jake did too. Alicia could stand against one of them, but not both.

There was a knock on the door and her doctor walked in. Dr. Aaron was a small, middle-aged woman with graying blond hair and kind green eyes. Audrey had known her since she was a kid, as she was also her mother's and Jessica's doctor.

"Audrey, how lovely to see you."

She smiled. "Sorry it's been longer than it ought to have been."

"It happens. What's important is that you're here now. I'm assuming you're here for blood work or a prenatal Pap?"

All the blood drained from Audrey's head and fell somewhere around her knees. "What?"

The doctor's smile froze. "There was hCG in your urine. I assumed you came to confirm pregnancy or get a checkup."

"I...I." Shit, it had been more than a month since her last period. "I've had a false positive before."

"Then we'd better do blood work to confirm or rule out pregnancy. Let's get you examined and then we'll get that blood sample."

"How long will it take?"

"I should have the results tomorrow if not the next day." Her smile was reassuring. "Don't get yourself all stressed just yet. How about you lie back and put your feet in the stirrups?"

On autopilot, Audrey did what she was told. Her mind seemed to be both blank and moving at a thousand miles a minute. Pregnant? She couldn't be. This was just a fake-out like before—like Jake's cyst.

But she'd gained a little weight, and she'd been queasy lately...

Fuck.

She couldn't be pregnant. She didn't *want* to be pregnant. As much as she liked helping kids, the idea of being responsible for how one turned out had always terrified her. She didn't want to change diapers and heat up bottles. She wanted her career.

"I hear your home for troubled kids is coming along great guns," Dr. Aaron commented as she began the exam.

Audrey expelled a deep breath, telling herself to relax. "It is. We're planning to open this fall. We already have a waiting list."

"That's fabulous news. Okay, I'm going to insert my fingers inside you and press down on your belly."

Staring at the ceiling, Audrey tried to wish away the warm, prickly feeling in her head. She was a grown-ass woman, not a teenager. She could handle this. There was just some pressure, nothing more. That didn't stop her from trying her best to zone out while Dr. Aaron did her thing.

Afterward, the doctor stripped off her gloves. "Okay, you can sit up."

"So?" Audrey asked, pushing herself up on the paper-covered table.

"I did feel a few things that are usually indicative of pregnancy, but I can't say for certain without blood work. We can do that here, if you like."

She nodded dumbly. This was really happening.

A short while later, with a bandage in the crook of her arm and a dazed expression on her face, Audrey made the drive back to the house. Just last week she'd given Jake hell about keeping things from her and now she was debating keeping this from him. Why have both of them freaking out? And wasn't it primarily *her* decision? That was what she tried to tell herself, but it didn't work.

She drove straight to Gracie's, barely noticing the cars in the driveway. The lunch crowd.

"Hey, Audrey. He's in the storeroom," Donalda, one of the few wait staff, said as she walked in.

"Thanks, Dee." Audrey knew every inch of Gracie's now, so she knew exactly where to go. She found him unboxing ketchup, loading the large cans onto a metal shelf.

"Hey. What are you doing here?" Jake's smile faded as he looked at her. "What's wrong?"

"I think I'm pregnant," she blurted.

Suddenly, her father popped up from behind some boxes. His gingery hair stuck out from beneath a ball cap, and a huge grin creased his rugged face. "Pregnant? Praise the Lord and pass the ammunition."

Audrey sagged against the door frame. "Well, fuck."

"Think Rusty will tell your mum?" Jake asked later, when they were nestled together in bed.

"He knows how to keep a secret," Audrey replied, absently stroking his bare chest. "I just hate that he knows."

"Because you don't want to have it?"

Something in his voice made her glance up. "I don't know what I want. What do you want?"

"It's not my body."

"*Jake.*"

"I'm serious. You are the one whose body will be taken over for nine months and then go through childbirth."

"But it's *our* decision. *Our* baby."

He looked as though she'd punched him. "Our baby. Jesus."

Audrey knew at that moment, without a doubt, that Jake wanted the baby. Maybe he wasn't even aware of how much he wanted it, but she could see it in his face, and it made her feel all the worse for feeling slightly sick over the news. It hadn't helped that her father had practically danced a jig in the backroom at Gracie's.

Why did everyone treat pregnancy like it was an awesome, fabulous thing? Not every woman wanted to be a mother. Not every man was determined to be a father.

Except, it seemed that Jake was, and that made her job all the more difficult, because she was 90 percent sure she didn't want the responsibility of motherhood. She didn't want to go through childbirth—and she sure as hell didn't want to go through the teen years, regardless of her PhD. With their luck she and Jake would spawn the first kid to ever be arrested in kindergarten.

"You're quiet," he said.

"I'm thinking."

"Whatever you decide to do, I'll support you."

"I don't want to make this decision alone."

"In the end, it has to be what you want, Aud. I want whatever you want."

That pissed her off enough that it took her hours to get to sleep. She couldn't argue it, because she knew it was true. Hers was the deciding vote, but would it kill him to at least be honest with her—and himself? If she had an abortion, would he despise her for getting rid of it? If she didn't have an abortion, would she end up despising him for keeping it? Worse, would she blame the kid?

God, she wished Gracie were still alive.

The following morning, Jake made breakfast and offered to stay home rather than work on the long list of things he had to do that day. Audrey told him to go. She had work to do, and she'd take his eyes out if she had to deal with his love and support all day. Sometimes, she wished he was more of an asshole.

Alone in the house, she powered up her laptop and logged into Twitter under the account she'd made up. HeadSick2017 had a job to do. She didn't want to do it, but neither Alisha nor Neve had given her much choice.

Looks like @LAPdawwg has an alibi for the night Tala was killed. She sucked in a deep breath. Alisha didn't know what she was getting into, but if Audrey didn't tweet about it, the kid would find a way to do it herself, and probably make it even worse. *@TrippyLish—was it love or a one-night stand?* T hen, she added the JusticeForTala hashtag so as many people as possible would see it, and posted before she could change her mind.

Within a few minutes the tweet got several reposts and comments. The news of Tala's murder had spread across the country now, and people from all over were watching the case—and their tiny little town. There had been the odd mention of Audrey's own scandal, but what was fresh in everyone's mind was the "Boy Scout" murder case and how it had made its mark on the area.

She was starting to think they should rename the place Cabot Cove, as they were getting almost as many murders as the fictional TV town. Or maybe Derry. Regardless, she had more important things to worry about than whether she'd brought bad luck down upon the place with her return home.

She had a little time before she had to go to the school, so she got in the car and drove to the hospital with the intention of checking in on Kendra. Yes, she was being nosy and hoping to get something useful out of the kid, but she was also genuinely concerned about her well-being.

On her way up to Kendra's room, she passed Kyle Granger in the corridor. He shot her a sullen look as he passed. Audrey didn't really know the kid, and she didn't think he knew her, but she was predisposed to disliking him for beating up Luke. Could he have a motive for killing Tala? Had she broken it off with him to go back to Luke? She'd already seen what Kyle could do with his fists and feet; stabbing someone wouldn't be hard for him—and it was often a substitute for sexual penetration.

When she reached the private room, she found it empty except for Kendra and Lucy, who had crawled onto the bed with her friend. The two of them were watching something on a tablet. They reminded her of when she and Maggie were young.

Audrey rapped her knuckles against the door frame. When the girls looked up, she smiled. "Can I come in?"

To say the two of them looked leery would be an understatement. Lucy flipped the cover over the tablet and slid off the bed to stand instead. She stood as stiff and watchful as a guard.

"Sure," Kendra said. She looked like hell. Her nose wasn't as swollen as it had been, but it was still bruised, as well as her eyes. Alisha had done a good job of breaking it. She was pale and drawn-looking, her hair in need of shampooing. Her eyes were heavy and glazed.

Audrey entered the room. "I won't stay long. I just wanted to see how you're feeling."

"Tired. Groggy. I don't remember much."

"I think that's pretty normal." She moved closer. "Has anyone been in to assess you?"

"You mean a shrink?" Lucy demanded. When Audrey nodded, she said, "She doesn't need one of those."

"It's standard," Audrey explained. "They need to know if an overdose was intentional or accidental."

"It was intenshun—intentional," Kendra replied. "But I didn't do it."

Tilting her head, Audrey considered the implication of her words. "You mean you were drugged?" She glanced at Lucy. T he redhead gave an almost imperceptible shake of her head. So Kendra was lying? Or didn't want to admit to having made a cry for help? An intentional overdose would probably lead to a longer hospital stay than an accidental one. But saying someone had drugged her took all responsibility off Kendra herself.

"I think it was the same person who killed Tala," Kendra went on, her voice thickening as her eyelids fluttered. She'd obviously been given something to help her sleep before Audrey arrived. "I'm going to tell Detective Graham."

Another tiny head shake.

Audrey began to understand—or at least she thought she did. Kendra had OD'ed in a desperate attempt to take suspicion off Luke.

"I'm sure she'll want to talk to you about what happened." As she moved closer to the bed, she noticed Lucy also moved closer to Kendra.

She was protecting her.

Audrey stopped a few feet away. Whatever had happened, Lucy obviously felt as though her friend needed someone at her back. She used to feel that way about Maggie. And Maggie had felt that way about her. When Everett Graham had shown up at Maggie's house that night and found Clint lying in a puddle of his own blood, his skull caved in, Maggie had stepped in front of Audrey, looked the cop right in the eye, and said, "I did it."

"She's still kind of out of it," Lucy said.

"I know...wha' happened," Kendra slurred. "I know the...truth."

"The truth about what?" Audrey asked.

"The night Tala died...Fucking asshole." Kendra closed her eyes. "I...know wha'...he did."

"What who did?" Audrey's heart picked up the pace. "What who did, Kendra?"

But the girl was out.

Lucy glanced at her friend, then at Audrey. "She saw Twitter this morning. There's a rumor that Luke was with Alisha that night."

Audrey nodded. "I heard that."

"Is it true?"

They had agreed not to reveal that Alisha had spoken to Neve, and Audrey really didn't want to discuss Alisha's business with this girl, so she hedged. "Alisha and I haven't had the chance to talk about it, but I know she cares about Luke very much."

"Yeah," came the acerbic reply. "I saw that."

Audrey shook her head. "Look, Lucy. I really shouldn't discuss it with you. I know both you and Kendra have been advised to stay away from Alisha, and I know what Kendra did to her. I'm trying to remain neutral, but to do that, I can't discuss one of you with the others."

She thought she might get attitude for that, but the girl lifted her chin. "I get it. It's just hard to see my best friend like this, you know?"

Audrey thought of Maggie and how her mental instability had gotten the best of her. "Yeah, I do." She managed a sympathetic smile, even though she thought the girl was hiding something. Then again, pretty much all teenage girls were hiding *something*. "I'll leave the two of you alone. Please tell Kendra I hope she's home soon."

Lucy nodded. "I will. Thanks."

As Audrey crossed the room, Kendra stirred in her sleep, making a sound of distress. She said something incoherent. Lucy's voice was soft, but it followed Audrey out of the room.

"Ssh. Don't worry—I won't tell."

CHAPTER TWENTY-ONE

Being the topic of gossip was not as easy as Alisha thought it would be. She wasn't used to being watched as she walked down the hall, and she certainly wasn't used to people laughing and whispering as she passed. It wasn't fun, but she could handle it. Really, all they were talking about was whether they thought she'd had sex with Luke. Not like it was a big deal.

But it had been a big deal. Bigger than she let on, and she hated it. She'd always thought virginity was an albatross around her neck—like that awful poem she'd had to read in English class. She never thought she'd be one of those girls who got emotional afterward, but she had. She'd cried. Luke had held her and stroked her back. He wanted to stay even when she told him he had to leave.

She'd been the one to say they should keep it a secret. That it had been a mistake. He didn't speak to her for a few days after that. It took her two days to realize that he wasn't a jerk, but that she had hurt his feelings.

What a way to start a relationship. She was so fucking backward. She'd slept with the guy, and now she was just starting to get around to dating him. If she could keep him out of prison, maybe they'd get to go on an actual date.

So, yeah. That was why she could handle the stares and whispers. It was for Luke. For her.

Lunch was almost over. She only had to make it through a few more hours and then she could go home. She'd checked Twitter just once since Audrey had posted that morning, and it was nuts. More people were debating the validity of the story than anything else. Some of them actually seemed angry that Luke might have an alibi. They didn't know him, but they wanted him to be guilty.

How had Audrey done it? she wondered as she opened her locker. Two girls giggled at her as they walked by. How had Audrey come back to this place after killing someone? It must have been fucking hell.

It only made Alisha love her more. Audrey was who she wanted to be when she got older. Alisha also loved her for the way she made Uncle Jake smile. She wanted a love like that someday. She didn't know if Luke was that one for her, but she cared about him—a lot.

Obviously, if she was letting Neve use her as bait.

Not that she really thought anything would come of it. At least not while both Kendra and Luke were in the hospital. It narrowed the field too much.

"Nice play, by the way."

She glanced around the edge of her locker door. "You really don't get the whole restraining-order thing, do you?"

Lucy shrugged. "I'm getting some books for Ken. You gonna call the cops?"

"I'm going to go to class."

"So, are they going to let Luke go now that you've got the whole planet talking about how you fucked him?"

"I honestly doubt the whole planet cares who I sleep with."

"Kendra does. Tala would."

That was a low blow. "Tala had already broken up with him—and she was doing Kyle, remember? Kendra had her chance and she blew it."

"So you figure you'll take a ride now, huh?"

"The question is, Lucy, why do *you* care so much? You still have a thing for Luke?"

The other girl blinked. "No. Of course not. Fuck, no."

"So, you're just upset on behalf of Tala and Kendra?"

Lucy hesitated, like she thought it was a trick question. "Yeah. Anyway, now everyone knows you're just another one of Luke's sluts."

"Guess that makes four of us," Alisha retorted. "Now, do I need to explain what staying the fuck away from me means, or should I just break your nose too?"

For a second, a smirk curved Lucy's lips, and Alisha thought she might actually take her up on it, but then she backed up. "My bad."

Alisha watched her walk away with a narrow gaze. It wasn't until she went to close her locker that she realized her hands were clenched into fists.

* * *

Search warrant in hand, Neve rang the bell at the Granger house, backed up by Vickie and two uniforms. She fully expected Elle to lose her shit when she saw them, and she was glad for the extra backup.

Only it wasn't Elle who answered the door, but Kendall, her husband. He had that ruddy, slightly puffy look of a man who drank too much and liked his steaks. He worked in finance, and looked it. A set of golf clubs sat beside the door, and he was dressed as though he planned to hit the course.

"What's this about?" he asked when he saw them. "My daughter is still in the hospital and my wife isn't here. We have nothing to discuss with you people." He looked at Neve as he spoke.

It was the "you people" that made her bristle. She'd heard variations on that before, with varying degrees of disdain. It didn't matter if he meant "cop" or even "nigger," the intonation was the same.

She shoved the warrant at him. "We're here to search the premises, Mr. Granger. Kindly wait outside with Trooper MacKay." MacKay was a young kid with a brush cut and a sunburned nose, but he was eager to learn the job.

Granger flushed even darker. "You can't do this. You have no right."

"The judge thought otherwise." She brushed past him to enter the house. "Please wait outside, sir."

"I'm going to call my lawyer!"

Neve gave him a gentle shove toward the door where MacKay waited to guide him the rest of the way. "You do that. You may need him when we're done."

Once the man was outside, she, Vickie, and the fourth trooper, Balfour, made their way upstairs. Kyle's bedroom was at the opposite end of the hall from his parents'. It was a large room with a heavy queen-size bed and matching dark wood furniture. The walls were painted a dark blue and there were framed posters of bands on all four. It was strangely neat for a young man his age, but not all college boys were slobs. Maybe the housekeeper cleaned his room as well as the rest of the house.

Vickie stood in the center as she pulled on her nitrile gloves. "If I were a frat boy, where would I keep my drugs?"

"Somewhere close but not obvious," answered Balfour, who wasn't long out of college himself.

"Speaking from experience, Jay?" Neve asked with a smile.

He grinned. "Of course not."

They each took a section and started searching. Neve took the closet—it was a huge walk-in with a wall of shelves and drawers.

"I have closet envy," she remarked, pulling on her own gloves. It was just as neat in there as it was out in the room. She started at the opposite wall and worked her way back, looking in pockets and shoes and bags and boxes. Behind a couple of boxes of sneakers that looked like they'd never been worn, she found a stack of pornographic magazines that featured transgender and intersex models. There were also a few dedicated to S&M. None of it was very hard-core or particularly disturbing. Everyone was fairly glossy and attractive and most of the acts depicted appeared consensual, if not totally staged. Highbrow fringe porn. She hadn't known it was a thing.

She put the transgender magazines in an evidence bag and continued her search. After finding condoms, lube, and an assortment of sex toys she really wished she hadn't seen, she finally found what she thought she was looking for. In one of the drawers was a small locked chest. She didn't see a key anywhere—Kyle probably had it on him—so she grabbed a jackknife that was also in the drawer and used the blade to pop the lock on the box.

"Eur-fucking-eka," she whispered. Then louder, "I found something!" She took the box out into the main room.

"Jesus," Vickie remarked when she peered inside. "The kid planning to open his own pharmacy?"

There was a bag of weed; some white powder Neve guessed was coke; a couple baggies of pills, one of which looked like antianxiety meds; and a couple small vials of clear liquid. One of them was only half full.

"That's got to be the GHB," she said, picking up the full one and holding it up to the light. The drug didn't have a smell, and she wasn't about to taste it. "The lab will be able to tell for sure." If it was, then her focus would definitely switch to Kyle and his sister. Kendra had gotten her hands on the stuff somehow, so either her brother had given it to her or she'd taken it, and one of them had probably given some to Tala the night she was killed. Kyle had been around that weekend with spring break, and he could have easily killed Tala before going back to school.

But what was his motive? Jealousy? Heartbreak that she'd tossed him over for Luke? Kyle didn't seem the kind to waste his time being brokenhearted, but maybe he was a better actor than she thought.

She put the vials into a baggie and gathered the other drugs as well. GHB was also sometimes available in pill or powder form, so she needed to have everything in the box tested.

"You guys find anything else?" she asked.

"He's got some porn on the computer," Balfour replied. "A lot of shemale stuff."

"Transgender," Neve corrected. "Or intersex. Shemale's a shitty term and I don't want to hear it, got it?" She'd known other cops who used the term, but that didn't make it right. She also knew cops that liked to drop the N-bomb on occasion and didn't care if she heard it.

He flushed. "Yes, ma'am. Sorry."

She clapped him on the shoulder. "Anything else on the computer?"

"I found some e-mails between him and the vic. I forwarded them to you. I didn't see anything that stood out—mostly sexy stuff."

She could tell from the lingering pink in his cheeks that it had embarrassed him to read it. "Good. Send me the photos as well."

Neve and Vickie finished going through the room while Balfour continued with the computer. It was almost an hour before they descended downstairs and outside, where MacKay and Kendall Granger waited.

Granger's lawyer had shown up. He was just as florid as his client, and twice as puffed up. "I'd like to know what this was all about, Detective."

Neve barely looked at him. "It's about murder. And GHB."

Something clanged. She turned in time to see Kyle Granger sprinting across the backyard toward the fence. Stupid, rich white boys.

They always ran.

Wednesday morning, Audrey went into the school to find someone unexpected waiting for her. Elle Granger's makeup and hair were perfect, but it was obvious she had been crying. Audrey couldn't help but feel some sympathy for her, despite the fact that she wasn't very likable.

She stood when Audrey approached her. Her shoes were Prada, which sparked a little envy in Audrey's gut. Or maybe that was just the baby. A bitter taste rose in the back of her throat, but she swallowed it back down. She was not going to puke on Elle Granger's exquisite designer shoes.

"I'm sorry to show up like this," Elle said. "Do you have a moment?"

Audrey nodded. She didn't have an appointment until nine thirty. "Come on in."

Elle followed her into the small office. Audrey closed the door and gestured to the love seat. "What can I do for you?"

"I don't know if you can do anything, to be honest," Elle admitted as she sat down. "I'm worried for my children, and obviously wondering what I did to make them as they are."

As they are. That was a strange turn of phrase, wasn't it? "What do you mean?"

Elle gave her a dubious look. "Surely you've heard that Detective Graham was at our house yesterday?"

Audrey shook her head, even though Yancy had mentioned it the night before. "I assume it had to do with Kendra's overdose?"

"I suppose it did. They found the drug she took in my son's closet—along with others."

Ah. So Kyle Granger had GHB. Had he given it to Tala, or had Kendra? "You didn't know that Kyle uses drugs?"

"Of course I suspected—he's in college, after all. But not to this extent, no. And to find this out after Kendra…" She frowned. "My daughter used to be my little angel. God, she was the perfect little girl."

Audrey inclined her head to one side as she leaned against the desk. She wondered how many drugs the other woman had done in college if she assumed all students partook. "Then what happened?"

Elle laughed, but there was little to no humor in it. "She became a teenager. She became obsessed with her looks and with boys. She became jealous of her friends. I tried telling myself it was normal teenage girl behavior."

"But?"

The woman's narrow shoulders sagged. It was obvious where Kendra had gotten her obsession with her physical appearance, but Audrey wasn't going to point it out. "She started abusing diet pills, and she began cutting herself. She also pulled out so much of her own hair that she had a bald patch. We could hide it with a little styling. We could hide the scars too, and some of the weight loss, but that's like putting a Band-Aid on a gunshot wound, right?"

She seemed to want Audrey to agree with her, so she nodded. "What did you do?"

"We got her into therapy, of course. The best we could find in the area. We even had videoconferences with doctors from New York. We got her on some medication, got her to eat normally. She stopped pulling her hair and cutting herself."

"That's good."

"Yes, but all of this attention on Kendra meant there was very little for Kyle. The next thing I know, we're at our summer home and the police pull into the drive. Kyle had wrecked his car. Luckily, the police know our family and didn't report it."

That was convenient. Jesus, it must be nice to have that kind of influence. "What happened then?"

"We put him in rehab, of course." She shook her head. "I thought he was fine. I thought they both were fine."

Something in her tone—a note of defeat—made Audrey frown. "But they weren't?"

Elle shook her head. "I've given them everything I could. I love my kids, Audrey. I really do, but I think I've also damaged them. There's mental illness in my family—my mother is bipolar, and I've been treated for depression several times over the years. I'm afraid I've passed it on to my kids."

"You can't blame yourself for that, Elle. Genetics are out of your control."

"I shouldn't have had kids, but Kendall wanted the perfect family." She said it with a degree of bitterness. "I've tried to protect them both because I feel so responsible for their problems, but I don't think I can protect them anymore. I think maybe I'm doing them more harm than good."

It was then that Audrey realized that Elle hadn't come to see her for her kids, she'd come to unburden herself. She was looking for Audrey to absolve her, or tell her it was okay to stop trying to mask the problem.

"Why did you come here, Elle?" She kept her voice low, but strong. It was the voice she often used to let some of the more vulnerable kids she'd interviewed know that she could handle whatever they needed to share.

The woman dabbed at the corners of her eyes with a tissue from the box on the coffee table. "When Kendra attacked Alisha in the hospital I knew something was wrong. I checked her medication and realized that she hadn't been taking it. It's not the kind of stuff you should just stop taking. There are side effects."

Audrey didn't know a lot about drugs—psychologists couldn't prescribe, and it had been a long time since she studied them. She was aware of some of the more popular and older drugs, but not like a psychiatrist would be, and for that reason, she didn't ask what Kendra had been taking. "So, you think going off her meds led to the violence with Alisha?"

"I know it did. You see, this wasn't the first time Kendra's stopped taking her medication without supervision."

It seemed like Elle needed her to ask in order to continue, so Audrey did. "She's been violent before?"

Elle nodded, her face pale beneath her makeup—it made her look almost garish. "Yes."

"What happened?"

A tear slid down her smooth cheek, carving a trail through the powder there. "She stabbed me with a hunting knife."

CHAPTER TWENTY-TWO

When Audrey called and told Neve that Elle Granger wanted to talk to her, Neve thought it was some kind of joke, but then she went to the high school and found the two of them waiting for her.

Elle refused to make any kind of statement or say anything on record. Everything Neve learned came from Audrey. Elle just sat there, silent and pale. It wasn't a good look for her, and Neve didn't take any enjoyment in seeing the woman so upset.

"Do you have a lot of hunting knives in your house, Elle?" she asked.

"Kendall has several," Audrey answered, her gaze locking with Neve's. Neither of them had to say anything else. T hey both knew what the other was thinking—it wasn't a big jump. Both Kendra and Kyle had access to hunting knives, and Kendra had been in Luke's bedroom. Having dated the kid, she'd know all about his collection of daggers and where he kept them.

"Where's your son? Where's Kyle?"

But Elle just shook her head. She didn't know.

When Neve left, she made sure she apologized loudly for interrupting Audrey and Elle's conversation and thanked Audrey for her help—just in case anyone was paying attention. She really didn't want people speculating as to why she was meeting with the two women, and gossip was a regional pastime, it sometimes seemed.

As soon as she got back into her car, she called Vickie. "Hey, Vick. You get anything on the knife we found at the Pelletier house?"

"Mm. It's handmade, apparently. I found the craftsman online. That pattern in the blade? Apparently it's Damascus steel or something. Can you believe it cost four hundred dollars?"

Having seen the inside of the Granger house, yes. "Find out who bought it."

"Already on it. I sent the guy a photo of the knife and asked for a list of clients in this area. He was very cooperative."

"Probably freaked out that one of his designs was used to kill a person. Turns out Kendall Granger collects hunting knives, and it seems Kendra likes to stab people with them—at least her mother."

"Shit."

"Isn't it?"

"Are you going to arrest her?"

"We don't have enough. I am going to cut Luke free, though. Prosecutor's dropping charges. It's looking more and more like he was framed—that whole knife thing and he's got an alibi for that night."

"You said yourself that we don't know the exact time of death, though."

"No, we don't. But if I'm letting Kendra walk around free, I need to let Luke do the same. Right now she's looking way more guilty than he is. Call me as soon as you find out about the knife." She hung up and headed toward the hospital. She wanted to talk to Luke about Kendra, but first she wanted to talk to Kendra herself. It was the perfect opportunity with Elle not watching over her daughter like a hawk.

She walked into Kendra's hospital room to find Lucy with her.

"Shouldn't you be in school?" she asked.

The redhead shot her a belligerent stare. "My mother knows where I am."

Neve really didn't care. "I need to talk to Kendra alone, please."

The girl straightened. "You can't."

The look Neve gave her was one she normally reserved for criminals who really pissed her off. "Yeah, I can. You need to leave the room."

Lucy turned to her friend. Kendra was still pale and bruised, but she looked like she was recovering well. Neve wondered what the psych evaluation had revealed and if the girl was going to be kept for any length of time. If there was no record of some of her previous behavior, the doctors wouldn't really have cause to keep her.

Kendra nodded. "It's okay, Luce."

Lucy didn't look happy about being dismissed. "I'll be right outside if you need me."

Just what did the girl think Neve was going to do?

When they were alone, Kendra surprised her by speaking first. "Guess you want to talk to me about the OD, huh?"

"We can start there," Neve allowed. "Did you get the drug from your brother? We found his stash."

Blue eyes opened wide, then went back to normal. "Yeah. He doesn't know that I know where he keeps it."

"Does he use GHB a lot?"

Kendra shrugged. "He used to when he was into sports."

It was used as an athletic enhancer. "What about recreationally?"

She blushed. "I heard him and Josh talking about how it made sex better."

Josh probably didn't know that Kyle was using it to have sex with Tala. "Did you ever give any to Tala?"

"Me?" She shook her head. "No."

Neve couldn't tell if she was lying. Of course, it was just as possible that Tala had gotten the drug from Kyle, or even from her own brother if he used it as well.

"Did you mean to take too much at school on Monday?"

The girl flushed even darker. "No."

Now that felt more like a lie. "Why did you take it?"

"I was upset over Luke."

"Over him being arrested, or that he'd hooked up with Alisha?"

All the pink in her face drained away. "What?"

She didn't know? Audrey had tweeted it the day before. It was all over town. Lucy had somehow managed to keep it from her.

"Alisha and Luke were together the night Tala disappeared."

Kendra shook her head. "No. That's not true."

"I'm afraid it is."

"No!" Kendra cried. "It's not true! She's lying!"

"Kendra…"

"I did not go through all of this just so he can end up with some white trash slut." The girl's eyes glittered like stones. "After all I've done for him, he cannot just fucking walk away from me."

Okay, this was getting a little too teen *Fatal Attraction* for Neve's liking, but still… "What did you do for him?"

"Lucy!" Kendra yelled.

Her friend rushed into the room. "Are you okay?"

"Why didn't you tell me Luke fucked Alisha?"

Lucy shot Neve a look that seemed to ask, *What have you done?* "It's just a rumor, Ken. Gossip."

Then, without warning, Kendra punched herself in the face. Just balled up her fist and smashed her already broken nose like her hand was the head of a hammer. She started screaming. And bleeding.

Neve and Lucy rushed her at the same time. Neve grabbed the hand that she was using to hurt herself and pinned it to the mattress while Lucy seized the other. Neve pressed the call button for the nurses, who came running a few seconds later. Kendra thrashed on the bed, her nose streaming blood, face red and puffy where she'd hit herself. She strained against them. She wasn't a very big girl, but rage gave her strength. Neve had to put her weight into it to keep her on the mattress.

"Get off me!" Kendra screamed as she pounded her heels into the bed. "Get the fuck off me!"

One of the nurses inserted a needle into Kendra's IV tube. Within seconds the girl quieted.

"I think maybe you should leave, Detective," she said.

Neve agreed. She looked at Lucy, who was wide-eyed and pallid. "Has she ever done anything like this before?"

The girl kept her gaze on her friend, who was whimpering now. She nodded. "It's this thing with Luke. It makes her crazy."

That was a fucking understatement. Neve would never admit it, but her knees were a little shaky as she left the hospital room. She'd never seen anyone lose it like that, not even when she worked in New York—and that was saying something.

In the elevator, she leaned against the cool wall and took a deep breath. By the time she reached Luke's room she felt more like herself. He looked good. His bruises were healing and it was obvious that they had lessened his pain meds. Both he and his mother looked surprised to see her.

"What is it?" Luke asked. "Did something happen to Alisha?"

His phone was on the table beside his bed. He'd probably seen the talk on Twitter. Had Alisha not told him what she was going to do?

"Alisha's fine," she told him. "We're dropping the charges against you."

Linda made a noise that was half laugh, half sob, while Luke looked like he might cry.

"I'll leave the two of you to celebrate in a moment," she told them. "But first, I need to ask if Kendra Granger has ever gotten violent with you."

Luke's good mood vanished. He glanced at his mother, then back to Neve. He nodded. "Once."

"What?" Linda rose to her feet. "Luke, what did that girl do?"

He rolled up the sleeve of his hospital gown to reveal a small scar high on his right shoulder. When he spoke, he looked right at Neve. "She stabbed me with a pair of nail scissors."

His mother gasped. Neve studied the mark. A little farther up the neck and she could have gotten his jugular. She took out her phone. "Do you mind if I take a photo?"

"Go for it."

"When did she do this to you?"

Luke looked up. "It was how she broke up with me."

It was the text from Luke that got Alisha through the rest of her day. When he told her that he was going to be getting out of the hospital the next day and that the charges against him had been dropped, it was the happiest moment she'd had in months. Even the stares and giggles—and people making digs about her relationship with Luke—couldn't dim it.

But then, eventually, came a wash of guilt. She'd slept with a friend's boyfriend, and then that same friend had been killed. Murdered. She didn't really feel like she had a right to be so happy.

She needed to make it right with Tala. She wasn't sure why

she felt she had to do it, but she did. She was pretty sure Audrey would understand, probably even Uncle Jake. So, when she left school that afternoon, she drove back to the Falls. T here was another car there when she arrived, but she really didn't pay much attention to it. She simply parked, locked up, and made her way down the shorter path that led to the bridge above the falls. It was the spot they would come to on occasion just to hang out. Tala had liked it back there, and Alisha did too. She hadn't been there since the park closed in October, though she knew it was a popular party spot.

She didn't get invited to a lot of parties, mostly because people were afraid of her uncle Jake. Once, a couple of boys from another town tried getting her drunk. Jake had found them and made them dig a couple of holes in the woods. The holes, he told them, were where he was going to put them if they ever came back.

They left that day and Alisha never saw them again. She had no doubt her uncle would keep his word. She had no evidence, but she didn't think it was a coincidence that Matt Jones, who had beaten not only Audrey but her mother as well, ended up being killed in prison. She was just surprised Jake hadn't wanted to kill the asshole himself.

As she picked her way along the sloping path, she felt a growing sense of unease. It was foolish, she told herself. Tala's body wasn't there anymore, and there was nothing to be afraid of. Still, her heart hammered as she stepped out onto the rocky cliff platform near the bridge. She had to stop and take a deep breath, and swipe the back of her hand across her forehead to wipe away the sweat that beaded there. It seemed so still. So close and quiet, despite the breeze in the trees, the birds singing, and the water bubbling below. There was a smell on the air—something wrong.

She didn't want to turn her head. She would see something horrible if she did. She made herself do it anyway.

Nothing. The bridge was perfectly clear. Shaking her head at herself, Alisha stepped onto the wooden planks. There was hardly any give as she walked across the chasm. Below, the falls crashed over the rocks to the bed below. The spray was cool on her forearms and overheated face. She stopped for a second in the middle to savor it. Had Tala stood in that same spot before she was killed? Had she run across this bridge trying to get away? Or had she crossed it with her killer, with no idea what was about to happen?

Alisha moved forward, trying not to think about her friend's last moments. Trying not to feel guilty about the fact that she might have very well been having sex with Luke at the exact moment Tala had been stabbed to death. There was no point in thinking about it. She would change it if she could, but she couldn't. And regardless of what she'd done with Luke, she hadn't been responsible for what someone else did to Tala. She knew that without anyone else having to tell her. But there was still that icky feeling of having taken advantage of Luke's broken heart. No, she hadn't forced him to be with her, and he said that he'd been starting to have feelings for her already by then, but they could have handled it better, and she knew it. Whatever happened between them now, she was going to be a lot more mindful of it.

The police tape was gone, but a lone piece of it fluttered from a tree branch not far from where the bridge ended. She saw the large boulders that lined the edge and knew that Tala's body had been found behind one of them, partially covered with rocks and sticks. That meant whoever had killed her had tried to protect her from the elements—or just wanted to hide her. If they'd really wanted to be rid of her, they should have just left her alone and let nature take care of it.

The thought rolled her stomach a bit. As she approached the area, her footsteps slowed. She didn't want to look. There was something there she didn't want to see—some trace of Tala. She just knew it.

And then she saw it—someone sitting on the ground near the spot where Tala had been found. It was Kyle Granger. He was leaning back against the rock, passed out. That had been his car in the parking lot.

"Kyle?" she said as she approached. She felt better now, knowing someone else was there. He didn't answer. He had to be out hard. "Kyle?"

Alisha froze just feet away from him. She could see him clearly now, and what she saw had her reaching for her phone in her bag. His skin was a strange color and his eyes stared straight ahead, unseeing.

Kyle Granger wasn't passed out. He was dead.

CHAPTER TWENTY-THREE

For the second time in two weeks, Neve stood over a body at the Falls. This one was at least in better condition, though dead was dead.

"Looks like an overdose," Charlotte commented.

"That wouldn't be surprising," Neve replied, hands on her hips. Although, given where he'd been found, he might have been murdered. Drugs made it hard to tell, which was why she still had her doubts about the guy who had beaten up Jake last fall. He turned up dead in his truck, which seemed entirely too convenient, but he'd been arrested for narcotics prior to that, so who knew for sure?

She turned to look at the girl standing on the bridge. She'd called Audrey, who stood beside Alisha, her arm around her shoulders. Neve assumed they'd told Yancy and Jake what was going on, but fortunately, neither of them had decided to show up. She didn't need more people messing up the scene.

It was creepy, him sitting against the same boulder that had obscured Tala's body. Had he known? Had he been the one to put her there after stabbing her with his father's knife? Or had he simply figured it out? Maybe he'd visited the scene before this. Maybe he'd visited Tala's body there over the winter.

There were a lot of maybes that Kyle Granger would never confirm or deny. There was no point in speculating until she got the autopsy results. But it certainly looked like the kid had committed suicide.

Neve batted at a fly that buzzed around her head. One of the rookies had done that thing where he put Vicks VapoRub under his nose to help counter the smell. His upper lip glistened in the sun. He looked like he might barf at any second. Huh. If he thought this was bad…

"Someone really ought to tell him using that stuff only opens the nasal passages more," Charlotte remarked, following her gaze.

Neve didn't know if that was true or not, but she'd take Charlotte's word for it. Personally, she found the only way to get through the smell of death was to get acclimatized to it ASAP and deal. There were worse things than decaying flesh—like porta-potties baking under the hot sun.

She left Charlotte and walked onto the bridge to where Audrey and Alisha stood. "You okay?" she asked the girl.

Alisha was pale, but she nodded. "His eyes were open."

"Yeah, that happens." She didn't know what else to say, except, "I'm sorry you had to see him like that."

"Me too."

"What were you doing back here?"

The girl blinked, as though she had forgotten. "Oh, it's stupid." Neve met her gaze and waited. "I was feeling guilty for getting together with Luke and I wanted to apologize to Tala. For some reason I thought this was the place to do it."

"That makes sense," Audrey offered, shooting a narrow glance in Neve's direction. "I sometimes visit the place where Maggie was killed."

Was that a dig about Bailey, or was Neve just PMSing way too hard? The thing that kept her and Audrey from being really good girlfriends was that they were always so on guard and defensive with each other. It hadn't always been that way, but then Audrey killed Clint and Neve became a cop and there was no way either of them could be totally at ease with each other, no matter how much they might wish otherwise.

"How long has he been here?" Alisha asked, her attention fixed on the corpse just feet away.

"Our death investigator figures he's been here since last night at least."

"Poor Elle," Audrey remarked. "After Kendra's overdose, this is going to be so hard on her."

"Losing a kid is hard, period." Neve frowned when Audrey winced. *What the hell was that about?*

"Have you notified her yet?"

Neve shook her head. "I'm not looking forward to it." She'd take Vickie with her. Telling parents their child was dead never got any easier. She supposed if it ever did, it was time for her to quit.

She'd go see Elle once they took Kyle away. She wanted to be able to tell the woman that it *looked* like an accident, because Elle was going to ask. They always did.

"Were there any other cars in the lot when you arrived?" Neve asked.

Alisha shook her head. "Just one. It was his, I guess."

She nodded. The plates were registered to Kendall. "And you didn't touch anything?"

"God, no!" The girl looked horrified at the idea. "I got to the edge of the bridge and I could tell he was dead. I didn't go any closer. I called you from where I'm standing right now. Believe me, I wanted to run the fuck away. Sorry."

Neve gave her a little smile. Now that she'd let Luke off the hook, Alisha seemed to think better of her if she was apologizing for swearing in front of her. "You did exactly the right thing. Go ahead and go home now. I know where to find you if I have any other questions."

"Are you okay to drive?" Audrey asked. "Or do you want to come with me, and we'll get your car later?"

"I want to go with you," Alisha replied. As grown-up as she sometimes seemed, she looked every bit a kid at that moment.

Neve said good-bye and watched the two of them walk away. Alisha had certainly been around a lot of death this past year. She hoped it didn't have an adverse effect on her. Hopefully Audrey would notice if it did, and be able to help.

She waited until Kyle's body was carried across the bridge and up the path to the upper parking lot, where the ambulance waited. Then she walked back to her car and got in. She sat there for a moment, with the windows down, trying to breathe in enough pine and damp to wash away the scent of death. When she could finally breathe without seeing Kyle's cloudy eyes, she started the engine and signaled for Vickie to follow her.

Then she went to tell yet another mother that her child was dead.

Alisha wanted to be alone, and Audrey didn't push it.

"Call me if you need anything."

"I will. Mum will probably be here any minute."

The resort that Jake owned and Yancy managed was only a mile or so farther back the road—right on the beach. It enabled Yancy to pop home when necessary, and there was usually someone there who could cover for her during the tourist season.

"Thanks for coming when I called."

Audrey smiled. "Anytime." They hugged and Alisha got out of the car. Audrey waited until she was inside the house to back out of the yard and drive away.

As soon as she got home, she checked for voice mail. There was one from Dr. Aaron. Heart hammering, she called the office. She was put on hold for a few minutes, and then a familiar voice picked up.

"Hello, Audrey. How are you today?"

"I'm fine, Dr. Aaron. Did the blood test results come back?"

"Yes, they did. Normally I would have you come in to the office, but I'm leaving for a bit of a vacation tomorrow."

"That's fine. What did the results show?"

"You're pregnant."

Audrey couldn't speak.

"Audrey?"

She made a squeaking noise. Jesus, this was ridiculous. "Okay."

"Are you all right?"

"I'm fine. It's just...it's a bit of a shock. I mean, we've taken precautions."

"Sometimes there's no denying biology. I'd like to send you for an ultrasound so we can determine just how far along you are. I know you told the nurse it had been at least a month since your last period, but based on what I felt during the exam, I'd say you're close to eight weeks along."

There was a roaring in Audrey's head that made it difficult for her to understand what Dr. Aaron was saying, even though she heard it perfectly well. "Okay."

"I'll have the clinic call you to make an appointment, all right?"

"Yes, that's fine." Eight weeks. Fuck. Could it really have been that long since her last period? Why the hell hadn't she been paying better attention? How could she have missed that? Was she stupid? Whenever she heard of women not knowing they were pregnant until they were a couple of months in, she always thought they had to be dumb not to notice; now she realized all you really had to be was busy. Busy and arrogantly confident in your choice of birth control.

"Audrey?"

"Yes?"

"Are you sure you're all right?"

"Yes. If you could have them call me for an appointment that would be great, thanks."

"Okay. We'll follow up after that. If you need anything, Dr. Fischer will be filling in for me while I'm gone."

Audrey mumbled something, said good-bye, and hung up. She stood there for a while, staring at the telephone as if it were somehow to blame for all of this.

And then she put her hand on her stomach, trying to see if she could feel the thing inside her. Maybe her belly was firmer, rounder. She couldn't really tell. She braced one hand on the wall by her head and took a breath. What were they going to do?

At one time the choice would have been easy. A thirty-something woman should not be struck with terror when she finds out she's pregnant, should she?

She wanted to call her sister, Jess, and talk to her about it, but she couldn't. Things were still a little strained between them, and this... this was a personal decision. Jess was a good mom, but as the oldest she would tell Audrey what she thought she should do, and Audrey didn't want to know what that was. This was her decision. Well, her own and Jake's. It was bad enough her father knew.

She picked up the receiver and dialed. He picked up on the second ring. "'Lo?"

"Hey, Dad." Her voice cracked.

There was a pause. "I'll be right there."

Audrey woke up in the middle of the night to find herself alone in bed. Jake's side of the bed was empty, though he'd been there when she fell asleep.

"Jake?"

No reply. He wasn't in the room or the en suite.

Frowning, she got out of bed and walked out into the hall. He wasn't in any of the additional bedrooms, so she went downstairs. There was a lamp on in the living room, so that was where she headed. As she entered the room, she opened her mouth to say something, then closed it again.

Jake slouched on the sofa, his head against the back cushions, mouth slightly open. He was asleep. In his lap was an open photo album. Another lay on the coffee table. Silently, Audrey approached.

The album on the table was old, open to reveal pictures of Jake, Lincoln, and Yancy when they were little—before their mother left their father. One of the photos showed the three of them sitting on the old porch swing, toddler Yancy between her big brothers. Audrey smiled at the sight of Jake in his shorts and T-shirt, his bangs cut crookedly. He looked so cute. So serious for a little kid. Lincoln, on the other hand, had a big grin on his face and looked as though he was missing a tooth.

She turned her attention to the album in his lap. The photos in it were newer. There was one of her taken shortly after she got out of Stillwater. God, she looked so young. So tough—in that way that only truly vulnerable girls could look.

Carefully, Audrey eased the book away from him, lifting it so she could better see. Next to the picture of her was one that made her heart skip a beat. It was Jake—long-haired and barefoot—sitting on the old sofa in that very room, holding a baby. He would have been about seventeen when it was taken.

She didn't have to remove the photo and check the back to know that the baby was Alisha; she could tell from the expression on Jake's face. Even then, at such a young age, he'd looked at his niece with such an expression of love and loyalty. She'd seen him look at the girl the same way so many times, but something about the photo made it difficult to swallow. She didn't need her PhD to figure out what.

Jake holding a baby. Not just any baby, but one he loved.

Audrey blinked her burning eyes. Earlier that evening, when she told him that she was indeed pregnant, he'd told her that whether or not she had the baby was up to her. She'd torn a strip off him for it, and then burst into tears. Talking to her father earlier hadn't helped. He told her that he and her mother had been terrified the first time they got pregnant—and the second, and the third. He had told her that he'd never wanted to be a father until he became one. And then he'd reminded her of just how much like him she was.

She had assumed that because Jake had helped raise Alisha that he already felt like a father. She assumed that was enough for him. She assumed being an aunt was enough for herself. She never really pictured herself as a mother. Really, she didn't think she'd be a very good one. But...

But seeing Jake with a baby made her want to bawl. She also wanted to brain him with the damn album and scream at him for making her so emotional. She wanted to blame him. Wanted him to wake the fuck up and tell her what to do, because she didn't want to make the wrong decision.

She didn't do any of these things. Instead, she lowered herself to the couch beside him and curled against his side. He stirred slightly when she put his arm across her shoulders and pulled her closer. She stared at the photo for a few minutes longer, then turned the page. The rest of the album was a chronicle of Alisha's childhood and Jake's involvement in it. Birthdays, Christmases, first days of school and class photos. Jake's hair changed, and both of them got older, but the love on his face when he looked at the kid always stayed the same.

Eventually, her eyelids grew heavy and started to close. Audrey leaned her head against Jake's shoulder and breathed in the scent of his skin mixed with clean cotton. The album was spread open across both their laps, to a page of photos of him teaching Alisha to play guitar, and taking her fishing.

Audrey bent her arm and twined her fingers with the ones that hung over her shoulder. She fell asleep with one hand holding Jake's, the other against her stomach, and the unanswerable question growing there.

CHAPTER TWENTY-FOUR

Kendall Granger, dazed and grieving, was all too cooperative. He showed Neve where he kept his knives, opened the box. When she showed him a photo of the knife used to kill Tala, he confirmed that it was indeed one of his. They dusted the display for prints to compare to those taken from the dagger chest in Luke's closet.

"Did my son kill Tala?" Elle asked, numbly. She had the look of a woman who was heavily medicated. She was probably blaming herself for this, and Neve had no way of making her feel better.

"I don't know," she replied honestly. They still had to check his prints, compare Kyle's blood to that found on Tala's glove. It didn't look good, given that he had access to the murder weapon and the drug found in Tala's system. The only thing he seemed to lack was motive. Had he killed her because she only used him as a booty call? It didn't seem to make sense, but like Audrey was always saying, people had killed for less.

"Kendra's evaluation is tomorrow," Elle announced. "I haven't told her yet, but she's going to find out. I don't know how she'll take it. I'd so like to bring her home."

After the scene in her room, Neve wasn't so certain Kendra would be getting out anytime soon. "I'm so sorry for your loss."

The other woman merely nodded, then turned and walked away like a zombie. Neve was frankly all too glad to be dismissed. As they left the house, she turned to Vickie. "I'm getting pressure to put this case to bed. There are going to be those who want to pin this on Kyle Granger and wrap it up in a neat little box."

"You don't think it was him?"

Neve glanced at her as she opened her car door. "Kyle's never been in Luke's room. Unless he had an accomplice, it wasn't him."

Vickie's eyes widened. "You think one of the girls did it."

Neve pursed her lips. "I think it was someone who could get close to both Luke and Tala, and that *wasn't* Kyle. Let me know as soon as you run those prints."

Vickie's phone blipped. She checked it. "Kendra's blood matches the type found on the glove. They're running a DNA comparison."

Neve swore under her breath. "Okay. Sit on that until we get Kyle's results. If we're going to put these people through more grief I want to be certain." She didn't particularly like the Grangers, but that didn't mean she got off on causing them pain. Which was almost too bad, because she had a feeling she was going to cause them a lot more before this was all over.

After school, Alisha drove immediately to Luke's house. He'd been released from the hospital and she was anxious to see him. The minute she rang the doorbell, however, a rush of awkwardness filled her.

What was she supposed to say? That she was glad he hadn't killed anyone? That Kyle's death was cosmic retribution? Maybe she could promise to be his one girlfriend who didn't seem to be fucking nuts? Was she stupid for even hoping their relationship had a chance?

Linda answered the door with a huge smile. "Alisha! We thought that might be you. Come on in."

It wasn't the first time she'd been in Luke's house, but it felt like it. It was the first time she was walking in as someone he was interested in. His girlfriend? God, his mother knew they'd had sex! Alisha wasn't sure she could look the woman in the eye.

"Luke is in the living room. Can I get you anything? A soda?"

"I'm good, thanks." Slowly, she walked to the living room and peeked inside. Luke was on the sofa in a T-shirt and sweatpants, watching TV. He still looked pretty rough, but she thought he was beautiful.

He turned his head, as though he felt her presence, and grinned. "Hi."

She smiled back—stupidly. "Hi."

"Are you going to come in, or just stand there?"

"Oh, right." She laughed self-consciously as she approached. Was she supposed to sit in a chair or beside him? Beside him, she thought, and carefully sat down on the sofa.

"I'm not made of glass," he joked. "You're not going to break me."

"Aren't you still sore?" she asked. "'Cause it looks freaking painful."

"If I tell you I'm fine, will you think I'm tough?"

"I'll think you're a liar."

"I still hurt pretty friggin' bad." They shared a grin. "I'm glad you're here."

"Me too."

His smile faded. "Do you think Kyle killed her?"

"I don't know why he would. But he was pretty messed up."

"We're all messed up. Doesn't seem to be a good reason to kill anyone."

"No," Alisha agreed. She looked down at her feet. What was she supposed to say? That she was glad if it was Kyle, because that meant it was over? She wanted to ask where they stood. If he wanted to be with her. All she could do, though, was sit there like an idiot.

Warm fingers curled over hers. She started, but didn't pull away. Instead, she lifted her gaze to Luke's. He was smiling at her, though it was hesitant.

"We've been doing this kind of backward," he said.

She nodded.

"I'd like to hug you but my ribs are still healing. Is it okay if I hold your hand?"

Alisha nodded, a little smile curving her lips. "Sure." She twined her fingers with his.

"And maybe I could kiss you?"

Her smile grew. "I don't know. You're moving pretty fast."

Luke grinned. "I thought I was being smooth."

She leaned closer, careful not to put her weight against his battered body. When his lips met hers, it was like someone had opened a door in her chest and released a thousand butterflies from it. It felt right, like his mouth had been made for hers.

He pulled back first, his breathing harsh and shallow. "Wow. I really wish I didn't have broken ribs right now."

She laughed. "Me too."

Squeezing her fingers, he leaned back, his bright blue gaze locked with hers. "I don't have a good track record as a boyfriend, you know that."

Alisha shrugged. "Maybe you were just waiting for me." She said it as a joke, but the look in his eyes when she said it made her breath catch.

"I think I was." Then he kissed her again and nothing else mattered.

Audrey didn't really want to drive over to Downeast to see Kendra Granger, but she could hardly turn down a grieving mother's request. Elle was a mess and in no condition to drive, and she said that Kendra had asked for Audrey specifically. How could she refuse? Yes, she had work to do regarding Grace Ridge, and she and Jake really needed to talk about the pregnancy, but at that moment, avoiding both seemed like the best choice.

Kendra was calm when Audrey walked in. Sedated, probably. She wondered what the doctors were doing to help her. Probably trying to get her meds sorted out and make sure she took them as she ought. Hopefully they had a psychiatrist seeing her. She couldn't believe Elle hadn't gotten one for her before this, given the family issues.

"Dr. Harte," she said, her voice little more than a cracked whisper. "You came."

"Your mother said you wanted to talk to me."

"I did. I do. Could you get me some water? The pills they gave me give me muck mouth."

Audrey smiled slightly at the term and poured the girl a small glass of water from the pitcher beside her bed. She helped her hold it, and Kendra gulped the contents down greedily.

"Thanks."

Perching on the side of the bed, Audrey gazed down at her. Kendra wasn't restrained, but she wasn't terribly concerned. She doubted the girl could lift her own head let alone attack her. She waited for her to speak.

"My brother's dead."

Audrey nodded. "I'm sorry."

"It wasn't suicide. Kyle wasn't depressed—not like that."

Audrey didn't say anything. She just smiled.

"He didn't kill Tala. He liked her. Really liked her." Her face darkened. "Everyone fucking liked her."

"Okay."

Shadowed eyes blinked, then rolled up to look at her. From the size of her pupils, there was no denying just how stoned the kid was. "I was really out of my mind that night."

A tremor of unease burrowed under Audrey's ribs. "What night?"

"The night Tala died. I don't remember anything."

"You were at a party."

"Was I?" She licked her lips and Audrey poured her more water. "Was I there the whole night?"

Brow wrinkling, Audrey set the glass aside. "I don't know. Were you?"

A slight shrug. "I thought so, but Lucy...Lucy says she couldn't find me when she first came back with Randy."

"Did she go looking for you?"

Kendra frowned. It was obvious she was trying to remember, but it just wasn't there. "I don't know." She closed her eyes.

Audrey hesitated. Silently, she counted to ten. Kendra didn't stir. Had she fallen asleep? Slowly, she moved to leave the bed.

"Do I have blood on my hands?"

Audrey jumped. Kendra looked up at her, eyes wide open now—or at least as wide as she could open them. "I look at them and sometimes I think there's blood."

Jesus. "There's nothing on your hands, Kendra."

"Good." And then. "I'm afraid I killed her."

"Why would you kill her? She was your friend."

"Sometimes I get really angry when I go off my meds. I was off them then. I've hurt people when I'm angry."

Yes, Alisha could vouch for that, as could Elle. "Kendra, if you think you hurt Tala, you need to talk to the police."

"Yeah." She sighed—a resigned sound.

Audrey tilted her head. "Kendra, did you take the knife from your father's collection?"

The girl thought about it. "I don't think so. I don't remember."

"Did you put it in Luke's room?"

"I don't remember that either. If I did it, wouldn't I remember?"

"I don't know." If the girl were more coherent, Audrey would probably say something about the brain sometimes trying to protect people by blocking memories, but there didn't seem to be any point.

A tear trickled from Kendra's eye down into her hair. "I hated her because she had Luke and she didn't seem to care. She was fucking my brother too. She only wanted Luke because Lucy and I had both dated him, and she knew I still liked him. What kind of friend does that?"

"I think maybe Tala was insecure," Audrey commented. "And she wanted to be like you and Lucy, her friends."

"I hated her. I still hate her." Another tear. "Oh, God. I killed her. Lucy was right."

"Sshh." Audrey calmed her before she could get too wound up. She pressed the buzzer for the nurse to come and give her something to make her sleep. She stayed with her until she knew it had taken effect. Then, and only then, did she decide it was time to go. She wasn't going to tell Neve what Kendra had said, but she might suggest Neve interview her when she was more herself. And she made a note to check in with the psychiatrist assigned by the hospital.

Outside Kendra's room she ran into Lucy. Wearing capris and a blouse, the girl looked summery and cool. She had a soda bottle in one hand and her phone in the other. "Oh, hey, Dr. Harte. What are you doing here?"

"Hi, Lucy. Kendra wanted to talk to me."

The girl glanced toward the room. "About what?"

"Just talk."

Closing the distance between them, Lucy looked hesitant. "I'm worried about her."

"The two of you are best friends, of course you're worried."

A scared gaze met hers. "No. I'm *really* worried. Some of the things she's been saying..."

"Like what?"

"Like..." Lucy glanced around, as though making certain they were alone. "Like she killed Tala. I told her she'd never do something like that, but...but I heard that the knife used to kill Tala belonged to Mr. Granger."

Audrey didn't bother to ask how she'd heard that. Gossip had a life of its own in Edgeport and the surrounding towns. "I heard that too."

"She was in Luke's room. She knows about his collection—everyone does." Tears filled her eyes. "What if she really did hurt Tala? I shouldn't have left her alone that night."

Audrey put her hand on the girl's shoulder. "None of us are responsible for the actions of others, Lucy. You can't claim fault for Kendra any more than she can for you."

The girl froze. "Did she say something about me?"

"Only that you were worried about her, as any friend would be." Audrey smiled. "Why don't you go sit with her? Here, give me that bottle. I'll get rid of it for you."

Lucy handed her the soda bottle. "Thanks. Yeah, I will go hang with her for a while. You think she'll be okay?"

She nodded. "I do."

Audrey said good-bye and made her way to the elevator. She waited until she was walking across the parking lot to call Neve, the soda bottle in her purse.

"Now's not a good time," Neve said when she picked up.

Audrey ignored her. "It's Lucy. She killed Tala."

CHAPTER TWENTY-FIVE

No offense, but I'm going to need more than just your gut to prove Lucy killed Tala," Neve said when she met Audrey a short time later at her house. "And why do you keep rubbing your stomach? You feeling okay?"

Audrey's hand froze over her abdomen. She looked down like she hadn't been aware of what she'd been doing. "Must have been something I ate. Look, it's more than my gut. It's professional opinion."

"Explain."

"First, here." She dug through her bag and handed Neve a soda bottle. "It was Lucy's. It's got her prints and her DNA."

Neve arched a brow. "Where'd you get that?"

"She gave it to me to toss out. Just take it."

Neve did. "Okay, now tell me what made you think she's guilty when Kendra's the one who's got the history of violence and mental health issues."

"It's simple, really. She sold Kendra out."

Neve frowned. "Because she's worried about her?"

"Because she implicated her. Look, a real friend would never do that. A real friend always has your back."

"You're speaking from experience."

"Damn straight. Maggie and I never turned on each other. Not when it mattered."

Neve didn't know the whole truth about the night Clint Jones was murdered and she didn't care to. A little while back, Audrey had helped her with a case that required spending time with a serial killer who wanted to know Audrey's story. She told him what he wanted to know, but Neve had no idea what she said, or how much of it was real. It was none of her business. At that moment, however, she wished she knew more.

"Think about it," Audrey said to her. "When you were a teenager, did you ever rat out your best friend?"

Neve shook her head. "No. If anything, I'd lie to protect her."

"That's what I'm talking about. As soon as I told Lucy I'd been talking to Kendra, she got squirrelly, like she thought maybe Kendra had implicated her. I think Lucy was covering her ass by throwing Kendra under the bus."

"That's harsh. What's her motive? She didn't seem to have a hate on for Tala, nor did she care that she was dating Luke."

"I don't know why she did it, but it wasn't a heat-of-the-moment kind of thing. She had to steal that knife, and that means she had intent."

Neve looked at her dubiously, then glanced at the bottle. "I guess I'd better run this against what we got off both knife cases and Tala's glove."

"You might want to do it quickly and quietly. If Lucy thinks we've figured her out, she might try to cover her tracks—

or take someone else down with her." Audrey chewed on her lower lip.

Neve's gaze narrowed. "You look constipated. What's up?"

Audrey met her gaze. "Remember when Jake slept with Maggie?"

"Like I'll ever forget. I thought you were going to kill one of them."

"I wanted to. That's why Maggie did it—to force me to confront her, because she knew sleeping with the guy I liked was the worst thing she could do."

"But if Lucy still has a thing for Luke, why go after Tala and not Kendra? Kendra dated him right after Lucy and Luke broke up."

"Because she didn't care that Kendra dated him. What she cared about was that Tala betrayed Kendra by dating Luke."

"If she's so loyal to Kendra, why turn on her?"

"Because Kendra doesn't appreciate what she did for her? Or because she's getting scared."

Neve shook her head. "That sounds like a soap opera plot."

Audrey's shoulders sagged a bit. "Maybe it does, but I'm telling you, Neve. Lucy did it."

"Because your gut."

"Because I know a killer when I look one in the eyes and they look back."

Her gaze was so direct Neve couldn't look away. As reluctant as she was to run with Audrey's theory, she had to admit it was as valid as any other she had pursued, plus she couldn't deny the fact that sometimes it really did take one to know one.

"All right," she said. "I'll see about getting prints off this bottle and test the DNA against the glove. Hopefully it will give us something to run with."

"And fast," Audrey added. "If Lucy feels cornered, there's no telling what she might do—or who she might hurt."

Neve considered that. "Like Luke's new girlfriend?"

Audrey's eyes widened. "Alisha."

Luke's mother and her boyfriend left them with homemade pizza and enough soda to drown a small country when they went out for dinner that night. Of course Alisha didn't mind staying with Luke until they got back. Linda acted like Alisha was the one doing *them* a favor.

"Does she really think we're going to eat all of this?" Alisha asked when she took the pizza out of the oven.

Luke smiled. "I can easily eat half of that by myself."

She shot him an envious glance. "Boys."

She got down plates and glasses and filled both for each of them. Then she made Luke go back to the living room and carried his food in for him.

"I'm not useless," he told her. "I can carry stuff without hurting myself."

In her family, fussing was how they showed they cared when they couldn't find the balls to say the words. "I know. Just let me do it."

He seemed to understand, because he didn't argue anymore. He just sat there and smiled at her in a way that made her insides tingle. She remembered that night in her room—his hands on her body...

"Be right back." She practically ran back to the kitchen, face hot. She wanted to be with him again, but the thought made her nervous. He was right—they were so backward. He'd already seen her naked; the rest should be easy, shouldn't it?

They were each into their second piece of pizza and well into their movie when Alisha got up to get them both more soda. She had just refilled both glasses when the doorbell rang. For a second, she entertained the idea of not answering, because she knew that whoever was on the other side wasn't someone she wanted to see.

When Luke appeared in the doorway between kitchen and living room, she knew she had no choice but to check. Of all the people it could have been when she opened the door, Lucy was not the one she expected to see.

"Hi," the girl said, with a small wave of her hand. She looked embarrassed. "I thought you'd probably be here. Can I come in?"

"What do you want?" Luke asked, suspiciously.

Lucy's pale cheeks pinkened. "To apologize. For me, and for Ken. She'd be with me if she weren't still in the hospital." When neither Alisha nor Luke spoke, she added, "Look, I don't want to be here any more than you want me. I'll make it quick."

Alisha glanced at Luke. He nodded. Against her better judgment, she stood back and let Lucy inside. As the redhead crossed the threshold into the house, Alisha bristled with distrust. She wanted to call Audrey, or even Neve, and that annoyed her. Seriously, she ought to be able to handle Lucy on her own.

Lucy saw the pizza and glasses on the counter. "Sorry to interrupt. Go ahead and eat."

Alisha didn't have much of an appetite, but she grabbed the pizza from the sideboard and followed as Luke turned to go back into the living room. Personally, she would have preferred to stay in the kitchen so Lucy didn't think she had an invitation to stay, but the girl was pouring herself a soda, so it was obvious she didn't care.

"What is that?"

Both Alisha and Luke glanced toward the TV as Lucy brushed past them. "*The Matrix*," Luke replied.

Lucy cast a tiny smile at Alisha as she sat down. She set three glasses of soda on the coffee table. "You actually like this stuff?"

"Yeah," Alisha admitted. "I do." And she resented the implication that she was only watching it because Luke wanted to. She wasn't the kind of girl who did things just because she thought it would make a boy happy. And she wasn't going to thank Lucy for bringing her a drink either. Fuck that. She shrugged.

"Okay. So, you guys heard about Kyle?" At Luke's nod, she continued. "Ken's wrecked over it. She can't believe it. You know the cops think it was intentional—that he killed himself because he felt so guilty for what he did to Tala."

Alisha didn't speak. She was waiting for Lucy to get to the point.

"I heard that," Luke said. "Look, Luce, I don't mean to be rude, but I'd like to get back to the movie."

She gave him a sad look. "Wow, that's harsh. I guess I deserve it after all that's happened. I'm sorry about all of it, Luke. So is Kendra. She knows she acted like a nut job. It's just that she's so crazy about you, she can't see straight. No offense, Lish."

Alisha didn't even blink. "No. Of course not."

"Kendra's going to have to get over it," Luke said. "I'm sorry she's hurt, but I'm with Alisha now, and nothing's going to change that."

Lucy glanced from one of them to the other. "So, you're official now?"

Alisha turned to Luke. It needed to come from him. He nodded. "We are."

"Well, nice for you two that something good came out of this. Meanwhile, Kendra has lost a friend, and her brother."

And Luke, Alisha added silently. *She's lost Luke.* "Is she okay?" she asked, because she couldn't help herself. She wasn't so cold that she didn't have some empathy for Kendra.

"No," Lucy responded. "She's really not. But she's sorry for what she did to you. We're both sorry, for everything."

Luke nodded. The two of them stared at Lucy, waiting to see if there was anything else. Apparently, there wasn't. The girl laughed self-consciously. "Okay, so I know when I'm not wanted. I told Kendra I'd be back tonight, so I guess I'd better go. Don't get up—I know where the door is."

Alisha watched her get up and followed her with her gaze as she left the room. She listened for the front door to close, but it wasn't until she heard Lucy's car pull out of the driveway that she spoke. "That was weird."

Luke took a drink of his soda. "Very. I guess it was good that she wanted to apologize in person, but it didn't really seem like much of an apology."

"It wasn't," Alisha agreed, also taking a drink. "She's gone now. Let's finish the movie. You still have pizza left."

He grinned at her, and even with the bruises she thought he was the sexiest thing she'd ever seen. He pressed a button on the remote and the movie continued. They talked and ate as the action played out.

About a quarter of an hour later, Alisha started to feel light-headed—like she'd been drinking. She turned to Luke. "Do you feel weird?"

He had an odd expression on his face. "I thought it was the painkillers. You feel it too?"

She nodded. Then she saw something out of the corner of her eye. It took her longer to turn her head than it should have, and the movement made her dizzy. There in the doorway was Lucy. She was smiling. Fear flashed through Alisha's mind, but it was quickly replaced by a heavy drowsiness she couldn't quite shake.

"What did you do?" she demanded, her tongue too thick for her mouth.

Lucy walked into the room. Luke stared at her. He tried to get up, but it was obvious he couldn't.

"A little GHB in your Coke," she chirped. "I got it from Kyle. He never did know how to measure dose properly."

"Why?" Alisha asked.

Lucy shot her a narrow look. "Because it makes it easier to

do what I need to do. You know, if you guys had said you were just friends, I might have not come back. I might have just let you sleep it off, but you had to flaunt the fact that you're together."

"What do you care?" Luke demanded. His voice was raspy and rough.

"*I* don't," Lucy replied. "Trust me, Luke, you didn't make that much of an impression on me when we were together, but apparently Kendra still can't get over you." She sighed.

"What are you going to do?" Alisha demanded.

"I'm going to fix the problem," was the cool, determined reply. "I'm going to fix it so Kendra doesn't have to obsess anymore."

It was then that Alisha realized the truth. This was the third time she'd found herself staring into the eyes of a murderer—she was beginning to recognize the signs. "You're going to kill me." Alisha knew she should struggle—should fight—but her arms and legs didn't want to move. On the coffee table her cell phone began to ring. It was Audrey's ring tone. If she could only reach it...

Lucy shook her head with a smile. "No, stupid. He'll just find someone else. You're as much his victim as me or Kendra ever were. I'm going to do what I should have done in the first place and make it so Kendra has no choice but to get the fuck over it." She nodded at Luke. "I'm going to kill *him*."

CHAPTER TWENTY-SIX

It keeps going to voice mail," Audrey said, ending the call. She was in the front seat of Neve's car as they tore down the road from Tripp's Cove. Neve hadn't put the siren on because she didn't want to draw attention.

"You're sure she's at Luke's?"

"Yes." Audrey gripped the armrest. "Jesus, the kid's a magnet for trouble."

"Wonder where she gets that?" Neve's tone was dry as they hit the main road. She pressed down on the gas as she handed Audrey her phone. "Try calling Lucy."

Audrey got the number but used her own phone to call. "Voice mail."

"Call Kendra. See if Lucy's with her."

Audrey dialed again. After a couple of rings Kendra picked up. "Hello?"

She sounded as though she'd been asleep. "Kendra, it's Audrey Harte."

"Dr. Harte?"

"Is Lucy with you?" It went against her training to jump

right to that point, but her concern for Alisha outweighed all other considerations.

"No. She left. She was mad at me because of Luke."

"Did she say where she was going?"

"She said she was going to fix everything."

"Was she going to Luke's house?"

"Don't know, but Dr. Harte? She scared me."

"Get some rest, Kendra. It's going to be okay."

"No, it's really not, but thanks." The girl hung up.

Audrey tried Alisha's number again, numb fingers fumbling the digits. "Lucy told Kendra she was going to fix everything."

"You think she means killing Alisha?"

"Maybe." The idea made bile rise in the back of Audrey's throat. "Or, maybe killing Luke."

"But then Kendra will never have him."

"If he's dead Kendra would have to let go of the idea of being with him again."

"That actually makes a twisted kind of sense."

"Kendra is Lucy's best friend. She can't give her what she wants, and she can't make Kendra do what she wants her to do, so she's going to eliminate the problem."

"Some best friend. She tried to implicate her."

"I think she just did that as a distraction. Lucy's not stupid. She has to know this is the end of the line for her."

Neve frowned as she took her eyes off the road long enough to glance at Audrey. "You know that makes her desperate, right?"

Audrey nodded, throat burning and tight. "I know." She just hoped Lucy didn't see Alisha as an obstacle.

As they approached Linda's house, Audrey spotted Alisha's car in the drive. Lucy's was parked just down the road—out of view of the house. The fear that churned in her stomach intensified. She had to get in there. She had to save Alisha.

Neve parked in the driveway and quickly got out of the car. "Stay behind me," she told Audrey. She knew her well enough not to tell her to stay out of the house.

Audrey did as she was told. Part of her wanted to run into the house, fists flying, but... she set her palm against her stomach with a frown.

She followed Neve up the front steps. The door was unlocked—like so many others in the area probably were at that time of day. Quietly, Neve turned the knob as she drew her weapon from its holster.

Audrey waited for her to step into the kitchen before she followed. Cautiously, she crossed the threshold. There was a pizza on the sideboard, partially eaten, and a drawer was open. She could hear the TV in the living room.

Neve was silent as a cat as she moved. Somehow she managed to seem both relaxed and ready for anything—a trait Audrey admired.

"Drop it," Neve said, as she turned into the next room.

Audrey looked over her shoulder. Alisha and Luke were on the sofa—unmoving. Tears streamed down Alisha's face. Lucy straddled Luke, a large kitchen knife in her hand. There was blood on the blade—and on Luke. It soaked through his T-shirt. She lifted her head to look at Neve.

"I'm almost done," she said. "Just give me a minute."

Her matter-of-fact tone was sharp and piercing in Audrey's ears. It was the voice of someone who had convinced herself she was doing the right thing—the only thing.

"Lucy," she said, moving to stand beside Neve. "Think about what you're doing."

The girl's determined gaze jumped to Audrey. "I *have* thought about it. All Kendra wanted was to get Luke back. I almost had it, and then he took up with Tala. He chose a girl that wasn't even really a girl over her. Do you have any idea how that made her feel?" She glanced at the boy beneath her. "You made her feel like dirt, you asshole. Worthless."

"So you killed Tala thinking Luke would go back to Kendra?" She'd been in the business too long, because it actually made sense on some level.

"Tala told me that part of the reason she liked Luke was that both Kendra and I had dated him. How fucked up is that? T hen I found out she'd been fucking Kyle." She shook her head. "It was like she was trying to rub Kendra's face in it. Tala had her boyfriend *and* her brother, and then she tried to be my friend, but I'm more loyal than some." She looked at Luke again.

"Kendra wouldn't want this."

The girl made a face. "Kendra doesn't know what's good for her. She'll figure it out with him gone."

"She'll never forgive you if you hurt him."

"Yes, she will," the girl said with a confident expression. "I'm her best friend." With that, she plunged the knife down.

Neve fired.

* * *

The entire town turned out for Tala's funeral a few days later. Even Luke was there—the wounds Lucy had inflicted on him had been shallow, meant to inflict the most pain before the killing blow.

Kendra was there too—a pale shadow of herself in the bright sunshine. She was still in the hospital and would be for a little while longer until the doctors decided she was mentally and emotionally ready to go home. The death of her brother had been added to Lucy's list of crimes. She claimed she hadn't meant to kill Kyle, and that she misjudged the dose. He'd wanted to go back the Falls to have a little ceremony for Tala, she said. When he got handsy, she drugged his drink. It was an accident.

An *accident*.

To Lucy, everything she'd done made sense. She'd done it for her best friend. It touched a little too close to home for Audrey's liking. She understood the girl wanting to protect Kendra. She understood that sort of loyalty. What she didn't understand was how Lucy decided to kill Tala. She could have done so many other things than kill her, but to Lucy, that had been the only option.

Neve had shot her in the arm—the one holding the knife. The girl had lain on the carpet, bleeding and crying—cursing them for stopping her. Her only remorse had been not finishing what she set out to do.

Audrey stood beside Jake, holding his hand. Alisha stood

between him and her mother, leaning into Yancy's side. Even Lincoln had shown up. A few times Audrey caught Alisha and Luke looking at each other. It reminded her of how she used to look at Jake when she had been that age. Funny, but Jake had looked at her the same way back then, she just hadn't seen it at the time. So much longing and emotion in those gazes. It wasn't quite as scary as a homicidal teenage girl, but close.

The school wanted to keep her on part time at least until the end of the school year, and she thought she might do it—so long as it didn't interfere with getting Grace Ridge ready to open. It was obvious that kids in the area needed someone to talk to, and it would make her feel as though she was giving back to her hometown.

After all, if she and Jake were going to raise their kid there, she wanted to make sure it was as safe as possible.

When the graveside service was over, Kendra approached Alisha. Audrey watched as the dark-haired girl apologized for everything she'd done. She seemed sincere.

Alisha offered up a small smile. "We're good," she said, and gave Kendra a brief hug. Then she added, "Luke and I are going to Fat Frank's. Do you want to come?"

Kendra shook her head. "I have to go back to the hospital, but thanks. And hey, I hope...I hope you guys work out."

Alisha stared at her for a moment, trying to find the lie in her words. Audrey did the same thing but found nothing. "T hanks."

Kendra walked away and Alisha sent Audrey a surprised glance. Audrey smiled. "Good job," she whispered.

Before leaving the cemetery, Audrey and Luke stopped by Maggie's grave. There was a bouquet of flowers starting to wilt leaning against the headstone, and the bracelet Audrey had left there months earlier had tarnished. At least no one had stolen it.

Audrey brushed a few blades of cut grass from the top of the headstone.

"Don't," Jake said.

She turned her head. "Don't what?"

"Don't compare you and Maggie to those girls."

"It's kind of hard not to. Lucy thought she was protecting her best friend."

His expression morphed into incredulity. "You think Lucy is like you?"

"Well, yeah."

He shook his head. "Aud, that kid is more like Maggie than you."

"What? No."

He took her hand and pulled her close. "Maggie was obsessed with you. A few years ago she got drunk at Gracie's and told me I was lucky that all she had to do was fuck me to get you away from me."

Audrey gaped at him. "You're lying."

Jake shook his head. "On Gran's grave. I laughed and asked what she would have done if it hadn't worked. She said you were the only person she'd ever kill for. She said I could never understand the bond between the two of you."

She swallowed. "What did you say?"

He smiled. "I told her it would take something stronger than her to destroy the bond between you and me." Then he kissed her, and all was right with the world.

A week later, the Harte and Tripp families gathered at Audrey and Jake's for dinner. Everyone brought a dish, and of course Jake had outdone himself in the kitchen. As the entire group—less Audrey's brother, David, who was in New York—sat around the table eating and laughing, Audrey took a moment to be thankful for the events that had brought her home a year earlier. If anyone had told her then that she would be living in Edgeport, starting her own business and about to marry Jake Tripp, she would have told them they were insane, especially if they told her she'd be pregnant and happy about it.

Two and a half months pregnant, to be exact. She knew that they were supposed to wait until the first trimester was up to announce it, but...

She tapped her fork against her glass to get their attention. Everyone looked at her—Jake, his siblings, her sister, her brother-in-law, their kids, and her parents. Even Alisha, who had resented having to leave her boyfriend for family dinner, looked at her expectantly. Which was punningly poetic, when she thought about it.

Audrey took Jake's hand and smiled at him. He grinned back before they turned to face their loved ones.

"We have something we want to tell you all."

ACKNOWLEDGMENTS

There are some people I need to thank for helping get this book out into the world. First of all, I want to thank Lindsey Hall for being such an amazing editor. You have been an absolute pleasure to work with on this series. Thanks so much for believing in it and supporting it. Big hugs.

Also, thanks to Stephen McCausland of the Maine State Police for answering my questions about procedure for Neve's scenes. If I got anything wrong or took liberties, that's all on me.

Thanks again to all of my friends who have gotten used to me being on deadline and accept the crazy.

Also, big thanks to my family for their support and never-ending font of inspiration.

I want to take a moment to thank all of the readers who have gotten behind this series and supported it. You all are fabulous and I love you to bits. Thanks for following Audrey's journey thus far.

And last, but not least, thank you to my husband, Steve. Just because.

MEET THE AUTHOR

As a child KATE KESSLER seemed to have a knack for finding trouble, and for it finding her. A former delinquent, Kate now prefers to write about trouble rather than cause it, and spends her day writing about why people do the things they do. She lives in New England with her husband.

if you enjoyed
FOUR OF A KIND
look out for
THE WALLS
by
Hollie Overton

Working on death row is far from Kristy Tucker's dream, but she is grateful for a job that allows her to support her son and ailing father.

When she meets Lance Dobson, Kristy begins to imagine a different kind of future. But after their wedding, she finds herself serving her own life sentence—one of abuse and constant terror.

But Kristy is a survivor, and as Lance's violence escalates, the inmates she's worked with have planted an idea she simply can't shake.

Now she must decide whether she'll risk everything to protect her family.

Does she have what it takes to commit the perfect crime?

CHAPTER ONE

Mom, move your butt or we're going to be late."

Kristy Tucker heard her son's voice, annoyance dripping from each syllable. She glanced at the clock and cursed under her breath.

"I'm coming, Ry," she said, quickly pulling her brown hair into a bun. She grabbed her purse and headed toward her bedroom door, nearly tripping over the edge of the fraying gray carpet. She steadied herself and raced downstairs toward the kitchen. No matter how hard Kristy tried—setting her alarm half an hour earlier, washing her hair the night before—she could never get her act together in the morning. And on execution days, forget about it.

Ryan, on the other hand, had been up for hours. At fourteen years old, Ryan was neat, orderly, and incredibly driven, the polar opposite of Kristy. She found her son seated at the dining table finishing his bowl of oatmeal, his sandy-brown hair neatly combed, and dressed in his usual uniform: pressed jeans, a collared black button-up shirt with a red-and-black-striped tie, and his beat-up old black cowhide boots. Texas hipster, Kristy dubbed Ryan's standard uniform. She loved how much care he put into his appearance but it did very little to help him fit in with the rednecks and jocks at school. She'd heard the whispers and teasing from kids and their parents. "That boy acts like he's too big for his britches," they'd said on more than one occasion. Kristy shouldered some of the blame. She was only seventeen when Ryan was born, *a baby raising a baby*, Pops used to say. She encouraged his differences, wanted her son to accomplish everything she hadn't.

"Hey, Pops, you owe me five bucks," Ryan said with a grin.

"Put it on my tab," Pops said.

"I'm afraid to ask. What was the bet?" Kristy asked as she grabbed her travel mug and filled it with coffee.

"How long it would take you to get ready this morning," Ryan said.

"I actually gave you the benefit of the doubt," Pops replied, shaking his head in dismay.

Kristy's father, Frank Tucker, let out a strangled laugh as he tugged on the oxygen cannula that snaked from his nose, down his body, and into a giant oxygen tank that kept his O_2 levels consistent. Only sixty-eight, Pops appeared much older, his hair wild and gray, rarely combed. A lifetime of chain-smoking had taken its toll, ravaged his lungs, and now he was basically a prisoner trapped inside his own home. But despite Pops's health challenges, his humor was still intact.

"If you'd set your alarm a few minutes earlier—" Pops began. Kristy cut him off, well aware that her morning routine was the bane of Pops's and Ryan's existence. She simply couldn't deal with their teasing.

"Not today, you two. I don't have it in me. C'mon, Ry. Let's go."

She grabbed her keys and turned to Pops. "Remember: no drugs and no hookers."

"I'm not making any promises," he said with a chuckle.

Kristy smiled. "I'll be back late. Let me know if you need anything from the store on my way home."

"I'll be fine, Kristy girl," Pops said. "You take care of yourself."

Kristy gave Pops a quick peck on the cheek and headed toward the front of the house, Ryan shuffling behind her. She opened the door and found herself greeted by a tidal wave of hot, humid air. Not even March and the temperatures were already soaring into the nineties.

She drove east along the 105, heading toward Conroe High School. An arm of the massive Lake Conroe shimmered in the morning sun as they whizzed by. Stretches of white wooden fences and green grass ushered them toward the city. In the passenger's seat, earbuds in, Ryan sat hunched over his refurbished second-generation iPhone, simultaneously listening to music and texting. Kristy's long hours working at the prison often meant that morning drop-off was the only chance she had to catch up with Ryan, which was why she normally enforced a strict no-cell-phone policy in the car.

But today she welcomed the silence, trying to brace herself for what lay ahead—interviews with death row inmates and the execution of a brutal killer and serial rapist. *Just another day at the office.* Kristy witnessed people die year after year. Yes, they were all convicted killers but it still wasn't normal. Besides, she knew it wasn't just work that was troubling her. Her life seemed stagnant, chronicling each month by Ryan's latest accomplishment or Pops's newest ailment. Some days she woke up with the sense that something terrible was going to happen. Today that feeling seemed worse. Kristy's *sense of impending doom* occurred before every tragic event in her life. Kristy sighed. She simply couldn't handle any bad news today.

Fifteen minutes later, Kristy pulled up a block and a half from Ryan's school. Lately, he hadn't wanted her to drop him at the front entrance. Kristy wasn't stupid. She knew Ryan was embarrassed by her beat-up old pickup. Or maybe he just wanted to assert his independence. She understood it intellectually, though her heart still hurt when she thought about Ryan pulling away from her. The downside to the two of them growing up together.

"You okay?" Ryan asked, eyes widening with worry. He'd always been a sensitive kid, overly concerned with what Kristy was thinking and feeling.

"Of course. Why wouldn't I be?" she asked.

"You can do something else. Get a new job."

Her smile faded. "Ry, don't start. I make decent money and get really good benefits."

"But you hate it."

"So what? Most people hate their jobs. That's why it's called work."

"Most people aren't committing murder," Ryan said pointedly, and it took everything in Kristy's mind not to lose her temper completely.

Kristy's job as a public information officer for the Texas Department of Criminal Justice required that she serve as mediator between inmates, the press, and the prison system.

Despite the challenges and the pressures, it also required that she act as a witness during executions.

Her job had always been hard on Ryan. She'd done her best to explain to him how the justice system in Texas worked: There were rules, and the men and women on death row had broken those rules in the worst possible way and they deserved to be punished. But Ryan had a tender heart and a curious nature. The older he got, the more he hated watching his mom stand up in front of TV cameras and talk about executions as if they were commonplace, like they weren't something that the rest of the world considered barbaric. Kristy had spent years listening to her son's passionate arguments. She'd assumed that it was just a phase, until last year when, eyeing the crowd on her walk to the death house chamber before an execution, she spotted him. There was her son in a crowd of protesters. She'd gasped, staring at him as he proudly waved a sign that read EXECUTE JUSTICE. NOT PEOPLE. Kristy wanted to rush over and tell Ryan to get his butt home, but she couldn't. She still had a job to do.

Quietly seething at her son's disobedience, she sat through the execution of Mitchell Hastings, a thirty-year-old drifter convicted of murdering his sister and her best friend, while Ryan stood outside the prison gates chanting, "No justice. No peace."

Deep down, Kristy was proud of Ryan for being so strong in his convictions. But if any of the reporters had caught wind that Kristy's own son was anti–death penalty, it would have been a PR nightmare. She could have lost her job. On the drive home that evening, Kristy told Ryan he was allowed

to have an opinion, but this type of behavior wasn't accept-
able. This was her livelihood. It was what kept the roof over
their heads and food on the table. Ryan respected that but
he wanted Kristy to look for a new job. Even now, months
later, he'd e-mail her job postings, with subject headings like
New Jobs. No Killing Involved. But she simply wasn't going to
indulge him today.

"You're going to be late," Kristy said. For once, Ryan didn't
push back.

"All right, Mama Bear, I'll see ya later," he said, grabbing
his backpack.

"Love you, Ry."

He didn't respond, climbing out of the truck and slamming
the door behind him. Kristy watched Ryan hurry down the
block, waiting until he turned around the corner. God, she
missed the days when she would drop him off and he would
throw his arms around her and say, *Mama, I love you more than
the moon and the stars and all the planets in the universe.* But that
didn't happen now. Fourteen-year-olds weren't exactly open
vessels of emotion.

Kristy navigated the pickup down the long stretch of high-
way, the miles clicking by, a pop-country tune playing on
the radio. She switched it off, not in the mood for overpro-
duced melodies. She made a left turn, gripping the steering
wheel, and headed toward the entrance of the prison where
her day would begin. Set on 472 acres and surrounded by
forests and fields, the Polunsky Unit in Livingston, Texas, was
an expansive complex connected by walkways and encircled
by two perimeter fences of razor wire with guard towers.

The buildings that housed Texas's male death row inmates were set apart from the others: three concrete rectangles with white roofs, each with a circular recreation area at the center. In total, the prison housed 2,936 inmates, 279 of them on death row.

Kristy made this drive once a week, arriving every Wednesday morning like clockwork, but she never acclimated to the work. She never grew accustomed to the stern guards with their rifles pointed in the tower above her, or the desperate inmates she met pleading their innocence and begging for her help, or the ones admitting their guilt without an ounce of remorse.

This wasn't Kristy's dream job. Not by a long shot. Knocked up at sixteen, Kristy vowed that even though she would be a teenage mother, she wouldn't be a statistic. She would do something with her life. She earned her GED and then, with Pops's encouragement, she took night classes at Sam Houston State. Kristy studied communications and psychology, working part-time in various administrative capacities at the prison to help pay the bills. Pops had been a prison guard and so had his father before him. Despite Kristy's insistence that she could find a job on her own, Pops kept harassing the head of the public information office and before Kristy even graduated from college, she'd landed a job as an assistant to one of the public information officers, or PIOs, as they were known.

Part of Kristy had hated the idea of being surrounded by criminals—men and women who had done terrible things—but she'd told herself it was temporary. She'd planned on going to graduate school, studying psychology, and becoming a social worker. She figured her experience in the prison system would be an added bonus on her résumé. Working with and getting to know the inmates strengthened that resolve, made her want to help those in need before they ended up behind bars.

But raising a kid was a nonstop, 24/7 job. Then Pops's health began to fail, and Kristy got a promotion and a raise and then another raise. Nine years later, she was still here, the graduate program applications growing dusty in her desk drawer.

Now this was her life, week in and week out—meeting with violent inmates, trying to make friends with jaded, disheartened reporters desperate to write something that mattered. These days, Kristy found herself skirting the truth when people asked what she did for a living. *I'm in public relations*, she would say, hoping they wouldn't probe, hoping she could make it sound more glamorous than it was.

She had to shake off this doomsday feeling. She had a long day of interviews with death row inmates ahead of her, and they would require every ounce of her emotional energy.

Each week, the prison held media visitation for death row inmates. Mondays were reserved for women incarcerated at the Mountain View Unit. Wednesdays were when the male inmates at the Polunsky Unit were interviewed. For two hours, reporters were able to visit with prisoners who had received prior approval from prison officials.

Kristy parked her truck and entered the Polunsky main gate. Guards waved and called out hello, busy opening packages and sorting mail, the ordinary nature of their tasks contrasting starkly with the people who would be receiving these deliveries.

Kristy went through the metal detectors and grabbed her bag on the other side. She was greeted by Bruce, one of her

favorite guards, a thirty-something redneck with liberal lean-
ings who liked discussing Nate Silver, *The Bachelorette*, and his
favorite, *Real Housewives*. Despite the friendly nature of the
staff, everyone here understood the dangers they faced when
they walked through these doors. You had to work hard to
keep the darkness and anxiety from seeping in, an ongoing
battle Kristy wasn't sure she'd ever win.

Bruce led her toward the warden's office. Kristy rarely went
to death row itself, but the reporters had been complaining
about the quality of her stock photos and she was tired of
hearing them bitch. Today, before her interviews began, she
had arranged with the warden to take new photos of death
row cells. Warden Gina Solomon greeted her warmly.

"Warden Solomon. How are you?" Kristy said.

The warden, late forties with a severe bowl cut and bright
green eyes, shook Kristy's hand. "How's the family doing?"
she asked.

"Can't complain," Kristy said. "My son just made the
debate team. First freshman to do that in ten years," Kristy
boasted, her motherly pride on full display.

Warden Solomon nodded. "That's nice."

But Kristy heard the false cheer in her voice. The warden's son was a star quarterback at Montgomery High School.
Kristy hated that she let it bother her. Who cared if anyone
else was impressed by Ryan?

"Should we get going?" Kristy asked, changing the subject, hoping to avoid the warden's enthusiastic stories about
this week's playoff game and her son's skills on the field.

Flanked by Bruce, they headed through the labyrinthine

halls of the prison, the two women chatting about the upcoming cold front. Weather was a popular topic for prison staff, everyone longing to be outside and away from these dark and depressing cells. They turned down a long corridor and the mechanized gates buzzed open. This was death row.

Kristy regarded the sign posted at the entrance to the cellblock: NOTICE. NO HOSTAGES WILL EXIT THROUGH THIS GATE. This sign served as a reminder that these inmates were not to be trusted, that in here, your life hung in a delicate balance.

Moving down the hallway, Kristy's senses were assaulted by a wave of smells that no amount of training could prepare you for: piss, shit, sweat, all of it mingling with a hopelessness and desperation so profound it seemed to seep into your bones.

"Take your time," the warden said. Kristy nodded, but she intended to finish this task as quickly as possible. She hastily snapped photos of the hallways and rows and rows of cells. Inmates' faces peered out through the tiny shatterproof windows on their cell doors. Some of them recognized her.

"Yo, Miz Tucker, my lawyer's got questions for you."

Some were heavily medicated and desperate.

"These motherfuckers are torturing me. You gotta get me help."

Others were lost causes.

"That's one fine piece of ass. Come here. I'll show you what a real man is like."

"I'll kill you, you motherfucking, cocksucking bitch. I'll kill all of you."

Not much shocked Kristy. Not anymore. She was used to hearing men talk like this. Inmates in prison weren't that different from regular folk. Some were kind and polite. Some were mentally ill and should never have been put on death row in the first place. Others were wretched, miserable souls with no chance of redemption. Sometimes it was hard to tell who was who. It had taken Kristy years to adjust, but their words no longer rattled her. As a PIO, she had to appear in control, unmovable.

She stepped into an empty cell and snapped more photos. Polunsky was often called "the hardest place to do time in Texas," and Kristy agreed. All the inmates were kept on lockdown twenty-two hours a day in these small solitary cells. Even their one hour a day of recreation was caged, no contact with any other inmate. With no access to phones or televisions and no contact visits, inmates were basically entombed in these cells. It was about as close to hell on earth as you could get. Kristy couldn't imagine being trapped behind these walls, day in and day out.

She scanned through the images on the digital camera she had borrowed from Ryan, checking to make sure they would suffice. Good enough. She couldn't wait to get the hell out of here. She craved sunlight and fresh air. Kristy stepped back into the hall where Warden Solomon and Bruce were waiting, and followed them back down the hall.

For some reason, right before they reached the exit, Kristy glanced over at one of the cells, inexplicably drawn to it. Through the tiny sliver of glass, she spotted an inmate, his body splayed out on the floor beside his state-issued cot. *Baby Killer Harris.* That's what the press and some of the guards called him. Kristy knew him as Clifton Harris. He had been sentenced eight years ago for killing his two young children.

"Jesus Christ, he's bleeding," Kristy said, turning toward

the warden. She hated how shrill and high-pitched her voice sounded, like this man had a paper cut and not wrists that were flayed open. The warden stepped forward, looking through the window to confirm that what Kristy was saying was true.

"Get some more officers down here. Now!" Warden Solomon shouted to Bruce, who pressed a button on his radio, the squawking sound echoing down the halls.

"Get back," the warden yelled at Kristy. The buzzer sounded and the cell door's lock opened. Unable to wrench her gaze from Clifton's pale face, his blue lips, his eyes rolling back in his head, Kristy rushed past the warden and pushed the door open, kneeling beside Clifton, touching his neck and searching for a pulse.

"Hold on, Clifton. Just hold on."

Clifton's eyes fluttered open, haunted, life slipping from them. A bloodstained hand reached out, grasping Kristy's wrist.

"Ms. Tucker, I can't do this no more. I can't," he said desperately, that same hand now reaching up to grab Kristy's collarbone. "Just let me go," Clifton begged, his hand starting to squeeze.

Kristy's breath caught in her throat. She remembered that sign at the entrance. NO HOSTAGES WILL EXIT THROUGH THIS GATE. She had rushed in here without thinking, worried that Clifton might die, desiring to help someone for a change, to do something instead of just being a bystander in her life. But Kristy realized in this moment that her unease, that sense of impending doom, had been an actual warning. With this convicted killer's hand around her throat, Kristy wondered if Ryan had been right all along, that by staying in this job, by accepting what they did here, Kristy had made a fatal mistake.